"Lindsey pens a riveting and emotive tale of a teenage boy who joins the Navy following the Japanese attack on Pearl Harbor and becomes a Navy underwater demolitions diver, clearing the water of hazards before amphibious assaults. It's a rare opportunity to observe the genesis of today's Naval Special Warfare."

- Ron McManus - Award winning author of *Libido's Twist* and *The Drone Enigma*

"A remarkable job! Lindsey's terrific writing provides incredibly distinct visuals. Lee "Stump" Kelley was definitely an amazing guy."

- Jim Curry, Lieutenant Colonel, USMC (Ret)

"Lindsey's command of the insights, military language, and history of the war was extremely impressive. I started the book and finished it in the same day-couldn't put it down. I couldn't wait to get to the next chapter, and the next, and the next. Congratulations on a masterful book. I expected much and got more than expected-much more. Thank you for letting me be exposed to things I didn't know, but thought I did."

- Terry Watto, Commander, USN (Ret)

Stump!
by Larry Allen Lindsey

© Copyright 2015 Larry Allen Lindsey
ISBN   978-1-940192-97-0

Published by

köehlerbooks™

210 60th Street
Virginia Beach, VA 23451
212-574-7939
www.koehlerbooks.com

bitlit
A free eBook edition is available
with the purchase of this print book.

CLEARLY PRINT YOUR NAME ABOVE IN UPPER CASE

Instructions to claim your free eBook edition:
1. Download the BitLit app for Android or iOS
2. Write your name in **UPPER CASE** on the line
3. Use the BitLit app to submit a photo
4. Download your eBook to any device

FOR LEE

To Steve Milgazo,
Fair winds &
a following sea,

[signature]

STUMP!

LARRY ALLEN LINDSEY

VIRGINIA BEACH
CAPE CHARLES

PREFACE

LEE KELLEY WAS my good friend and neighbor. A truly amazing man, he lived life to the fullest. Never content to take the easy way out, when life pushed he pushed back—to the day he died. And I was honored to care for him during his last few weeks, painful though they were. Although we were a generation apart, we were banded brothers of sorts. He, a frogman from World War II. Me, a river rat from Vietnam.

For ten years we went to dinner every Monday, and invariably our waitress would ask if we were father and son. Mainly because we both shaved our heads, sported moustaches, and our faces looked a little bit alike. Lee would wink and say, "Nah, he's just my little brother." Even though he had some twenty-plus years on me and I was a full head taller.

At seventeen Lee enlisted in the Navy—shortly after the sneak attack on Pearl Harbor. When he completed his frogman training he served in some of the bloodiest actions of his war. Blowing up obstructions all over the Pacific, he and his team of *naked warriors* were always the first to hit the beach. He was even waiting on shore when General Douglas MacArthur made his famous *I shall return* landing.

Born in a trunk to Vaudevillian parents, as a toddler Lee literally had to sing for his supper. After the war he became a vital part of the Atlas space program, hobnobbing with astronauts and rocket scientists, including the ex-Nazi camera hog Werner von Braun.

This book is a compilation of Lee Kelley's colorful war stories, many of which were told to me on his deathbed. Sixteen million Americans served in World War II and "Stump" is one of the more than fifteen million who are no longer with us. I miss Lee more than mere words can express, and hopefully this meager attempt will help keep alive the memory of this gallant patriot.

ONE

ANOTHER AMPHIBIOUS LANDING, another devastated shoreline, more bodies drifting away with the tide. Lee "Stump" Kelley had seen enough death to last a dozen lifetimes. And up until last month he'd forced himself to shrug it all off. People died in a war. It was the nature of the beast and there was nothing he could do about it. Shedding a tear wouldn't bring the dead back to life. But as he stood in that far corner of a once pristine beach, now sullied by the unforgiving tread of a thousand war machines, his eyes began to well up. Staring into the last vestiges of a blood red sun, this time the hollow imbalance in the pit of his stomach wouldn't go away. Swallowing hard he felt as if he were adrift on a sea of shattered glass. Never before had he felt so alone, so beyond hope.

First Athos, now Porthos—two of the Three Musketeers were now gone. In the short span of a month Lee had lost his two best friends, his right and left arms. Killed before either had reached their nineteenth birthday, both had met violent and gruesome ends on two remote Philippine beaches ten thousand miles from their homeland. Twenty-eight days ago it had been Hillbilly. Yesterday it was Frenchie's turn.

Taking another swig of tepid San Miguel, Stump plopped his tired butt into the sand. It was late in the evening on a Tuesday,

October 1, 1944. Then again it could have been a Wednesday. In the middle of an overly long war, time seemed to overlap into a never-ending string of nameless days.

The multi-colored label on the dark bottle in his hand spelled out *beer* in Tagalog, but the liquid tasted more like panther piss. A far cry from his favorite back in Ohio—Hey Mabel! *Black Label!* The night before, he and his team of light-fingered frogmen had *appropriated* a case of the foul smelling stuff from a detachment of British soldiers, snatching it from their tent when their backs were turned. And it would have been a shame to waste the fruits of their labor, especially in this God-forsaken corner of the world. No matter how bad it tasted.

Lee had nothing but admiration for the Brits, but they sure were a strange lot. He could stomach most of their strange eating habits—blood pudding, spotted dick (now there was a name you didn't mess with), and even bangers—a type of water sausage that had an alarming propensity to explode when cooked. But how those Limeys could drink their beer warm was beyond him. Beer was supposed to be served ice cold, out of a frosty mug, not warm as bath water. And at this low point in his life—a life that was rapidly careening down the road to Miserable—he would have sold his soul for a long, tall, cold one. As if he had much of a soul left after all the shit he'd seen and done.

The war in the Pacific was finally turning in America's favor, but at the moment that was little consolation to Lee. His bosom buddies were now dead. Four weeks to the day, his fellow go-fer Hillbilly Parsons had been blown to smithereens on the beaches of Tacloban, a once picturesque fishing village on the Gulf of Leyte. Like too many other little villages in the Philippines, it had taken the American fleet all of a day to reduce the place to rubble.

Six foot two and strong as a bull, Hillbilly had been involved in yet another night-diving operation when he was ripped apart in only eight feet of water. One second he had been alive and kicking, looking forward to another so-called beer as he planted his last charge. And in the blink of an eye he'd been turned into a reddish cloud of chum drifting away with the current. Ten pounds of tetro is powerful stuff. Especially when it explodes a foot in front of your face. Normally stable when tetro isn't attached to primacord, something must have gone terribly wrong. Whatever it was, it cost Hillbilly and his partner their lives. The only saving grace, they never knew what hit them.

Pursing his lips, Lee inhaled deeply through his nose. Mixed with the ever-present tang of salt air floated a hint of scorched iron and singed hair. Once again the all-too-familiar smell of warmed-over death left a rancid tinge in the back of his throat. A second swallow of beer could not wash the sickening taste away. Nor would a third.

At least Hillbilly got his wish, thought Lee. *The big galoot always said he wanted to go quick. Die with his boots on.*

Shaking his head Lee looked out across the bay. Then slowly scanned left towards a distant island. Just beyond where the surf began to break, a flock of seagulls was circling the carcass of a large dead fish floating belly up in the water. It could have been a grouper, or even a shark. Maybe a blue tip. Oblivious to the wars of men, the air-borne scavengers couldn't have cared less how many soldiers had died on this beach the day before.

To the hungry birds humans were noisy, mindless creatures, who the previous morning had turned the surf red as far as the eye could see with their infernal thundersticks. During the insanity it seemed destruction would reign supreme, that the entire island would be devastated for generations to come.

But it had taken Mother Nature less than a day to wash most of the blood and guts away. All that remained were a few of man's broken tanks dotting the shoreline. Soon to be rusted out hulks, they stood in mute testimony to yet another of man's follies as they slowly sank into the muck. But in her infinite wisdom Ma Nature would take care of those broken pieces of war, too. It would only take her longer. Iron always took longer than flesh. And whereas the human race had a limited amount of soldiers to sacrifice on these foreign shores, Nature had an unlimited amount of time. Such were the costly vagaries of war.

TWO

THINKING BACK ON Hillbilly's easy laugh, Lee cracked a wistful smile.

Of course he probably would have preferred to die of a massive heart attack. Brought on by making mad monkey love to a big breasted redhead. Son of a gun always had a thing for red hair. At least then he would have met his Maker with a goofy grin on his face. And there would have been something of him left to bury.

Lee had been devastated by Hillbilly's death. Still was. At the time he thought the world couldn't hit him with a worse heartache. But yesterday had proved him wrong. When the chief told him Frenchie Lafourche had drowned in Manila Bay, at first he couldn't believe it. Not Frenchie the indestructible. He was the best swimmer in their frogman class. Even better than Lee—and Lee had set a few meet records in high school. With lungs like a dolphin, Frenchie could hold his breath underwater a full two minutes. *Frenchie drowned?* It just wasn't possible. No way on God's good green earth that could have happened to Frenchie. But somehow it did. Recent history had taught Lee that in a war like this, when your number was up, your number was up.

Too many *if onlys* must have lined up against Frenchie to drown him like that. *If only* that Jap patrol boat hadn't taken a direct hit and sunk in Manila Bay. *If only* it hadn't shifted with Frenchie trapped inside. *If only* he hadn't been hooked by that jagged strip of metal. *If only* his partner hadn't been chased away by that giant hammerhead shark.

But when the chief showed him Frenchie's diving knife, Lee knew it was all too true. Frenchie never let that knife out of his sight.

An inch taller than Hillbilly and blessed with cat-quick reflexes, Frenchie never said much. Didn't have to. Never one to pick a fight—but the first to end one—he was front-and-center the man you wanted on your side in a bar room brawl. His steel-eyed stare could wither a grizzly bear. That, and the ever present knife he stashed in his jersey flap pocket. A quick flash of its gleaming blade and in half a second he'd pop off the top button of a guy's shirt—without drawing a drop of blood. It never failed to drain the starch out of even the most belligerent drunk.

That damn switchblade saved my sorry ass on more than one occasion. Especially that time on Market Street in downtown San Diego. Hadn't been for Frenchie, those four Marines would have pounded me into the floor.

Nudged by the memory, Lee reached into his back pocket for his wallet. Pulled out a faded photograph, the only one he carried. Ever so carefully he unfolded the yellowed piece of paper. Taken three years ago on the day he graduated from underwater demolition class, it was a snapshot of him and his two buds in their dress whites on the beach at Coronado. What a proud event that had been! Frogman training had been a bitch—harder than anything Lee had been put through in his yet young life—but they all passed with flying colors.

Hillbilly on the left, Frenchie on the right, and Lee in the middle—as always. Flanked by the two giant oaks, it was easy to see why Lee was nicknamed "Stump." Even though he was standing on his tiptoes, he was still a head shorter than both of his friends. His eyes brimming with moisture, more memories came flashing back. Time seemed to stand still as one after another, visions of their many liberties together cascaded through his mind.

"Good times," he said softly.

After a few minutes Lee refolded the photo then returned it

to its place of honor in his wallet. Looking out to sea again he caught a glimpse of the sun settling onto the horizon, two hands high beneath a pair of feathered clouds. As it sank its rays began to shimmer the bay with broad strokes of crimson. Farther out to sea a whimsical breeze pickled the surface with a now-and-then whitecap. Off to his right a colorful reef—resplendent in its blues, yellows, greens, and reds—provided a perfect backdrop. If it hadn't been for the dregs of war piled up all around him, the scene might have been idyllic, a tropical paradise most Americans would have paid big bucks to visit. Ironically for Lee, his trip hadn't cost him a plugged nickel. Just his two best friends.

THREE

FIFTY YARDS TO Lee's left a half-submerged Higgins boat rocked to the beat of the incoming waves, its bottom ripped open by one of the many jumping jacks the Japs had planted in the surf. Three railroad tracks welded together at the center, the simple device could pop through the sheet metal of any landing craft as easily as an opener slices open a can of beans. Lapping over the boat's starboard railing a small flotilla of litter bobbed in and out with the surf. Here, a shredded life jacket, smashed wooden pallet, broken rifle stock; there, a torn helmet liner, empty rations carton, solitary working glove.

Farther up the beach was a bulldozed pile of ashes. Half again taller than a man, it smoldered in the late afternoon sun, marking the last vestiges of this morning's funeral pyre. A thin wisp of smoke flagged the last resting place of the bones of hundreds of Japan's finest.

Serves the bastards right. Sons of bitches got what they deserved. Especially after what they did to us at Pearl.

Lee grudgingly respected the enemy's dedication. To a man they stood their ground and died in droves when the Americans clamored ashore. Either they were some of the bravest soldiers he'd ever seen, or the dumbest.

Over his right shoulder half a jeep rested on its back. Scorched a dull carbon black, its tires had melted off their rims. What was left of the frame looked like a cracked egg. Its splintered drive shaft pointed straight up towards the sky like a defiant flagpole. All it lacked was a white flag to signify it had finally given up the ghost.

All the king's horses and all the king's men, mused Lee. *For sure that jeep has seen its last days. So too has its driver.*

The jeep's shattered windshield was twisted to one side, like a plucked wing. Streaked with blood it told an all too familiar tale. From the tracks in the sand it appeared the driver had been making a mad dash for a distant dune, seeking protection from incoming enemy mortar fire. He'd probably taken a direct hit when he slowed to avoid that nearby palm tree. Given the position of the wreckage it didn't take much for Lee to imagine the scene.

Poor guy probably never saw it coming. One second you're hauling ass up the beach heading for cover, your heart pumping to beat the band... the next, pieces of you and your jeep are tumbling ass over tea kettle in the air. An hour later some corpsman scrambles up to jam your dog tags between your teeth. That is if you had any teeth left.

It was a far cry from the visions of glory that danced through Lee's head when he raised his right hand to enlist in Cleveland. A naïve dream, he had learned the hard way that there was no glory in war, just blood and death. Like his own president, Lee had now seen war and he hated it.

Blood, sweat, and tears, sighed Lee, thinking more of Churchill than FDR. *An ocean of blood and a bucket of tears. And I can't even begin to count the sweat.*

All he and his two buddies had wanted to do when they joined up was to kill Japs. Payback for what they pulled off at Pearl.

Killing Japs? Pay them back? Easier said than done.

And now Frenchie was gone too. According to the chief he'd been laying a charge when he snagged his knee clear to the bone on a sharp piece of metal in that sunken patrol boat. Always a battler, Frenchie nearly tore his leg off when he finally pulled himself free. Probably bled to death trying to get to that hatch just two feet out of his reach.

Two feet or two miles. When you get right down to it, what difference did it make? Stone cold dead was still stone cold dead. When they finally brought Frenchie up he was the color of a shucked clam and the fish had gotten to his right eye. Par for the course for a Navy frogman in World War II. Lee knew it was just the cost of doing business over here. Churning away in the pit of his stomach like a bucket sloshing over with acid was a double dose of empty. First Hillbilly and now Frenchie. Two chunks of his heart had been ripped out. They were like family. Better actually, since he was closer to them than he was to either of his self-centered parents, who time after time had disappointed him. And were destined to do so in the future.

If bad things happened in threes—and in this war they seemed to come up in sevens, eights and nines—that meant Lee was next. Just three lowly sailors? Who in their carefree young lives probably downed too many beers and chased way too many women? In the infinite and unfathomable scheme of things over here, how much could they matter?

At this point Lee felt resolved to his fate. In fact he almost yearned for it. At least then he wouldn't have to stare at one more mutilated body. Or smell the stench of rotting flesh every time he took a breath. Hillbilly and Frenchie had been his sky hooks, the solitary reasons he'd been able to keep some semblance of sanity in all this madness.

"You sure picked a doozy of a war to land in, Kelley," he mumbled into his sweat soaked jersey. "Now what?"

Hopped up on saki the Japs were willing to do anything for that buck-toothed emperor of theirs, dying in wave after wave of banzai attacks if need be. They'd caught the United States with its pants down at Pearl and had slaughtered thousands of innocent civilians in their mad dash across the Philippines. The sons-of-bitches marched to a different beat, that was for sure, and in the beginning the allies lost hundreds of lives adjusting to their brutal cadence. But if anything, the American G.I. had proved to be a resilient cuss and a fast learner. When fighting a ruthless enemy you can't play by the rules, so he learned to shoot first and ask questions later. And now that MacArthur was *returning* as promised, the shoe was suddenly on the other foot. In retaking Manila, Mac's army had been instructed to shoot anything that moved. And let God sort out what's left. Downing the last of his tepid beer, Lee leaned back in the sand.

Kill or be killed... that's the ticket. I guess war isn't really an alternative, but the total lack thereof.

Savoring the warmth—if not the taste—of the alcohol as it burned a path down his throat, a sardonic grin snickered onto his face.

"Oh, so now you're spouting philosophy, Kelley?" he said. "Careful, numb nuts, you'll give yourself a headache. Somewhere out there there's a bullet with your name on it so why not end all the suspense. Just put your trusty pistol in your mouth and pull the trigger. Send a slug in that muddled brain of yours."

Looking down at the San Miguel label he had to laugh. A 45 caliber was a messy bullet. Left a two foot hole coming out.

"Yeah, right, asshole. I can just hear the death notification officer's words when he delivers what's left of your body. *Sorry, Mrs. Kelley, but the top of your son's head is missing.*"

Sometimes gallows humor was the only way to keep from losing it. With a shake of his head Lee stood and grabbed the empty beer bottle by its neck. Then with a grunt and a mighty heave, he hurled it towards the setting sun. Splashing down thirty yards out in the surf, it bobbed twice before disappearing beneath the surface with a resounding "PLOOP!"

For the longest time he watched the ripples dissipate with the incoming tide. Finally he looked towards the horizon, in the vague direction of America. Sucking a deep breath in through his nose he scratched his head. Then picked up a handful of sand to let it trickle through his fingers. Watching the particles fan out in the breeze a single question ran through his mind.

How in hell did I end up way over here?

FOUR

A FEW WEEKS before Halloween, every kid in Elyria who owned a pair of ice skates began to pray for snow. And since there were few ponds on the west side of Cleveland, every year when the mercury dipped below freezing for a few days the local fire department flooded a section of the town park to provide the neighborhood with a makeshift hockey rink. Although tufts of grass jutted up here and there, the ice was at least playable. If you avoided the soft spots in front of both goals.

Just thirteen and the shortest man on his squad, Lee Kelley was flying down the right side of the rink when a high stick to the chest sent him sprawling across the ice face first. The blind side body check had been so hard it knocked both of his skates clean off. No surprise there, held together by three yards of duct tape they were on their last legs anyway. After sliding a good ten yards on his chin Lee rolled over twice, then popped right back up. Mad as a wet hen.

"What the hell!" he growled, tonguing a loose tooth.

"Geez, Lee," said Tommy Hutchins, skating over. "You're bleeding like a stuck pig. That cut's gonna need a couple of stitches."

Tough as nails and royally pissed off, Lee dabbed at his chin with a sleeve then waved Tommy off. Spitting a bloody loogie into the snow he stink-eyed the kid in the tattered brown sweater. The one with the *high stick.*

"Nah, I'll just slap a bandage on it. Let me at the son-of-a-bitch!"

On his second trip down the ice Lee's eyes never left the brown sweater. Swinging wide to gather momentum he lowered a calculated right shoulder to cartwheel the kid over the nearest snow drift—and into the thorniest crabapple tree on the block. A clean shot, but payback was a bitch. As they always were in these pickup games.

As a high school senior Lee "Stump" Kelley stood an exalted five feet five-and-a-half inches. If he stood up straight and craned his neck, on a good day he might stretch that to five six. An all-around good athlete, his quick wit and gift of gab had garnered him *Most Popular* honors in the class yearbook. Along with Most Likely to Succeed. This despite being born in a trunk to Vaudevillian parents and having to sing for his supper the first three years of his life.

Lee's father—also five foot five—played clarinet, told the requisite corny jokes on stage and squandered his money on flashy clothes, Jack Daniels, and fast cars. And even a few faster women when his wife wasn't looking. In a top hat and black face—and wearing a pair of over-sized white glasses—his most risqué line was rather tepid by today's standards.

The snake's forbidden apple didn't drive Eve from paradise. It was Adam's green pair. Badda-bing!

Not averse to running a con game now and then, the senior Kelley was a carny through and through. Living life on a hedonistic slant, he was all grasshopper, no ant. It came as no surprise, then, that his first heart-to-heart with his only son reflected his *me-first* outlook.

"Lee, there are two kinds of people on this sorry-ass planet. There are those that give. And there are those that take. And we are definitely takers."

Still naïve to the world's harsh ways, four-year-old Lee had trouble incorporating the concept.

"But, Pop, Grampa says it's better to give than to receive. And whenever he takes me to church the Sunday school teacher always tells us it's good to be charitable."

"Oh, that's just his Bible thumpin' ways. You know he's always flappin' his gums about some damn scripture. Sometimes I think he missed his calling. Old coot should have been a preacher. Charity begins at home, son. Besides if everyone went around giving, there'd be nobody left to receive."

It was a philosophy that would come back to haunt Lee later in life.

Five foot two and eyes of blue, Lee's equally spend-thrift mother played drums, hoofed in the chorus, and would eventually divorce her bounder of a husband before her son became a teenager. She and her younger sister performed duets as the "Dove Sisters," singing "My Blue Heaven" to adequate reviews. Looking a bit like America's Sweetheart, Mary Pickford—and possessing *great gams*—in 1930 Mom relished the limelight of Vaudeville but harbored aspirations of becoming a movie star. Those dreams died a lingering death five years later when the demand for barnstorming entertainers petered out.

Lee's Bible toting grandfather—the relative he liked the most—played a mean trombone and a gentle cello. Standing tall in a long coat and a straw hat, his stage routine consisted of talking about creation while tearing pieces from a folded newspaper. When he got to his punch line he would unfold a string of crosses and snowflakes. The only Kelley with a marketable talent, Grandpa ended up playing with Paul Whiteman, a famous band leader of the era.

In school Lee's twinkling eye and devilish grin made him a hit with the girls. So much so that later in life he would enjoy three marriages—and weather three divorces. Simply put, Lee loved the ladies and the ladies loved him.

A freestyler on his high school swim team, at sixteen Lee weighed a lean, mean hundred and forty pounds soaking wet. Swimming kept Kelley lean—and secondarily clean—but his favorite sport of ice hockey made him mean. Mean enough to tolerate the nickname Stump. A few years after the doctor sewed that chin of his up however, he took an errant puck to his right cheekbone. Hard enough to knock out two teeth and cave in his orbital socket. After regaining consciousness he found himself gravitating towards sports without sticks and ice. And especially pucks. Although swimming wasn't half as much fun as hockey, it required fewer trips to the dentist—an important consideration to his financially strapped parents who had trouble coming up with the price of a new pair of skates.

FIVE

FIVE MONTHS AND eighteen days after Lee Kelley's seventeenth birthday, his world was about to be turned upside down. Along with everyone else's for that matter. Two hundred miles northeast of Hawaii, early in the morning a squadron of one hundred eighty-four war planes lifted off into the pre-dawn gloom from six Japanese aircraft carriers. Their fleet had set sail from their homeland last month in response to an American oil embargo. Which had been in retaliation for Japan's invasion of Indo-China. A final escalation in a dangerous game of political chess, the sabre rattling had been going on for over a year.

Heading this first attack wave was a moustached lieutenant commander named Mitsuo Fujida. Hanging beneath the fuselage of his Nakajima B5N was one of the new type 51 torpedoes, equipped with a special wooden device attached to its fins. Designed to stabilize the torpedo in flight then shed itself on impact with the water, it would keep the weapon from plunging to its normal depth of a hundred feet. Since Pearl Harbor was only forty feet deep in most places, that would have rendered the torpedo useless. Unfortunately for the Americans, the device would work like a charm and the torpedo would sink the *USS Arizona*.

"Commander, I've picked up a faint commercial radio channel. It's hard to make out, but I think it's music. Maybe coming from Honolulu."

The navigator in the bomber's three man crew, Chief Warrant Officer Hideo Watari, was the pessimist of the group. The one who prayed the most—and lingered the longest in front of his shrine before take-off—he was positive he'd never see his family again.

"Turn it up so we can all hear it," replied Fujida. After listening to a few strains a relieved smile blossomed beneath his moustache. "That's definitely Hawaiian music. Hone in on that signal. It appears the Americans have given us an engraved invitation."

A few minutes later—and right on schedule—a dark green shape on the ocean materialized beneath a string of puffy white clouds ahead of their left wing. Oahu. Sending an electric shock up his spine, the sight set Fujida's fingers a-tingle on the stick. Battle hardened from the campaign in China, he was one of the most experienced pilots in the world. But he still had to fight off the heady feeling.

Easy, Mitsuo. Now is not the time to get overly excited. Control your emotions. This is what you've been training for. You know what to do. Break radio silence and get the squadron into attack formation.

"Come left to two-eight-zero. Drop to two hundred feet and maintain your speed."

Simple and as practiced a hundred times before. Now all he had to do was wait for the go ahead from command. It would come at seven forty-nine and consist of three words. When Watari heard them through his receiver his mouth went dry and he had to swallow twice before conveying them to his superior.

"Commander... TO! TO! TO!" (Charge! Charge! Charge!)

"Excellent! Now we attack!"

"Sir," said Watari, concern in his voice. "Do you really think we can succeed in this?"

"Our leaders have given us an outstanding plan. If we carry it out I'm sure we'll be successful. The Americans are weak and morally bankrupt. All they want to do is drink, gamble, and jitterbug. They have no heart for battle. Besides, they're the ones who pushed us into this war."

"But so much depends on the element of surprise."

"We've been lucky so far and I see no reason why our luck would change. Sometimes you're like an old woman, Hideo. You worry too much. The divine wind is with us."

When they crested the last ridge on their approach into Pearl Harbor, Fujida's words rang true.

"See, I told you. Not a single enemy plane in the sky. And no anti-aircraft fire. As the Americans like to say, we've caught them with their pants down."

It was a Sunday, December 7, 1941, a day that would live in infamy and cost over twenty-three hundred Americans their lives.

SIX

A YEAR AHEAD of Lee Kelley in school, Chuck Vandusen was a teammate on the swim team. As tall as Lee was short, and wise to the ways of the world—at least to those of a sleepy whistle stop town in northeast Ohio—Chuck was his mentor, his idol. A suave upperclassman, he showed Lee the intricacies of pursuing the eligible females in school without getting your face slapped. So when Vandusen enlisted in the Marines in 1942 it was only natural that Lee thought about joining up. Elyria wasn't exactly a happening place, and given what was going on in the rest of the world, it seemed like the patriotic thing to do.

The clincher came when Vandusen returned on a week's leave after basic training. Parading around in his dress blues he cut such a dashing figure, starry-eyed girls two blocks away were falling into a dead swoon. The creases on his dress blues looked sharp enough to slice bread and you could actually see the cracks between your teeth in his spit polished shoes. Beyond impressed, young Lee made up his mind then and there that nothing would stop him from following in Chuck's awesome footsteps. Come hell and/or high water, this Kelley was going to turn leatherneck.

After convincing his father to sign the required parental consent form, it was time to trot his eager butt down to the local recruiter and raise his right hand. Not even his best friend—who had serious reservations about Stump becoming a grunt—could sway his resolve. Class valedictorian, unlike Lee Jack wasn't swayed by flashy uniforms and the prospect of getting laid. He never did anything without thinking it through ten times over. Articulate in everything he did, his penchant for using big words could either impress or confuse his friends. Watching Lee struggle with the only tie he owned, Jack shook his head, a concerned look washing over his face.

"I hope you're not serious about this, Lee. You aren't actually thinking about joining the Marines, are you?"

"Yep. I've thought it over and it's my only choice." Tugging at the lop-sided mess at his throat, Lee scrunched up his nose. "Damn! I can never get the hang of these stupid things."

"But, the Marines?" continued Jack. "I'm as gung ho as the next guy, but let's get serious. You got a death wish or something? They're the first to come under fire. And Chuck himself called their basic training the supreme ball buster."

"You've seen me on the ice so you know I ain't no candy-ass. I can take anything the Marines dish out. And then some. Besides, if Chuck can make it through, so can I." Lee gave his tie another yank, turning it into a Gordian knot even Ulysses couldn't master. "And if I wait too long there won't be any Japs left to shoot."

"A commendable sentiment, but there are more plausible alternatives to accomplish your objective. With a lot less risk, I might add."

Jack looked out the window for a second to calculate his next words. At this point he wanted to avoid any more big ones. And knowing Lee's quick temper he didn't want to come up with the wrong ones. Worried that he'd unleashed his potent vocabulary too soon, he took time to regroup.

"Look. I'll be the first to admit I'm not the hero type. But neither do I consider myself to be a coward. When it comes to blood, I have a very simple philosophy—one that so far has served me quite well in times of peril. Simply put, blood belongs on the inside of your body, not the outside."

Lee had to laugh. Sometimes he didn't understand Jack's droll sense of humor—or his highfalutin words—but they always made him stop and think.

"'Plausible alternatives,'" he said, mocking his friend's erudition. "Like what?"

"Like joining the Navy instead."

"Me? Become a sailor? I hate their friggin' uniforms. Bell-bottom trousers with thirteen buttons? By the time you get all those suckers undone you've already pissed your pants. And those white hats they wear look like over-sized Dixie cups."

"The Navy may not be as fashionable as the Marines, but they're also a lot less fatal."

Lee gave his tie one last tug. Frustrated, he tossed the uneven ends to one side. Crooked as the damn thing was, it would have to do.

"If it's such a smart *alternative,* Jack... why don't YOU join the Navy?"

"As a matter of fact, I intend to. I made the decision last week after talking it over with my parents. And they both agreed it was a logical choice. More so than the Marines anyway."

"Well, shiver me timbers! You son of gun! You've been holding out on me, buddy. How come you didn't tell me you were thinking about enlisting?"

"You know me, ol' steady-as-she-goes Jack. I had to mull it over, examine all the aspects. *Angels fearing to tread where fools rush in...* That sort of thing."

"Same old feet-on-the-ground Jack Conners. Wait a minute! Are you telling me in that roundabout way of yours that I'd be a fool to join the Marines?"

"Who, me?" grinned Jack. "No, I'd never say that. Not in those exact words anyway." Cocking his head to the right, he crossed his arms. "At any rate... the Navy recruiting office is in downtown Cleveland, right next to the Marine's. I thought we could ride the bus down together and sign up at the same time."

Lee's grin blossomed into an ear-to-ear smile.

"Sounds like a workable plan to me. As long as you promise to can the pep talk about the Navy. I don't care what you say, there ain't never gonna be no Dixie cup perched on Lee Kelley's head."

A twinkle in his eye, Jack went palms up.

"Despite the triple negative, I hear you loud and clear, my friend."

SEVEN

THE BEST LAID plans of mice and especially men... on a hot Indian summer day, Lee and Jack were greeted in the city by a line that stretched out of the Marine recruiting office, down the block and around the corner. Despite the unseasonably warm weather, apparently they weren't the only patriotic Buckeyes eager to join up. His throat already parched, Lee cast a wary eye at the depressingly long line.

"I guess we should have brought something to drink while we're waiting."

"Would you look at the size of that line?" whistled Jack, also well beyond thirsty. "On the positive side however, there's no line outside the Navy office. Are you sure you don't want to change your mind and join up with me?

"Not on your life," grumbled Lee, calculating his ever-expanding line. In ten seconds it had grown ten feet. "Aw, crap. At this rate it's gonna take me all day just to get to the damn door."

Shielding his eyes from the blazing sun, Jack removed his cap to dab at his forehead. Mad dogs and Englishmen, heat radiated off the sidewalk in waves, parboiling anyone dumb enough to be caught outdoors. To make matters worse, the surrounding buildings seemed to hoard their shade, looming down on the wilted pair with suffocating disdain. For at least one of the two it was going to be a long day. After wiping his brow Jack replaced his cap.

"Looks like you're in for a hell of a wait, Lee. Sorry to bail on you, buddy, but I think I'll extricate this frail body of mine from the sun's ravages."

"You're deserting me in this heat? I thought we were in this together."

"Hey, you're the one who chose the Marines. Not me. I love you like a brother, but let's be practical. It doesn't make much sense for both of us to languish out here in this broiling heat."

"Some friend you turned out to be."

"A friend who also happens to be a realist at heart. After all, you're the one who's hell bent on becoming a jarhead. Luck of the draw, you can't hold it against me if I chose the service with no waiting."

Watching this exchange from the comfort of his cool office was a gunnersmate first class. Dressed in his Navy dress whites and a veteran of the recruiting wars, Dan Eubanks was sharp enough to recognize a golden opportunity. Especially on a hot day in downtown Cleveland. And when opportunity knocked, Eubanks always listened.

After pinching off his half-smoked Lucky Strike between a pair of wetted fingers, Dan tucked the still-warm butt into his jersey flap pocket. Waste not, want not, he'd finish it later. Snatching his rolled *Dixie cup* from the hat rack he tilted it to a jaunty angle on his head. Definitely non-regulation, the tilt was more appealing to your run-of-the-mill—and hopefully impressionable—teenager.

A quick look in the wall mirror verified his three rows of ribbons were squared away. Sucking in his gut he gave the bottom of his jersey a tug. Then made sure his bell-bottoms were hanging straight and that his buttons were properly fastened. All thirteen of them. His final assessment: Not as impressive as a Marine in his dress blues, but presentable at least.

Opening the hardworking refrigerator behind his desk he kept stocked for just such an occasion, he grabbed two ice-cold bottles of Coca Cola. Then with a well-practiced smile on his face he headed out into the midday sun. Time to go fishing; the Navy had two more on the line. If all went well, come sundown he'd have both their signatures on the dotted line.

EIGHT

FISH IN A rain barrel, when the recruiter swooped in for the kill the two teenagers from Elyria didn't stand a tinker's chance of escaping his clutches. At least poor Lee Kelley didn't. Game over already—swab jockeys two, jarheads zero. Since Jack had already made up his mind to join the Navy he probably shouldn't have counted as a kill, but Eubanks wasn't about to quibble. Licking his lips as he approached, the recruiter's trained eye sized up his prey. The taller one had the jib of a sailor and would be no trouble. Money in the bank, he was already on his way to boot camp. The shorter of the two, however, looked to be the real problem. He had that certain glint in his eye, that unmistakable "Semper Fi" bravado that set the Marines apart from the Navy.

GM1 Dan Eubanks had seen that look many times before. And although he would never admit to it, deep down he respected the swagger, the cockiness, that aura of invincibility, in fact the whole package Marines seemed to exude from every pore. But he also took it as a challenge. A personal call to battle, if you will. One that he relished, that made the game worth playing. And given the impressive number of recruits he had already *stolen* from the Marines, it was a game he won more often than not.

Although New York City born and bred, Eubanks had gone to great pains to hide his citified background. He discovered early on in the dog-eat-dog business of recruiting that a Bronx accent did not play well in most parts of the country, and especially not here in the Midwest. Brandishing his two bottles of ice cold Coke—now dripping enticing beads of moisture—he let loose his first broadside.

"Hey fellas, how's it going?"

Wiping his brow with one of the bottles, he calculated the height of the sun before continuing.

"Whooee! It's hotter'n blazes out here! These two bottles of pop were going to waste in my fridge and I thought you two might be able to put them to better use. And if you've got the time, it's a whole lot cooler in my office. Maybe we could suck down a coke or two and shoot the breeze while you wait your turn. The Marines are a great branch of service—hard chargers every last one of them—but they do stand in line a lot." A quick nod towards the competition's office. "And that line over there doesn't seem to be getting any shorter."

Spider to the fly, Eubanks had chosen his first words carefully. In the Midwest a carbonated beverage was referred to as *pop,* not soda like they called it in the Bronx. And no self-respecting New Yorker would ever spend a single solitary second *shooting the breeze.* Anywhere. Anytime.

"An excellent suggestion," piped up Jack. "Matter of fact, I was just heading your way."

"Thinking about joining the Navy, are you?" Eubanks noted the lad hadn't said "we." The challenge was on.

"Yes, sir, I am."

Salivating now, the eager recruiter extended both palms to shake Jack's hand.

"Glad to hear it! Name's Dan Eubanks, Gunnersmate First Class. And I'm just the man to fix you right up. Only you don't have to call me 'sir.' There ain't no bars on my collar. Unlike most khaki-asses, I work for a living."

Never having heard the time-tested jibe at officers before, both recruits laughed.

"What's your name, son?"

"Jack. Jack Conners."

"Ah, yes. A strong Irish name if ever I heard one." Turning his attention to Lee. "And yours, lad?"

"Lee Kelley."

Raising an appraising eyebrow, Eubanks shook Lee's hand with equal vigor.

"Two Irishmen in the same morning? Must be my lucky day. I'm half Irish myself, on the maternal side of the family tree."

Since Eubanks' mother came from Belgrade and not Dublin, this last bit of information wasn't exactly true. But as two wet-behind-the-ears Ohio boys were about to find out, all was fair in love and the recruiting wars.

"How about you, Lee? Thinking about joining the Navy, too?"

Lee didn't hesitate. Puffing out his chest he craned his neck to five foot six.

"Nope. It's definitely the Marines for me."

"Excellent choice. I'd never bad mouth the Corps because they'd just kick my ass. And I'd probably deserve it. No doubt they'll make a man out of you. Maybe even a hero. And just between you, me, and that lamp post over there... they've got some killer uniforms." A quick wink, and he looked down at his bell-bottoms. "Much better looking than ours, sorry to say."

More laughter from his prey.

"Of course..." continued Eubanks, "life in the Navy is a whole lot easier than the Marines. Gobs safer, too. And we do feed a hell of a lot better. Even the Marines have to admit there's nothing like Navy chow. Sure you don't want to reconsider?"

"Sorry, my mind's made up."

"Ah, well," grinned Eubanks, "I thought it might be. I can tell you're a man who sticks by his guns. Can't blame a guy for trying, though. But the offer still stands. You can drink your *pop* while Jack fills out a few forms. Maybe jaw a spell with me."

Again a New Yorker would never be caught dead *jawing a spell*. Most times he wouldn't give a stranger the time of day.

Now dry-as-a-bone thirsty, Lee found it hard to resist.

"Um... well, maybe. But only for a few minutes. I don't want to miss my turn."

"I promise the moment that line starts to move I'll turn you loose," grinned Eubanks. "As you soon will learn, the Marines wait for nobody."

The Navy, on the other hand, had all the patience in the world.

NINE

WHILE JACK STRUGGLED with paperwork in the Navy office—and Lee drank his Coca Cola—Eubanks decided to shift gears and move on to plan B.

"Tell me, Lee... do you have any special hobbies or pastimes, maybe sports you played in high school?"

"Well... I played a lot of ice hockey as a kid. And I was on our local swim team. Won a few medals even."

Bingo! Just the angle Eubanks was looking for.

"Swimming, you say. What a coincidence! I know you have your heart set on joining the Marines, but the Navy has a special deal they're offering to accomplished swimmers. And I'm here to tell you, since you were on the swim team you more than qualify."

"Special deal?"

Snake oil salesman that he was—like all recruiters had to be—Eubanks knew that although he now had his foot firmly in the door, he had to tread softly.

Easy on the hard sell, he cautioned himself. *Don't get too pushy.*

"I'm sure the Marines would appreciate a guy with your talents, Lee... but for someone who likes the water as much as you do, this offer might be too good to pass up. Ever hear of frogmen? If you're looking for adventure—and a way to WOW the girls back home—it's the only way to go."

"Frogmen?"

"Guys that wear snorkels and fins. They scout out the underwater terrain for amphibious landings, even before the Marines gear up."

"Sounds kinda dangerous. Not that I'm afraid, or anything."

"Not as much as you might think. It's a lot safer than hitting the beaches under fire. Most of a frogman's work is done at night, under the cover of darkness. The Japs may fight like friggin' maniacs, but they can't shoot what they can't see."

"Sounds interesting," Lee had to admit. "But I think I still prefer the Marines. Hitting the beach doesn't scare me none. I just want to kill Japs."

"I'm not one to blow smoke up your butt," said Eubanks, preparing to do just that. "However, it's a well-known fact that what frogmen do is just as vital to the war effort as the Marines. Even the most gung-ho leatherneck has to admit they've already saved hundreds of Marine lives. Maybe thousands."

"That many?" said Lee, intrigued now.

"If you don't believe me you can look it up in the war ledgers. Without the information provided by Navy frogmen a lot more of this country's finest would have perished on some distant tropical beach."

"Geez... I had no idea."

Time to reel the young man in, Eubanks slowly tightened the line.

"Frogmen are a new concept in warfare. A breed apart, they're fast developing their own esprit de corps. So far they've been unsung heroes, but not for long. Their fame is spreading and now is a good time to get in on the ground floor. Be part of history, so to speak."

Unashamed at stringing so many patriotic clichés together in one breath, Eubanks would have hummed The Star Spangled Banner in the background if he thought it would work to his advantage.

"In addition..." he continued, "there are certain perks to being tagged for frogman training while you're going through boot camp."

"Certain perks? Like what?" asked Lee, his resolution wavering a smidgeon.

"Like getting out of all the shit details. No standing midnight watches on a freezing grinder. No cleaning heads. No mess cook duty. Hardly any marching. Frogmen even have their own private galley so there's no waiting in line for chow."

When no further comment was forthcoming from Lee, Eubanks was smart enough to back off and let the stew bubble.

"Look..." he said finally. "I won't kid you. Although it's not half as tough as the Marines, our boot camp is still no stroll in the park. I sure wouldn't want to go through it again. But it's less of a hassle when you're slated to be a frogman. Hell, they even have their own swim team that travels all over the country. Where would you like to spend Christmas? On a sunny beach somewhere in Florida? Or standing garbage can watch in the middle of winter at Great Lakes? With the Hawk blowing in off Lake Michigan, whistling up your pant legs to freeze your butt off?"

Long story short... On a hot humid fall day in Cleveland, Ohio, a depressingly long line—abetted by a resourceful pitch from a determined gunnersmate—torpedoed Lee "Stump" Kelley's dream of becoming a United States Marine. As a consequence both he and Jack Conners would suffer through Navy boot camp together wearing the dreaded *Dixie cups*. Jack however, would suffer the most. Forced to endure the wintery winds blowing off the lake every night, he froze his skinny behind off. And as a non-swimmer designated for submarine school, he had to endure the full range of "shit details" for the duration, cleaning hundreds of backed-up toilets and marching at least a hundred miles.

To make matters worse, upon graduation poor Jack had to travel to the equally chilly shores of Groton, Connecticut to complete his military training. Where he continued to freeze his ass off.

After Great Lakes however, Lucky Lee—unfrozen and well-rested—found himself bound for the sun-drenched shores of southern California.

TEN

NEWLY CHEVRONED WITH his second stripe, Seaman Apprentice Lee Kelley's first big-time train ride turned out to be a real eye opener. And much longer than expected. Two days prior to graduation from boot camp he'd looked up San Diego in the base library at Great Lakes. It was supposed to have been two thousand miles from Chicago—as the crow flies. At least according to the map in the weathered thirty-year-old Atlas. So it shouldn't have taken him two weeks to get there. But it did.

Traveling day and night, roughly calculated that meant his train averaged a tortoise's foot over five miles an hour—a less than exhilarating speed more characteristic of a snail crawl than a crow flying. Halfway through the never-ending journey an increasingly impatient Lee Kelley thought seriously about getting out and walking the rest of the way to California.

"Hell..." he grumbled, "I used to ride my bike faster than this on my paper route back home. And that was uphill, with a full load in my basket."

The trip had begun deep in the bowels of the windy city's Union Train Station. On that last Saturday of December Lee and one hundred and fifty nine other frogman candidates were herded into a string of six reconditioned cattle cars. Although several windows had been cut into the sides, the boarded-over slats were still visible in many places. An over-worked conductor claimed the cars had been thoroughly cleaned, fumigated and disinfected. That the walls were spray painted twice and all the flooring replaced. But two coats of paint and an eighth of an inch of cheap linoleum hadn't been enough. An underlying bouquet of manure would accompany Lee all the way to the West Coast. Sardined into bunks stacked six deep, each night he would hit the rack with the faint aroma of wet hay and bovine excrement tickling his nose.

Add to that the concentrated body odor of dozens of sweaty, snoring sailors and it was easy to see why he spent many sleepless hours flat on his back, listening to the steady click-clack of railroad tracks. For those first few nights everyone in his car was excited about being bound for underwater demolition training—UDT for short. So in the beginning he and his buddies could force themselves to overlook the less than stellar sleeping arrangements. After all, how long could one train ride last? However, pulling off the mainline five times a day to make way for faster freight trains headed east quickly gnawed away at their resolve.

To pass the time during these protracted delays—all of which dragged on for at least an hour—at first Lee kept a running count of the Sherman tanks whizzing by on flatbeds, seemingly only inches from his nose. When his ongoing tally reached a thousand he lost both count and interest. Had he been able to compare the number of tanks heading west, he would have come to the conclusion that the country's industrial might was concentrating first on the war in Europe. And he would have been right. Current scuttlebutt had it that the Allies were planning something big in France—something to kick that asshole Hitler all the way back to Berlin. So it seemed only logical that if an invasion of the mainland was in the works, they'd need all the armor and big guns the United States could muster.

Frogmen? Not so much. Although they would prove essential to the eventual invasion of Normandy, they'd freeze their butts off in the process. Rough seas and frigid temperatures made the English Channel dangerous for even the hardiest of swimmers—a fact not lost on Lee. Having shivered through enough winters to last a lifetime, he thanked his lucky stars he was headed for sunny California, and not dark and dreary England. After enduring Great Lakes in the dead of winter, if he never saw another snowflake it would be too soon.

ELEVEN

AFTER GARY, JOLIET, and Rock Island—three lackluster towns plunked down on an indiscriminate landscape—the rolling terrain of Illinois finally gave way to the flat plains of Iowa. Which in turn gave way to the even flatter plains of Nebraska—and its never-ending horizons of corn, corn, and more corn. With maybe a few sheaves of wheat thrown in for good measure. Des Moines, Omaha, and Lincoln—after the war Lee would be able to say that at least he'd been there. Truth be told however, having slept through all three he couldn't distinguish one from the other.

Two hundred miles into Nebraska the neatly manicured fields seemed to meld into one monotonous blur. One can take just so many waves of grain—no matter how amber they are. If it hadn't been for their ongoing poker games, several dog-eared paperbacks making the rounds, and the tall tales swapped about girlfriends past and present, he and his two new-found friends would have been bored to tears.

A man of few words, Frenchie LaFourche was what old timers south of the Mason-Dixon Line called a tall, dark drink of water. Raised by Cajun parents deep in the confines of Louisiana's Atchafalaya Swamp, his skin approximated the texture and hue of a ten-year-old wallet. As he liked to tell it, his bluish eyes could be traced to a Melungeon great, great, great grandfather who may have shinnied up the family tree a few years after the Civil War. Trained in diapers to gig frogs from a flat-bottomed pirogue, by the time Frenchie reached puberty he'd already mastered the art of knife throwing. When he turned fifteen—the same year he lost his father to Big Jake, the biggest, meanest alligator in the bayou—he could pin a horsefly to the outhouse door at ten paces.

Having lived all his life at an elevation less than ten feet above a swamp, when the train crossed into Colorado Frenchie wasn't sure what he was looking at in the distance. At first he thought they were clouds.

"Jumpin' Jehosaphat! Them's gotta be some giant thunderheads up ahead. From the size of 'em we gonna get ourselves drenched. I guarantee it."

Pronounced *garr-wrong-tea,* his drawl was thick enough to cut with his own sharp knife.

William H. Parsons, Lee's second new friend, shook his head as he let out a deep-throated chuckle.

"Hell... those ain't no clouds, Frenchie. Them's mountains. And damn big'uns from the looks of them. I should know. I lived on one all my life. Though not half that size, I have to admit."

Bill "Hillbilly" Parsons was just that. Having spent all of his eighteen years hunting 'possum in the Yew Range just north of Droop, West Virginia, he was well acquainted with mountains. An easy six foot two he was maybe half an inch shorter than Frenchie, but outweighed him by at least twenty pounds—all of it muscle. Barrel chested with hands the size of ham hocks, Hillbilly's right cross could punch through a brick wall. If you were lucky enough to dodge that thunderous right hand, his lightning quick left jab would buckle your knees.

No one messed with Hillbilly Parsons and his two fists of iron. Or Frenchie La Fourche and his flashing blade.

Tugging at an ear, Lee cocked his head to the right. Then pulled out his trusty pocket Atlas. The only thing his mother had mailed to him at boot camp.

"You just might be right, Hillbilly. According to this map, those are the Rocky Mountains. Says here they're over fifteen thousand feet high."

Scratching his cheek, Hillbilly let out a slow, shrill whistle.

"Fifteen thousand feet? Well. I'll. Be. Damned. If those are what they call mountains in these parts... then I guess I grew up on a piddly-ass hill."

Not entirely convinced, Frenchie glanced down at his watch.

"Mountains, you say? We'll just see about that. It's two o'clock now. So, if they really *are* mountains we should probably make their foothills before dinner. That is, if we don't get pulled over ten times in the process."

But four hours later their train was still chugging along on the flat and level. Apparently in the wild, and wide open west distances were deceiving. Especially to three fledgling sailors who had lived all their lives east of the Mississippi River. By the time they started to climb, their dinner—something resembling cold meat loaf—was a distant rumbling in their bellies, and the sun had long ago dropped below the western horizon. Ten hours later, when it rose again to the east, the train was still climbing, its engine huffing and puffing along at a very pedestrian four miles an hour.

Back and forth, forth and back—when a sign marking the Continental Divide finally appeared in their windows, six reconditioned cattle cars crammed full of sweaty young men let out a collective cheer. And Lee's was the loudest.

"It's about damn time! Maybe now we can pick up some speed."

But if anything, the ride down the mountain took even longer. As any good railroad man knows, on a steep slope a runaway locomotive spells nothing but disaster. So, for a solid day and a half it was first gear all the way and heavy on the brakes. By the time they reached the flatlands of Arizona, every sailor on that train had had their fill of mountains. And that included Hillbilly.

According to Lee's Atlas, from there it was clear sailing to the Pacific coast. They still had to make their way across the Santa Rosa Range, but after the mind-blowing Rockies it would be a walk in the park. Even the ungodly hundred degree temperatures radiating from mile after mile of desert sand couldn't dampen Lee's spirits. The locals called it a *dry heat,* but compared to the oppressive humidity of a Cleveland summer, the weather was almost refreshing. At least it set the stage for that fabled city in the sun called San Diego.

TWELVE

CONDUCTOR HAROLD "CHUBS" McCauley was fast running out of patience. With his job, with his life in general, and especially with this bunch of hayseed sailors. Juvenile delinquents, every last one of them. Thank God this wearisome train ride was finally coming to an end. Ever since September these cross-country trips had been a gigantic pain in his ass. During his fifteen years working for the Northern Pacific Railroad he'd never had a worse stretch of duty. Life on the rails was never easy, but over the past two weeks these clowns had forced Chubs to work his tail off.

If one more pimply-faced kid under a Dixie cup so much as looks at me cross-eyed...

Pulling out his pocket watch he wiped his brow. They were running over six hours late. Par for the course on this damn train.

"Wake up, all you jacktar wannabes! End of the fucking line! Drop your cocks and grab your socks!"

Chubs, too, had been in the service way back when. He, too, had learned the appropriate lingo.

A retired Army sergeant—who'd spent most of World War I bogged down in the ankle-deep mud of the damn trenches surrounding Flanders Field—his current pique was understandable. During *The Big One* he thought anyone who served on a ship was a snot-nosed slacker. A pansy-ass who never came close to a real fight. Still thought so, in fact. Sailors had it too easy. They never had to go *over the top,* charging headlong into a screaming hell called *No Man's Land.* Or have their lungs turned to mush by mustard gas. Or flop face down into the mud when the shells began to fly. Or live butts-to-nuts with wet, hungry rats the size of dogs. Dry, warm bunks every night? Three hot meals a day? Showers anytime they wanted one? All the time being protected by a ship's six inch armor plating? What a bunch of goddamn wimps!

Deep down however, what bothered McCauley most was the fact that he'd never had the good sense to join the Navy himself back in the spring of 1916. If he had, maybe he wouldn't be walking around with a limp today—courtesy of a jagged chunk of the Kaiser's finest shrapnel. And he definitely wouldn't be hacking up phlegm every time he lit up a cigarette. Or hear that infernal ringing in his ears whenever things got real quiet at night.

If wishes were fishes... he muttered to himself as he re-checked his watch.

Thank goodness he wouldn't have to listen to one more fuzz-faced whelp caterwaul about how he missed home, his mommy, or his high school sweetheart. At least until the next go-around. If he wasn't so close to retirement he might have thought about packing it in, telling the Navy to kiss off, and seeking employment elsewhere. With most of the country's able-bodied men heading off to war he'd probably be able to write his own ticket. But despite all the shit he'd been through recently, at heart he was a railroad man and couldn't imagine working a job that didn't involve giant iron wheels. Old dogs, new tricks. That sort of thing.

Chubs wasn't entirely without feelings however. Despite his distaste for anyone wearing bell bottoms, he considered it cruel and unusual punishment to cram so many young kids into these rolling sardine cans—even if they were messy no-account sailors. Talk about a pig sty! It would take him and his crew a full day of back-breaking work to swab out these cattle cars. Pocketing his watch, he reached over to raise the nearest window blind.

"Tracks stop here, fellas," he said, the edge to his voice softening a bit. "Sun's coming up and this is as far as we go. From here on you'll have to walk. Welcome to San Diego."

Heading for the caboose—and his second cup of coffee—he added his standard parting thought. One that he doled out at the end of each trip.

"Watch where you stick your peckers. You ain't in Kansas anymore."

Considering what lay ahead for his passengers, it was passably good advice. Advice he was sure most of them would ignore in the weeks to come. As had the four train loads of sailors before them.

As he was heading through the door Chubs McCauley shook his head. Then let out a sigh.

Should have saved my breath. I might as well have peed into the wind.

THIRTEEN

CRANING HIS NECK to gape at the tall palm tree across the tracks, Lee almost tripped on the last step as he was coming off the train. Leaning his scuffed-up duffel bag against a nearby stanchion, he couldn't believe his eyes. Or any of his other senses for that matter. It was as if he'd landed on a different planet. San Diego's train station didn't look all that different from the one he'd boarded three months ago back in Cleveland. Same tired wood, same black scuff marks on the worn tile floor, same ominous barricade where the train tracks came to an abrupt halt. Even the lone hot dog vendor looked vaguely familiar. But that was where the similarities ended.

Instead of a bone-chilling wind slicing off a brown and always frozen Lake Erie, he was caressed by a balmy breeze wafting across the biggest bay he'd ever seen. Instead of barren, ice-laden oaks—gently swaying palm trees lined the streets. Gone was the never-ending grey cloud depression that seemed to linger over northeastern Ohio six months out of the year. In its place a dazzling sun hung high in an incredibly blue sky. Mid-January, and the flowers were still in full and radiant bloom. Back home this time of year anything hinting of color had long ago hibernated for the winter. Never to be seen or smelled again until a distant spring when his street turned into a river of mud.

April showers brought May flowers, but it also messed up the roads.

"Can you believe this place?" mumbled Lee to no one in particular. "It's as warm as Florida but not half as muggy."

"Has to be close to eighty degrees," offered Hillbilly.

"This time of day down in the Atch' I'd be sweating like a stuck pig," added Frenchie.

"That's because you spend half your time dodging alligators," said Lee. "I could definitely get used to weather like this. Everything looks so green. Even you two jokers."

Said Frenchie, "Before I left for boot camp I looked up San Diego in the parish library almanac. It said they have to buy most of their water from another state. Colorado, maybe. Even had to build a string of canals to get it here from the mountains. Irrigation... I think they call it. Maybe that's why things are in bloom this time of year."

"Payin' for your rain?" Hillbilly clicked his tongue. "If that don't beat all."

Tilting his head back he pointed to a huge patchwork net hanging forty feet above their heads.

"Then again, that thing up there could be the reason we all look a tad green."

Lee used his cap to shield his eyes from the bright sun.

"I heard they were camouflaging cities up and down the west coast—what with California being the closest to Japan. But, damn! That has to be the biggest stretch of fabric I've ever seen. There must be a million square yards worth hanging above us."

After hitching up his pants, Frenchie tugged at his chin.

"And then some. I don't know about you two, but I ain't sure I'm gonna cotton to living under no giant green blanket. Makes me fell kinda claws... tro... You know, cooped up."

"Claustrophobic," said Lee, shouldering his duffel bag.

"Yeah, that's it."

"Better get used to it, Swampman. Because we're stuck here for the next two months. It bothers me too, but I don't think they're gonna take it down anytime soon just because it gives the three of us the willies."

Lee slapped his cap against his thigh. Then put it back on his head.

"That being settled... First thing we have to do is check in at the amphib base. According to our orders it's on some island called Coronado."

"Second thing we do is take a long, hot shower," snorted Hillbilly. "After that damn train ride you guys stink like a pig waller. And I probably smell worse."

Lee took a whiff of his own armpit.

"Phew! You got that right. And after we clean up maybe we should hit the nearest beach to work on our tans. We look like three buckets of white paint. Can't catch us no surfer girls that way."

"Sounds like a workable plan to me," said Hillbilly.

"Agreed," nodded Frenchie.

FOURTEEN

SAN DIEGO—HOME to the largest naval base in the Pacific—was by far the most paranoid settlement in California when it came to the prospect of being attacked by Japan. After the infamy of December Seventh the city launched a frenzy of construction to establish defensive measures up and down its shoreline. If the Japs could bomb Hawaii without warning, they sure as hell could slither across the rest of an undefended ocean to invade southern California.

Although the Navy's carrier fleet at Pearl had escaped destruction, all eight of its Pacific battleships had been knocked out of commission. Two were destined to lie at the bottom of the bay forever. Since San Diego was first and foremost a Navy town—and also the center of what was left of the fleet—it seemed logical that its worried citizenry would consider their fair city a prime target for Japan's advancing minions.

A day after the sneak attack on Pearl San Diego's town council voted unanimously to drape a camouflage net over the Cortez Hotel, the city's tallest building. At first a modest endeavor, the project ended up stretching for miles in either direction. The net eventually covered all of downtown, turning its citizens—and three newly arrived frogmen—a hazy shade of green during the day.

Although the Cortez was considered a valuable historic landmark—and therefore worth protecting—the more productive result of their efforts was to hide the huge Consolidated-Vultec complex located at Lindbergh Field. Working home to over forty thousand employees, the plant produced the B-24 Liberator bomber and the PBY Catalina seaplane, both essential flying machines in the war.

Thanks to hundreds of seamstresses working feverishly around the clock on a gazillion yards of netting, within the short span of two weeks the entire factory was covered in camouflage. An impressive civic achievement for all San Diegans. However, since Consolidated was still within spitting distance of the uncovered warships anchored in the bay, she was probably vulnerable to air attacks for the duration.

While volunteers strung the camouflage the Army carved out a series of gun batteries out on Point Loma, the elevated peninsula that guarded the entrance to San Diego Bay. Pointing ever westward over the Pacific, two sixteen inch battleship-sized cannons were buried into the nosebleed cliffs. Along with two eight-inchers, six six-inchers, and a whole host of lesser caliber anti-aircraft gun emplacements.

When the frantic construction was finally completed the town's politically savvy mayor thumped his chest, stuck out his jaw, and in a flag-waving ceremony proudly proclaimed that "if any Jap warship dares to peek its sorry ass over the horizon it will be blown out of the water faster than a fart blows away in the wind." A dairy farmer from El Cajon with a flair for the dramatic, he'd been elected in a landslide. Despite his foul mouth.

With daily blackouts and strict rationing a wartime way of life, San Diegans were reassured when they looked up from their pristine beaches to see the hills bristling with so much steel. At the end of the war however—four long years later—those same citizens were even more relieved that the feared "yellow threat" had never materialized on this side of the ocean. And that not one of their bristling big guns had to be fired in anger.

Under the comforting shadow of those giant sixteen inchers, during their first two weeks in San Diego Lee, Hillbilly, and Frenchie toiled on the beach from before dawn to well after sunset. After swimming several miles in the choppy bay, hefting heavy logs over his head, and running in the sand until his calves nearly exploded, Lee could barely crawl out of the chilling surf. Battered and bruised that first night, it took his last ounce of strength to flop fully clothed onto his bunk, too tired to take off his water-logged boots.

"Sweet Jesus," he groaned, "I hurt in places I didn't know I had places."

"Sorry," rasped Frenchie, his voice barely above a whisper. "I can't hear a word you're saying. My ears are still clogged full of salt water."

On his rack Hillbilly coughed up a briny loogie. Spat it on the floor. When he tried to sit up his back went into spasms. Giving up he rolled back down to stare at the overhead. But his eyes kept going in and out of focus, so for a few seconds he had to grapple with his bearings.

"Where the hell am I," he sighed. "Am I still alive? I sure as shootin' hope not. 'Cause ain't no way this poor country boy can go through this shit again tomorrow."

"Tomorrow?" moaned Lee. "Oh! My! God! We're all gonna die."

FIFTEEN

WELL BEFORE THE sun even thought about making its appearance, day two broke to more agony for Lee—not quite as painful as day one, but still well within the realm of torture. That morning it took a solid hour to work the kinks out of his aching muscles. Halfway through the first exercise his lungs started to burn again and the cramps had returned. Bent over and gasping for breath, for the third time in less than an hour he found himself wishing he were back home in Ohio, tucked into his nice warm bed. With no visions of cold hard sand dancing through his head. Once again that nagging question of yesterday reared its ugly head.

What the hell am I doing here? I didn't sign up for all this pain and misery.

Day three turned out to be more of the same. But by then at least he was able to get his boots off at night. On a more positive note, by week's end the stitch in his side had subsided to a tolerable level and he was no longer walking with a limp. He even dared to think that with the Lord's blessing—and a smidgeonette of luck—he might even be able to survive the next two months.

"Hell," he said into the mirror, "if Hillbilly and Frenchie can take all this crap, so can I."

That night all three were even able to joke about their aches and pains.

"I've spent so much time in the water my hands are looking like prunes," said Hillbilly, kicking off his boots. "I must be turning into a damn fish."

Scratching his neck, Frenchie sucked air in through his teeth.

"I hear what you're saying, Mountain Man. I think I've sprouted gills."

"They might come in handy if and when we're sent overseas," said Lee.

"Just a matter of time," said Hillbilly. "Scuttlebutt has it the Navy's trying to take back a string of islands in the Pacific. To get our bombers close enough to hit the Japanese mainland. If the rumor's true, South Seas here we come."

"About damn time we took it to those slant eyes," nodded Lee. "I don't care where they send us, as long as it's someplace with warmer water. I don't know about you two yahoos, but I'm getting sick and tired of freezing my ass off in this California surf. I thought San Diego was supposed to be the land of sun and soft sandy beaches. Hell, Lake Erie was better than this."

"You'd think a place with so much sunshine would have warmer water," added Frenchie. "Maybe the ocean currents have something to do with it."

"All I know..." Lee put a palm to his throat. "I've had it up to here with swimming a mile before dawn. And if I have to run that damn obstacle course one more time, I think I'll puke."

"Like you did the first three times, Stump?"

"Up yours, Frenchie. At least I waited until I finished the damn thing. And as long as we're keeping tabs... Someone I know tossed his cookies halfway through the course. At the top of the ladder climb, of all places. That was quite a show you put on up there, Swampman."

"You got me there, little feller. But I only puked once."

"Hell," laughed Hillbilly, adding his two cents worth. "I got both you slackers beat. This ol' country bumpkin didn't puke at all."

"Yeah," grinned Lee, "but that's because you've spent your entire life on a slant. Your stomach is used to climbing. Me and

Frenchie are flatlanders, so it's not a fair comparison. Only thing we ever got to climb was a step ladder."

"At least the course hardened us up real quick like," said Frenchie, flexing a bicep. "I don't think I've ever been in better shape. I guess we all are. Even Stump's got himself a few muscles now. Short and stringy though they may be."

"Gag me with a spoon," said Lee, sticking his finger down his throat. "The big man from Louisiana hacks up another of his hilarious *short* jokes. How about coming up with some new material? At least something original. Good things come in little packages, you know. And quit calling me *Stump*. Besides, when we finally get down to the serious business of killing Japs... you two tall piles of shit are gonna make bigger targets than me. When it comes to the prospects of getting shot, I like my chances a whole lot better."

Although spoken in jest, Lee's jibe had an immediate effect. Especially on himself. And for several seconds the smiles on three faces hung awkwardly in space. None of them was sure which of Lee's off-the-cuff phrases had the more sobering effect. "Killing Japs" or "bigger targets."

It was obvious to anyone with half a brain what their class was being trained to do. Eliminate the enemy by any means possible. Recruiting posters could euphemistically claim that they were being groomed to "make the world safe for democracy" or to "protect America's home shores," but in reality they were being trained to blow something up. Or someone. Not so obvious however, was the other side of that patriotic coin. They were also being trained to avoid *being* killed.

Up until this point none of them had given much thought to the disturbing fact that there was an outside chance that after they finished their training they might not return from overseas. At least in one piece. And given the current successes of the imperial Japanese forces, that chance might not be so *outside*.

Expelling a deep breath through puffed-out cheeks, Frenchie rubbed the back of his neck.

"Nice going, Lee. *Killing and getting shot?* Way to throw a wet blanket on the party."

"Yeah, Stump," agreed Hillbilly. "Talk about dragging a feller down. You sure know how to gloom up the conversation."

Despite the sudden hollow in the pit of his stomach Lee tried to slough off the whole disturbing business with a wave of his hand.

"What's the big deal, guys? Of course there's gonna be some killing involved. What are we supposed to do? Turn the other cheek, walk up to the yellow fuckers and shake their goddamn hands? *That's OK, Mr. Tojo, we forgive you for bombing the hell out of us at Pearl?* Personally I can't wait to stick to the slant-eyed bastards!"

Shocked by the overdose of bravado spewing from his mouth Lee blinked twice. Clopping his mouth shut a puzzled look slid slowly onto his face.

"Whoa..." he said finally. "Where the hell did all THAT come from?"

"Way to go, little man," laughed Frenchie. "I didn't know you had it in you."

"Neither did I."

Despite their forced smiles, the sobering topic still hung heavy over the trio. It was as if a giant vacuum had sucked all the air out of the room. For a few seconds no one knew what to say. The first to regain his voice, Hillbilly scratched his head as he swallowed the lump in his throat.

"Other than a 'possum or two I ain't never taken a life before. Leastwise nothing halfway human. What's more, I don't know if killing another human being is in my nature."

Frenchie flipped opened his switchblade. Tweaked the tip with a thumbnail.

"I'm sure when the bullets start to fly—and your life's on the line—the killing gumption will come to you real quick."

"*You* ever kill anyone with that pig stabber of yours?" asked Lee.

"Can't say that I have. But I bit off an ear or two in bar fights. Fair fights they were, too. And I did slice off some drunk's middle finger when he came at me with a broken beer bottle. Purely a matter of self-defense, it was either him or me. Time comes, we'll all know what to do."

"But how can you be so cock sure of yourself? Ears and fingers don't come close to taking a life."

Lee aimed a thin lipped half-smile in Hillbilly's direction.

Shot a doubtful eyebrow towards the ceiling.

"For that matter, neither does bagging all the 'possums in West Virginia."

Brown stained and always three minutes slow, the heretofore unheard clock on the wall began to tick off time in audible chunks. Swimming in thoughts of his own mortality Lee became mesmerized by the suddenly emphatic time piece. After ten, maybe twenty seconds he had to clear his throat.

"Enough of this depressing crap! Tonight's our first liberty in weeks and we should be concentrating on the task at hand. And that, my two, tall, horny friends is getting our tender young asses laid."

"You got that right," said Frenchie, relieved to be able to laugh again. "Time to chase us up some females. Preferably of the pretty kind."

"But more importantly..." corrected Lee, "of the *willing* kind."

Sporting a devilish grin Hillbilly raised an imaginary glass.

"I'll drink to that!"

SIXTEEN

AND DRINK THEY did. The moment the three frogmen trainees hit the War Zone—San Diego's infamous bar district— they all had beer bottles in their hand. Since none of them had wasted their hard-earned wages on cigarettes they could afford to drink their fill.

For men trained to live in and under the water the ability to hold your breath was vital. And tobacco had an adverse effect on your lung capacity. Therefore most frogmen exchanged their cigarette rations to non-suspecting Marines for money to buy beer. The first time an instructor caught a trace of tobacco on a frogman's breath he was submitted to an unpleasant experience called a G.I. shower. The second time he was shown the door and transferred to the nearest rusty ship. Where he could expect to chip paint for the duration.

With money in their pockets and mischief on their minds, before their first liberty was half over Hillbilly, Stump, and Frenchie were well into their scuppers. They had fallen in and out of love at least once and been in two fights.

The first had been little more than a good-natured wrestling match with three other classmates. A couple of shoves, a torn tunic, and that was about it. After a few slaps on the back they toasted each other with a round of beers and the tussle was promptly forgotten.

However, the *confrontation* with six Marines—a given when squids and jarheads frequent the same bar—was more substantial. Bottles were smashed, punches thrown, lips split, and two noses broken. Since Hillbilly and Frenchie were by far the largest and strongest of the combatants, the Navy held its own despite the lopsided odds. And although Lee was the smallest, in the beginning he gave as good as he got. His experience wielding a hockey stick came in handy, but it was still six against three.

Sensing the tide was turning against them, Frenchie pulled out his big equalizer. Calling forth the most ferocious Cajun grunt he could muster, he snatched his switchblade from his flap pocket and flipped it open with a loud click. Then with a backhand sweep of his arm he hurled it halfway across the room into a dartboard hanging on the far wall. Dead center bulls-eye. When his knife hit that board with a resounding *thunk* hostilities came to an abrupt halt and you could hear a pin drop in that bar.

"Enough of this shit!" growled Frenchie. "I forgot what we're fighting about. And I'm too tuckered out to keep this crap up much longer."

Tossing his head back he ran a hand through his hair as he walked slowly across the room to retrieve his knife. Tugging at his neckerchief he squared his shoulders and sucked a breath in through his nose. Taking his time he raised one eyebrow and snickered up a cavalier grin from the left side of his mouth.

"Besides... all this tomfoolery is cutting into my boozin' time. And isn't that what we're all here for? That and chasin' women?"

Flummoxed by the Navy's sudden change of tactics, the six Marines just stood there. After searching each other's faces for a few seconds, the one wearing corporal stripes bent over to suck wind. When he finally stood up again he too was wearing a grin.

"Now that you mention it, swabee, I'm kinda tuckered myself."

"Next round's on me!" proclaimed Lee.

Three saloons and the entire contents of their wallets later, the three frogmen found three semi-attractive females who were at least halfway *willing*. Frenchie loved blondes, and eventually got to second base with his. Hillbilly had a thing for redheads, but since they were in short supply—probably due to the sun-drenched clime—he had to settle for a curvaceous brunette with almond shaped eyes. More persistent than his knife-wielding buddy, he got thrown out sliding into third.

Lee, however, knocked it out of the park. Never one to quibble about specifics when it came to getting laid, towards the end of the evening he lowered his standards a few notches and ended up rounding the bases with a foul-mouthed, slightly overweight secretary who turned him every which way but loose.

Broke and blissfully oblivious to the ball buster of an obstacle course lurking in their immediate future, around half past one all three downed their last beer at the end of the strip and headed back to the Broadway pier. Singing "Anchors Away" at the top of their lungs—in a key never before endured by the human ear—arm in arm they boarded the last ferry back to Coronado.

Their final chorus could be heard all the way to Tijuana.

SEVENTEEN

THE MORNING AFTER the night before, Hillbilly awoke with the mother of all hangovers. When one drinks five double shots of whiskey then chugs over a dozen beers in the short span of two hours one can pretty much expect to be saddled with a pounding headache. Along with a queasy stomach, bird cage mouth, and double vision. All topped off by a couple of pink elephants waltzing across the ceiling wearing purple tutus.

Staggering out of the third bar on Broadway he'd had trouble remembering his name, much less what he was drinking at the time. Mainly because he'd been challenged to try something called a *Skip and Go Naked.* Over the lips, under the gums, look out stomach, here she comes—consisting of three kinds of mind-numbing rum separated by thin layers of powdered sugar, the drink was aptly named. After downing the potent combination Hillbilly stripped to his shorts on the nearest table and began to sing the Battle Hymn of the Republic to the appreciative cheers of a well-soused crowd. His Sally Rand imitation got him promptly tossed out the front door by two burly bouncers.

But as bad as Hillbilly was feeling that morning, Lee felt ten times worse. The only one to hit a homer that first liberty, come the painful first crack of dawn he was dead to the world. When those first raw notes of reveille sounded, what was left of his brains was splattered across the barracks wall. His teeth throbbed in cadence to his pounding heart and his mouth tasted like he'd been sucking on a sweaty sock all night. Even his hair hurt. When he tried to move it felt like someone had tied an anvil to his testicles. His eyes a fuzzy shade of red, when he was finally able to force them open they refused to focus on anything farther away than a foot. Dog-ass tired, it took the concerted effort of his two large muscular friends to pry him out of his rack.

"Come on, Lee," pleaded Hillbilly, still half in the bag himself. "Get your sorry ass out of that bunk. We're already late and they're gonna put us on report if we don't make muster."

"Go away," groaned Lee. "Let me die in peace. I think I'm gonna be sick again."

Misery loving company, Hillbilly had to laugh. But when he did his skull almost exploded.

"Oh, my aching head," he moaned. "I think I just popped an eyeball."

"What a pair of cream puffs," smirked Frenchie, no worse for the wear. Although he'd had just as much to drink, he was stone cold sober. A moonshine drinker since puberty, his ability to hold his liquor was already the stuff of legends. And the pride of the barracks.

"Well, hell... My little sister could drink you two lightweights under the table. And she's only twelve years old. Those who play gotta pay the Piper my friends."

Casting a nervous eye towards the nearest wastebasket Lee cradled his head in both hands.

"Jesus... I feel like I've been flattened by a steam roller. I swear to God—and anyone else who might be listening—I'll never drink again."

That bleary-eyed statement had been mumbled by hungover sailors since the beginning of time. Vowed by many, it would be kept by none. Including one sick-as-a-dog seaman apprentice named Lee "Stump" Kelley.

"Hillbilly's right about not making muster, Stump," continued Frenchie. "And it'll be damned nigh impossible to tap Miss Thunder Thighs again if you get your horny butt restricted to base."

"I'm not sure he'd want to," said Hillbilly. "Even if he sobers up."

"Hey..." mumbled Lee. "She wasn't that bad."

"Says you. Did you get a good gander at that face of hers? My watch stopped the minute she walked into the room. And those pock marks? They probably came from being touched with ten foot poles."

"That, or she plays goalie for a dart team," added Frenchie.

"Have a little respect for my secretary friend. She may not have been much to look at but she was great in bed. I think. After we left the bar together I can't remember much of anything."

Lee lurched for the basket and made it just in time.

"Besides..." he managed from the bottom of the barrel, "the worst sex I ever had was marvelous. And come to think of it, Hillbilly... you're one to talk. Your so-called lady was no great shakes either."

"At least mine couldn't out cuss me."

"Easy, fellas," said Frenchie, "you can't put the toothpaste back in the tube. Forget about last night. That ship has sailed. You'd better focus on how you're going to make it through the morning. Lee? You're as pale as a sheet. And you don't look much better, Hillbilly. If I were a betting man I'd lay odds neither of you survive the obstacle course."

EIGHTEEN

BUT SURVIVE, HILLBILLY did. If barely. In the middle of the course he got his right boot tangled in the rope ladder, causing him to flounder upside down for a full minute. Shouting and waving his arms around he looked like a drunken orangutan. Rallying finally, he managed to extricate himself from the ladder's clutches—and stagger across the finish line in his worst time ever.

Lee, however, wasn't so lucky. Green to the gills and sweating buckets in the heartless sunshine, he found himself reeling back and forth at the starting line. Sticking out like a sore thumb—and with no place to hide—he knew he was going to get reamed a new one.

"What the hell's wrong with you, Kelley?" snarled the drill instructor.

Throwing back his shoulders Lee made a feeble attempt to snap to attention. Big mistake, he had to close his eyes. With pin points of light shooting across the inside of his eyelids he got dizzy again and had to glom onto the guy next to him for support.

"Nothing, Chief!" he yelled. Even bigger mistake, the sound of his loud voice elevated the pain between his ears to *seeing Jesus* levels. "Uh... maybe I got a touch of the flu," he added, whispering now.

"Flu, my ass! You're still fucking drunk!"

"My stomach's just a little bit upset, that's all. I'm sure I can handle—"

But that was all Lee could manage. Beginning at his toes and rolling upward through his torso and into his throat, a rumbling heave deposited the remnants of last night's dinner in the sand. And onto the chief's spit-polished left boot. Been there, done that, the chief fought off a knowing grin.

"Oh no you don't, dickwad! You're not going to mess up my nice clean beach with your buzzard barf! Haul your sorry ass back to the barracks! And if it takes more than five hours to get your balls back in place I'll put your worthless hide on report! *Do I make myself clear?*"

"Yes, sir," nodded Lee as he staggered off in the vague direction of his bunk. He ended up puking his guts out in the barracks but at least he didn't die that day. Even though he wanted to at times. Bottom line, the following weekend he got the chance to hook up with his foul-mouthed secretary again.

Lucky him.

NINETEEN

AFTER THAT FIRST disastrous liberty things fell into an easier routine for the three friends. With the passage of each day the rigors of training became less and less painful. Either the drill instructors decided to show mercy and backed off, or, more likely, Lee, Hillbilly, and Frenchie toughened up. After two weeks the obstacle course didn't seem so daunting and the daily surf swims so long. Even the water didn't feel so cold. And in the female department—after three weeks of merely stepping up to the plate—Hillbilly and Frenchie began to challenge Lee for the batting title.

Near the end of training Frenchie was designated an underwater demolition technician. Largely because of his steady hands and expertise with a knife. Loosely translated he was a guy with fins and a snorkel whose specialty was exploding things on and under the water.

Lee and Hillbilly in turn were classified as underwater equipment specialists—swimmers who handled the various paraphernalia required to blow those same things up. In other words they were aquatic *go-fers,* equally important but not quite as glamorous as UDTs.

After a quick graduation ceremony—and the requisite round of picture taking—the three packed their duffel bags, said farewell to San Diego's sunny shores and boarded a crowded transport ship bound for Hawaii. But not before one last raucous night on the town to toast the beautiful and willing women of southern California. Of which there had been many.

A month into their training Lee had tired of his secretary's potty mouth and he moved on to calmer pastures. After two weeks of hit-and-miss propositions he settled on a diminutive third-grade teacher from National City who possessed a quick wit and more refined vocabulary. Not as vigorous in bed as the secretary, at least she was someone he could talk to.

During their final weeks Hillbilly finally struck pay dirt and corralled his dream girl. Even though her raspberry tresses probably came from a bottle.

As their boat was pulling out of the harbor the schoolteacher, the redhead, and Frenchie's current blonde were all on the pier waving their tearful goodbyes.

TWENTY

A RUST BUCKET that may have seen duty in the Spanish American War, their transport was the largest conglomeration of nuts and bolts Frenchie had ever seen. Stretching from one end of the pier to the other, its monstrous smoke stack towered a hundred feet over his head. Craning his neck he couldn't see the top.

"That thing makes my daddy's rowboat look like a toothpick."

"Let's hope she rides better than a toothpick," said Lee. "'Cause I can tell from her lines that tub ain't no speed queen. It's gonna take us forever to reach Hawaii. Probably even longer than that damn train ride."

Reconfigured twice and currently classified as an APA, thankfully the *USS Deliverance* did prove to be more seaworthy than a toothpick. But not by much. With bunks piled eight deep in the hold, its accommodations were considerably less than first class. To make matters worse every nook and cranny was stacked with provisions so there was hardly any room to breathe. Every time Lee turned around he was bumping into cans of this, boxes of that. With so many people crammed on board, apparently the Navy couldn't chance running out of food.

It took a while for the three west bound sailors to adjust to the constantly pitching decks. It seemed as if their innards were always sloshing from one hip to the other. But after that first sleepless night they were finally able to catch a few winks.

"Thank God we got our sea legs back in San Diego," said Hillbilly. "Although I sure do wish this here big boat would settle down a bit."

On the positive side, the ship's rolling motion did provide the trio with their main source of amusement during the early stages of the cruise. After that first evening meal—when the *Deliverance* finally cleared the break wall and got down to some serious rocking and rolling—Lee and his buddies strolled back to the fantail coffee cups in hand to watch the show.

A company of Marines talked a big game when they swaggered on board earlier in the day. The moment they hit the gangplank they were flapping their gums about how much tougher they were than Navy *pukes*. As the hours passed their insults got longer, more colorful, and less printable. "Fucking pansies," "limp-dick assholes."

Halfway through dinner however—after the seas had kicked up nicely—the worm turned and those very same Marines began to sing a different tune. For most it took a single bite of the greasy, undercooked ham the Navy cooks had so thoughtfully prepared. For others it was the smell of grilled onions wafting through the mess decks. First by one's and two's—and then by six's and seven's—almost the entire company ended up on the fantail to hang over the railing. Sick as dogs, they all began to belt out the gut-wrenching gospel from the book of *Ralph*. And feed the fishes with that small portion of dinner they'd been able to get down.

Their sudden change in attitude came as no surprise to the revenge-minded cooks on board—who, like all sailors everywhere, had taken offense to being called *pukes*. A well-known fact to stewburners on every ship in the US Navy, the aroma of sizzling grease was a surefire way to upset the constitution of any seasick Marine. No matter how tough he thought he was.

For several days Lee, Hillbilly, and Frenchie took great pride in grading the Marines' expulsive efforts. In the beginning a few nauseated jarheads gave it the old heave ho, but toward the end most could only dribble their half-digested meals down the side of the ship.

"Not much on distance," said Lee. "But I'll give the skinny one on the end a B-plus for volume. I didn't know the human stomach could hold that much slop."

Watching the action with a grimace on his face Frenchie pinched off his nose. Tilting his head to one side he hissed a lungful of air in through his teeth.

"I'm afraid I'll have to knock him down on artistic content, though. Too many greens in the mix—it looks like he's been grazing in a cow pasture."

When the depleted Marine turned and started to shuffle back to his sleeping compartment, Hillbilly hit him with a departing catcall.

"Who's a *puke* now, Mr. Tough Guy?"

By the end of the week most of the Marines had learned to subsist on a diet of crackers and water. Or not eat at all. With little amusement left on the fantail Lee and his buddies decided to take a stroll through the Marine quarters. Eating raw sardines from a can.

"These things are mighty tasty," said Hillbilly, biting off an oily fish head. "But they sure are slimy."

Frenchie held up one to let the oil drip between his knuckles.

"Yeah... and this damn fish juice gets all over everything."

"And then there IS that fishy smell," said Lee, holding up the largest sardine he could find. "But once you get past the stink they ain't half bad. Any of you jarheads care for a bite?"

That cleared the compartment in no time flat. And for the rest of the voyage every Marine onboard gave the three frogmen a wide berth.

TWENTY-ONE

TRANSIT TIME TO Hawaii was officially recorded as twenty-one days, five hours and twenty two minutes. Bucking strong easterly headwinds and loaded down to the gunnels, the *Deliverance* didn't set any speed records on the passage. The two tons of barnacles attached to her hull below the waterline didn't help. Much to the dismay of every Marine onboard, the ship arrived a day late. In the end it cost the Navy roughly two hundred and sixty thousand gallons of fuel to get its passengers across the ocean. And over twenty thousand half-eaten meals. When he first sighted land Hillbilly let out with a *West-by-God-Virginny* whoop.

"Whooee! Honolulu here we come! Sun, surf, and Waikiki Beach! Warm water at last. No more freezing our nuts off."

"Don't forget all those wahinis waiting for us," added Frenchie.

"I hate to rain on your parade, guys," said Lee. "But this bucket of rusting bolts ain't taking us anywhere near Honolulu."

"Whaddya mean?" frowned Hillbilly. "My orders specifically state *Hawaii*. Yours, too."

"Yeah, but Honolulu is on the island of Oahu. We're headed for the naval base at Hilo. And Hilo's on Hawaii, the big island to the southeast. At least two hundred nautical and very unswimmable miles from Honolulu."

"You mean there's more than one Hawaiian Island?"

"Seven, to be exact. But don't worry, the water will be warm. And I'm sure we can scrounge up more than a few *wahinis.*"

"Damn! I was looking forward to surfing the North Shore."

"Easy, big fella. Just because you managed to survive a boogie board in San Diego doesn't mean you can run with the big boys in Hawaii. Those thirty foot waves would eat you alive. But if you've got your heart set on wiping out at Waimea Bay I'm sure we can hop a shuttle flight when we're on leave."

But for the next month at least, none of the three would have the chance to even think about taking leave. Their training at Hilo may not have been as physically demanding as San Diego—after all they were no longer shave-tail recruits—but it was twice as intense. And ten times more demanding.

Whereas San Diego had been aimed at getting them physically ready for what lay ahead, Hilo's sole purpose was to make them smarter. And that meant a whole range of boats, boats, and more boats. Of various shapes and sizes. At one end was the small inflatable—a frogman's version of the jeep. At the other, larger end were the minesweepers and destroyers. And somewhere in between was the ubiquitous and all-important LCVP.

A Landing Craft Vehicular and Personnel was a flat-bottomed, rectangular plywood box covered with a thin layer of sheet metal. Originally designed to navigate the swamps and marshlands of southeastern America, in rough seas the gangly device bobbed up and down like a hyperactive cork. Despite its skittish nature over twenty thousand of the capricious vehicles were built during the war. Short on lines but long on both adaptability and especially durability, the LCVP—or Higgins boat as she came to be known—would see duty on the French beaches of Normandy, the Italian shores of Anzio, and all over the Pacific. Or wherever the top brass thought about making an amphibious landing. By the time Japan surrendered, the craft's workhorse contributions had proved so vital that Eisenhower himself lauded its designer, Andrew Higgins, as "the man who won the war for us."

Mindless of such accolades, for the next month Lee,

Hillbilly, and Frenchie were destined to spend countless hours being ferried about in one of Mr. Higgins's ill-riding creations. Whether they liked it or not.

TWENTY-TWO

MASTER CHIEF MICHAEL P. Hargrove had racked up nearly thirty years in the Navy, most of it at sea. Figuring he'd infused enough salt water into his veins, in late November of 1941 he decided to submit his retirement papers. It was a dreaded process for any died-in-the-wool lifer, but he'd spent too many years away from his family and was reluctant to subject them to another deployment. For almost three decades the Navy had been the only life Hargrove had ever known. Or ever wanted to know. And although he tried to hide his ingrained fear of never wearing the uniform again, deep down the prospect of becoming a nine-to-five civilian scared the living bejesus out of him.

Because of that fear, when the Japs attacked Pearl Harbor he didn't hesitate to re-enlist for one more go-around. Never one to shirk his duty he pigeon-holed his plans to buy a rocking chair, kissed his long-suffering wife goodbye once more—and hopefully for the last time—made ready to set to sea again. A crackerjack gunnersmate with hash marks up past his elbow, he was itching to get at least one Zero in his cross hairs before hanging it up.

Due to his advanced years however—and the fact that his eyesight wasn't what it once was—the Navy in its infinite wisdom decided he would be more productive as an instructor than behind the trigger of a forty millimeter. At first Mike wasn't too pleased with his assignment—"Hell, I'm twice the man I used to be!"—but after a few beers and the requisite amount of grumbling—dutiful sailor that he was—he snapped off a salute, said "Aye, aye," and got down to the tricky business of putting newly designated frogmen through their paces.

This would be his third class pushing *pollywogs* through the wringer and he was getting better at it. No longer recruit poster material, Hargrove's hairline had receded two inches beneath his crumpled chief's hat. Farther south he sported a King Neptune beer belly that had begun to sag over his belt buckle. Dunlop's Disease, old-timers called it. Criss-crossed with cavernous wrinkles, his leathery face approximated the texture of a ten year old catcher's mitt. With about the same shape. Mike looked every one of his forty-seven years, and then some. But woe be unto anyone who dared call the chief *old*. Officers and enlisted alike.

A fierce competitive fire still burned in Mike's gut and any recruit foolhardy enough to challenge his authority—or question his girth—was laid low by a single withering glance. Like a fiery broadside from a veteran battlewagon, Hargrove's evil eye could shrivel the scrotum of every sailor within a two block radius. Lee therefore took seriously the warning he received from one of Mike's outgoing class.

"Chief Hargrove is fair, but he's hard as nails. Whatever you do, don't look the son of a bitch square in the eye. He'll turn you to stone in a heartbeat."

Waiting for the chief to speak, Lee had his eyes locked straight ahead, his shoulders back, his jaws clamped tight. And of course he was all ears as The Man approached.

By now Hargrove had his routine down pat. First came the deliberate stroll as he gave his new charges a quick once over. Turning his back on the class he slowly looked to the heavens. Shaking his head he puffed out his chest. Hitched up his pants.

"Why me, Lord?" he muttered. Loud enough to be heard in the back row. "Is it too much to ask to send me some *real* sailors?"

Five seconds passed. Quickly turned into ten. Then twenty. A practiced scowl on his face the chief finally turned around.

Pursing his lips he stepped off into an even slower stroll to "stink-eye" anyone he thought had potential.

The three on the end of the first row caught his attention. A pipsqueak flanked by two tall timbers. The big guys had a look about them that said they could handle themselves in a tight situation. Given time they might even be worth his effort. At least they seemed to be in shape. From the size of their biceps they could probably take anything he could dish out. In and out of the water.

But it was the little guy who really stuck out. He had that special glint in his eye more common to Marines than sailors. He also had that certain chip on his shoulder—the one that said not only could he take it but he could also dish some back. That meant *short stuff* bore close watching. Gobs of potential there, but on the flip side he could also be tons of trouble.

TWENTY-THREE

"GENTLEMEN," HARGROVE SAID at last. "And I use that term loosely. The boat you see floating so peacefully before you is what the Navy calls an LCVP. She's a landing craft used to transport small vehicles and personnel. But I prefer to call her by her maiden name, a Higgins boat. During the next three weeks you will get to know every nut, every bolt, every inch of tin and timber on her thirty-six foot frame. She may not be much to look at—and she does tend to pitch about in rough seas—but she'll get you to where you want to go under any and all kinds of conditions. Hopefully in one piece."

Letting those tidbits sink in, he took a sip of coffee from perhaps the dirtiest cup in the Hawaiian Islands. Black and thick as mud—just the way he liked it—the hot liquid burned all the way down. Just enough to kick start this morning's lecture.

"Despite her good looks some of you will come to love her. Others will hate her guts. The choice is up to you. The one thing you *all* will do—and the one thing I demand above all—is that you respect her with a capital R. Come hell *and* high water. That is if you want to come back from overseas with all your appendages attached. And that includes your pecker.

"Since her bottom is as flat as your momma's kitchen table

she has only a three foot draft. That enables her to operate in shallow water. Eighteen inches if push comes to shove, and her skipper doesn't mind scraping bottom. Fully loaded at high tide she can haul six thousand pounds of cargo to and from the beach. Personnel-wise that equates to thirty-six seasick Marines complete with rifles and full battle gear. If you pack them in like cord wood—which the Navy has a tendency to do."

After draining the last of his coffee the Chief wiped the cup out with an oily rag. Taking his time—the class wasn't going anywhere—he secured the cup to a loop in his dungaree work pants. Eying the threesome on the end he retrieved a soiled pack of Chesterfields from the front pocket of his blue work shirt and shook out a cigarette. Last one, he crushed the pack then wedged it into his empty cup. Taking more time to light up, for good measure he cast another stink eye in short stuff's direction. The little guy seemed to be standing taller. Napoleon complex? Maybe.

"A bit of fatherly advice," continued Hargrove. "If you ever have to hitch a ride with thirty-six seasick Marines in one of these things make sure you're in the last row. It's been my experience that ninety-nine times out of a hundred, jarheads never come close to getting their sea legs. And when ol' Henrietta here gets to rocking and rolling they tend to puke their guts out. All over the poor dumb schnook in front of them. Take my word for it. You don't want to be that poor dumb schnook. In addition, when that ramp goes down and the bullets start to fly it's much better for your health if you're as far aft as you can be."

The chief took off his cap. Wiped the back of his neck with that dirty rag.

"Which brings me to why you limp-dicks are standing in front of me today. I'm about to let you in on a nasty little secret. You didn't hear it from me, but last November the Navy made a humongous blunder on Tarawa. No one upstairs will cop to it officially, but it was what the top brass call a *tactical miscalculation.* I prefer to call it a major fuck up. One that cost a bunch of lives. Simply put, the whole damn operation was a major disaster from the git-go. Due to a lack of proper planning a line of LCVPs deposited a company of Marines in water ten feet deep."

Hargrove cleared his throat. Spat on the pier. Waiting for the other shoe to drop the class held its collective breath.

"Loaded down with all that gear over half of the poor dumb bastards didn't even make it to the beach. And most of those who didn't drown were picked off by Jap snipers as they floundered in the surf. Some said hidden coral formations prevented the boats from reaching shore. Others blamed it on the strong currents, or lack of proper maps. When the finger pointing finally stopped, Admiral Turner blew his top and issued an edict that henceforth no landings would be made without adequate underwater charting. And that's where you jaspers come in."

TWENTY-FOUR

AFTER BLOWING A perfect smoke ring Hargrove took the time to watch it twist away in the breeze. And let the tension build.

"Henrietta here packs a 225 horsepower diesel engine in her bowels. When empty, which is most of the time you will be riding her, she can motor along at a steady twelve knots. Nine knots fully loaded and headed for shore. Normally she's manned by a three man crew. One to drive the boat and two to operate the thirty caliber machine guns mounted on her railings. She has a reversed curve area mid-ship with two flat-planed sections flanking a tunnel on her bottom that protects her propeller. This enables her to retract from the beach after discharging cargo."

With a long final drag Hargrove finished his cigarette. Flipping it to the pier he ground the butt out with his boot. Narrowing his eyes to slits, he looked left, then slowly right.

"Any questions?" he growled.

Smart enough to realize that at this point dead silence was called for, the class kept their mouths shut. Except for one dim bulb in the second row.

Hiram Smithisler—the second son of a South Georgia peanut farmer—never made it past the sixth grade. Smart, he was not. Book 'larnin' or otherwise. His ability to hold his breath underwater overruled his tendency to ask stupid questions. And the fact that he couldn't read or write.

"Hate to bother you, sir... But I'm a teeny bit confused."

Hargrove read the man's nametag.

"I'm a chief, Smithisler. Not a damn officer." Puffing out his cheeks he cast his second *Why me, Lord?* look of the day skyward. "OK, rook, what's your question?"

"Um, I was just thinking..."

Dangerous proposition, thought Hargrove.

"... all those big boats we'll be riding out at sea..."

"Ships! We call them ships in this man's navy."

"Sorry. Ships. Anyhowsomever, I hear tell we'll be steaming over some pretty deep spots. More than a mile deep in places."

"So?"

"Well... It seems to me that when you have to drop anchor way out there it's gonna take a lot of chain to hit bottom. It's gotta be a *fur piece* down."

Hargrove's mouth sagged. His eyes blinked.

"Where are you going with this, Smithisler? I haven't got all day."

"It also seems to me most ships won't have enough room to store all that anchor chain."

Turning his back on the class once more, Hargrove struggled to keep from laughing. His gut reaction was to chew Smithisler out for being so damn dumb. But that would have been too easy.

"Glad you asked that question, seaman," he said with the straightest face he could manage. "Whenever the Navy sends one of its ships over one of those *deep spots* as you call them, its captain puts in a requisition for a special barge to store all the extra chain. If it's a real big ship, and they're gonna cross over a really deep spot he might ask for two barges."

A few snickers and a lot of grins from the rest of the class. Smithisler's eyes filled with wide-eyed innocence.

"Really?"

"Of course not, you idiot! No one drops anchor in the middle of the fucking ocean!"

At least Smithisler was refreshing. And his off-the-wall question would make for a round of laughs down at the chief's club.

"Anyone else got a bee in their bonnet?"

"No, sir!" from the entire class. Including one red-faced seaman recruit.

"Out-fucking-standing! Maybe there's hope for you dickwads after all. If there's no more stupid questions, this lecture's over. Now let's get to work."

TWENTY-FIVE

IN THE WEEKS to come Lee got to know *Henrietta* inside and out. Having no choice in the matter he became familiar with her most intimate details, her personality, her every quirk. What she could do and what she couldn't do.

He learned how to drive her and fire the thirty caliber machine guns. He learned how to dislodge her from a hidden sand bar in shallow water in case her driver fell asleep at the wheel. He learned how to "kick" start her balky gears when her ramp refused to drop. How to goose an over-heated engine back to life. How to jury rig a jammed rudder. How to patch sheet metal if her hull got ripped open by an underwater obstruction.

Most importantly, he became adept at jumping on and off her decks from every angle imaginable. In all kinds of weather, at any speed. Loaded down with all kinds of gear. Day or night.

Exhausted from his first night exercise on Henrietta, Lee tossed his salt-encrusted gear into the nearest corner. After following suit Hillbilly knocked his flashlight against the palm of his hand. Shook it twice.

"Damn! Don't these things ever work?"

"Only when you don't need them," replied Lee. "Like most things in this navy. Mine went on the fritz, too."

"Good thing there was a full moon out tonight or I wouldn't have been able to see my hand in front of my face."

"It wasn't the moon, Hillbilly. It's what they call surf luminescence. Something to do with tiny phosphorescent critters in the water."

"You been sneaking off to the library again, Stump?"

"Don't knock it. You could stand to hit the books now and then." Lee shot Frenchie a raised eyebrow. "You, too, Swampman."

"I swear on my pappy's grave," grumbled Frenchie, "if and when I make it back to the states I'm gonna scuttle every Higgins boat I run across. So help me, God."

"Sounds like a plan to me," nodded Lee. "I'll be Sancho Panza to your Don Quixote."

"Don who?"

"Old Spanish guy. Tilted at windmills."

"Well, if you're so damn smart, Lee... what was all that growling and groaning I kept hearing underwater? You never hear that kind of ruckus during the day."

"That was probably the ocean floor reacting to the tides. With maybe a few mating calls thrown in for good measure."

"Ah... fish fucking. That explains it."

"I thought it was kind of peaceful. As if the sea was singing me a lullaby."

"Lullaby my ass!" snorted Hillbilly. "Whatever it was it gave me the creeps. If I never go night diving again it'll be too soon."

"Nothing to be afraid of, big guy," said Lee. "And you'd better get used to it. From what I hear most of our diving is going to be at night. I have to admit though, I nearly shit my drawers when that tail fin swam out of sight."

"Tail fin?"

"It happened about fifteen feet down. Just before my light went out I caught a glimpse of this huge fin in the distance. And from what I could see before everything went black, that fin was attached to one big fish. Had to be a shark. Maybe a ten-footer. Probably sniffing my backside, deciding if it wanted to take a bite out of me."

Hillbilly shook his head as he sucked wind.

"Damnation! Ain't that a shit and a half?"

"I'm here to tell you I almost did. Good thing for me that shark didn't like what he was smelling."

Frenchie broke out a crooked grin.

"Sucker probably thought you weren't worth the effort, Stump. Half a mouthful of mostly gristle? Why bother?"

"Yeah, right, Frenchie. As if you're not full of hot air. You're just lucky I didn't ring the dinner bell in your direction. I'm sure Mr. Mouth-full-of-teeth would have appreciated some down home Cajun cooking."

A worried look sliding onto his face, Hillbilly rubbed his chin.

"Suppose he came back, Lee. What would you have done then?"

"That's a no-brainer," said Lee, stifling a chuckle. "I'd have calmly pulled out my knife and cut you on the leg. Then swum like hell when you started to bleed."

"No, seriously."

"You mean after I messed my pants again? Well... according to what I read in a book, a shark has no real brain, just two ganglia on either side of its snout. They also have no skulls. So they're vulnerable to shocks of any kind. If you rap them on the nose hard enough they'll get disoriented and swim away. Theoretically."

"Theoretically?"

"I haven't had the misfortune to test the theory out yet. Nor do I ever want to."

From his rack Frenchie let out a slow whistle.

"Sharks, barracudas, moray eels, poisonous jelly fish... they all can do the evil deed on you."

"Yeah," nodded Lee, "but at least you can see those guys coming. The critter that really scares the daylight out of me is the stonefish. More than any shark anyway."

"Stonefish can't be more dangerous than a great white."

"Moreso. They say the venom packed into the spines on a stonefish is the most powerful on earth. What's worse is that the ugly suckers bury themselves in the sand. Can't even see them until it's too late. Weren't you listening during the chief's last lecture? *Step on the son of a bitch and he'll make the last ten seconds of your life very unpleasant.* Even if rescuers are able to drag your choking ass to the surface you're destined for a toe tag."

"Holy shit! I'll never fall asleep in class again."

And true to his word, for the next twenty-six days Frenchie took great pains to be wide awake and bushy-tailed whenever the chief opened his mouth. And every time he went diving he kept at least one eye peeled for the dreaded, all-powerful stonefish.

When the frogmen finished their Hawaiian training the Navy split the class right down the middle. The first half received orders to the Pacific Ocean Area Fleet commanded by Admiral Chester Nimitz. Stump, Frenchie. Hillbilly—and seventy-seven others—were attached to the amphibious support group under the direction of General Douglas MacArthur.

Now part of "Mac's Navy" the trio boarded their second troop transport in as many months. Their new destination: Milne Bay in New Guinea. Soon they would be involved in helping a corn-cob-pipe-smoking general fill his historic promise of "I shall return."

TWENTY-SIX

HAVING READ UP on the Philippines, Lee had braced himself for the heat and humidity. But this was ridiculous, beyond anything he could have prepared himself for. Ten steps onto the pier his jersey was already sopping wet and sweat was dripping off his nose like a leaky faucet. The air was so muggy, every time he took a breath it felt as if he were sucking down a wad of warm, wet cotton. He wasn't breathing so much as swallowing. And for those first few seconds he thought he would gag. Glancing up at the scorching sun he let his duffel bag slide off his shoulder. In the stifling heat the damn thing weighed a ton. Wiping his brow he took off his water-logged Dixie cup to wring it out.

"Jesus H. Christ!" he said with a shake of his head, "We've landed in a goddamn furnace. Hell couldn't be much hotter than this."

Scanning the pier for the nearest shade, Frenchie added his own lamentation.

"Hellsfire! And I thought Louisiana was bad. This place is worse than the damn swamp in August. I'm drowning in my own sweat."

"I'm melting, I'm melting," laughed Lee, trying to make the best of it. "And we're nowhere near Oz."

"Shit, Stump, there's not enough of you to make a decent puddle." Shading his eyes Frenchie nodded towards the Quonset hut at the end of the pier. "I don't know about you and Hillbilly... but this tin man is gonna haul his French-fried butt out of the damn sun."

And the three promptly hauled ass down the pier, panting all the way. Unfortunately, the hut turned out to be even hotter. No relief to be found inside, its curved metal sheeting acted like a king-sized oven. Piled high with hundreds of large canvas mail bags the wooden floor radiated heat, par-boiling Lee the second he stepped through the door. Hillbilly was so shocked by the sudden blast of hot air he let out a gasp. It was as if they'd staggered into Hell on earth.

"You'll get used to the heat, fellers," said the hut's only inhabitant, a shirtless sailor in frayed khaki shorts. Clearly the local mailman, he sported a burnt sienna tan and a shaved head—obvious necessities in the hot climate. His right hand propelled a large black fan back and forth in front of his face without stopping.

"Name's Burt. Welcome to Milne Bay, vacation paradise of the civilized world."

Lee peaked a dubious eyebrow.

"You call this inferno *civilized?*"

"Don't knock it. It's a damn sight better than most places you froggies are headed for. As I said, you get used to it after a while. In a week or two it'll almost seem livable. Emphasis on the *almost.*"

"How'd you know we were frogmen?'

"The flippers attached to your bags are a dead giveaway. I didn't mean no disrespect. Better you than me I say, I sure couldn't do what you guys do. Hell, I can barely swim."

Burt swatted away a gigantic flying insect trying to land on his filthy, sweat-encrusted cap. It flapped for a few seconds then fluttered to the floor at Lee's feet.

"What the hell is that thing?" he cried.

"Aw, that's only a harmless water beetle. It's mating season and they're everywhere this time of year. Trying to screw anything that moves. Including my damn cap."

Lee raised his boot to squash the critter but it skittered away.

Making a rustling racket as it went.

"Don't step on him!" cautioned Burt. "It'll only make him mad."

"Cripes... are they all that big?"

"Nah, that's just a baby. His daddy's twice that size. Poppa usually comes around after evening chow to beg for scraps. I call him Hercules."

"You can tell one bug from another?"

"Hard not to. 'Specially since Herc took to wearing those red sandals of his. Not too fashionable, but they sure look comfortable."

"Yeah, right. Pull on my other leg while you're at it."

"Scoff if you must, but they come in real handy when the supply ship is late and food gets scarce around here. Which happens a lot on this side of the island. There's plenty of protein under those hard shells. Once you pull of the legs and get past the crunch, they don't taste half bad. Fry 'em up in a pan of hot butter, add a pinch of salt—maybe a little ketchup—and they're downright delicious. You should try one sometime. It'll put hair on your chest."

"Thanks, but no thanks," said Lee. "I think I'll pass on the insect lunch. No offense, but I'd rather chow down on that dirty hat of yours."

During the next few days Lee learned the hard way that Burt was only halfway joking. Every morning he had to shake six or seven water bugs out of his bedroll, some of them eight inchers. Apparently Hercules and his clan fancied the body heat generated by a sleeping sailor. Thankfully while Lee was there the island's supply of C-rats never dipped to a level where he had to contemplate dining on one of the monster beetles.

He was just getting used to his six-legged bedfellows when he found himself onboard an ocean-going minesweeper bound for Mindanao. There he and his buddies made several quick—and unfortunately for Hillbilly—nighttime surveys of its southern shores. Their findings were less than encouraging. With the disaster at Tarawa fresh on his mind, MacArthur wisely decided to avoid the island entirely. The projected cost in men and material was just too damn high. He and his staff of advisors felt it would be more efficient to bypass Mindinao and merely starve the enemy troops there by cutting off their supply lines. Never one to look a gift horse in the mouth, Lee had to agree.

"Fine with me. It makes our job a hell of a lot easier."

"And a lot less dangerous," added Hillbilly. "Without no food, in a few months the Nips will be so weak we can take the whole damn island for a few handfuls of rice. Without firing a damn shot."

"I'll drink to that," said Frenchie. "Of course I'll drink to anything that doesn't involve me getting killed."

After a series of soft landings Lee and his buddies found themselves with some down time on their hands. With no operations in their immediate future, they worked on their tans, drank more than their fair share of beer, and wore the numbers off two decks of cards playing poker. It wasn't until the second week of October, 1944 that Lee saw his first real action of the war. It would be in the Gulf of Leyte, on the beaches of Tacloban. And it would scare the crap out of him.

After reading his orders out loud, Lee gave Hillbilly a playful thump in the arm. Hard enough to get his attention, but not hard enough to draw retaliation. He had seen the big man end a bar fight with a single blow from that crashing right hand of his, and he didn't want to take any chances. Even when Hillbilly was joking around he could raise a serious bruise.

"About damn time!" crowed the mountain man. "I've had it up to here with sitting around on our duffs. Now it's our turn to dish out some serious shit."

"Look out, Hirohito!" grinned Frenchie, "Tokyo, here we come!"

TWENTY-SEVEN

IT WAS THE third minesweeper he'd ridden in as many months and Lee had already forgotten its number. Easy to do since it had been drenched with camouflage a year ago. He wasn't sure the scrappy little vessel even had a name.

Tabbed a *belligerent looking yacht wearing grey paint* by a wise-ass journalist back home, the hundred and thirty foot almost-a-ship was proving to be a work horse in the Pacific. So much so, that by the end of the war five hundred and sixty of the "scrappy little yachts" had rolled out of America's shipyards.

Packing a forward forty millimeter tandem gun and two fifty calibers aft, minesweeps provided the perfect platform to launch and protect frogmen. In addition their shallow draft was a big plus in getting them close to the beach. On the negative side, however, when the seas turned iffy they changed into a first class seasick machine. And when they fired up the twin diesels it became a veritable hot box below decks, one that radiated heat all over the ship. It got so hot down in the engine room that you could fry an egg on any exposed metal surface. A cliché perhaps, but one hundred percent accurate. Lee even tried it once. Even though the egg was uneatable due to all the oily dirt it absorbed, it fried up in less than a minute. Burned to a crisp in two.

The never ending heat and cramped quarter were the main reasons Lee took to sleeping topside, stripped to his shorts—and sometimes naked—on his bedroll. That wasn't all bad news though. Lying there after a hard day's work, staring up at the stars, enjoying the cool evening breezes, the experience was almost pleasant. All things considered.

Tonight however there was little time for sleeping. The sweep had already dropped anchor and was slowly swinging with the tide. Soon her transom would point towards the southernmost beach at Tacloban City. A thriving settlement before the Japanese invaded, a few years back Tacloban's blazing lights could be seen miles out to sea—a beckoning sight to heavily laden trading ships all over these islands. Eighteen months ago, however, the war had reduced her once captivating skyline to little more than a dark hump on the horizon, lusterless and foreboding. Given the Japanese presence, Tacloban was now a port to be avoided at all costs.

Clouds now and then slid across the night sky, playing peek-a-boo with a crescent moon. Casting just enough light across the inky waters to see where you were going, at least it didn't give away the sweep's position. Perfect conditions for the frogmen's mission.

Standing on the fantail already suited up in their gear, Lee, Frenchie, and Hillbilly were chomping at the bit as they listened to Lieutenant Tom Jackson give his spiel. As the projected beachmaster he had the weight of the world on his shoulders. For the next few days he would be in charge of directing the beach landing. Basically an aquatic traffic cop, it was a job few men could handle. And even fewer would want to.

A no-nonsense mustang from Hattiesburg, Mississippi, Jackson and his drawl got right to the point. He'd worked his way up through the ranks the hard way and he wasn't about to take any guff from anyone. And especially not from three wise-cracking frogmen.

"Listen up! I don't want any heroics tonight. The Navy has spent too much time and money on training you froggies to lose any of you your first time under the gun. You won't be of any further use to Uncle Sam if you get yourself killed doing something stupid. Y'all get in, make your charts, lay your charges, then haul ass. The fleet has shelled the hell out of that beach for two days straight now so hopefully you won't run into any shit out there. Then again, who knows? You can never trust the Japs. Everyone knows what happened at Iwo so keep your head on a swivel."

Sucking in a lungful of salt air, Jackson looked out to sea. Took off his cap and scratched his head.

"It may just be my creaky old bones talking back to me, but I got myself a sneaky suspicion there might be a few Nips layin' low on us. The bastards have a tendency to burrow into the sand when the shells start to fly, then pop up when least expected. That means there may be a sniper or two hidden in the bushes. You start taking any fire, give us a quick holler over the wireless."

The lieutenant took a draining swig from his coffee cup, the one he'd had as a chief. Even though he'd been an officer for over two years now, he'd never upgraded his china. Coffee just seemed to taste better out of it.

"While you're in the water we'll keep our guns trained on the shoreline," he said, nodding towards the beach. "And if a slant-eye so much as sneezes in your general direction we'll blow his yellow ass to kingdom come. If I were you I wouldn't even think about using those popgun pistols you've been issued. Under these conditions you couldn't hit white in a snowstorm. Besides, your muzzle flash would only give your position away. And piss off any Jap in the area. So leave the hard stuff to us."

Jackson wiped out his cup. Then secured it to a belt loop. Rubbing the back of his neck, he took a few seconds to survey the twelve men standing before him. The adventurous half of him—the one that was itching for a fight—wished he could go with them. The other—more intelligent half—was thankful he didn't have to.

"Okay, men. I've said my piece. Put your boats in the water. The sooner you get to it, the sooner we can haul our butts outta here."

TWENTY-EIGHT

AS THE LUCK of the draw would have it, Lee, Frenchie, and Hillbilly had ended up on different teams. Then again, it could have been Navy policy. According to the powers that be, too many close friends could muddy up the teamwork. Frenchie, as the UDT, was in charge of his own team, while Hillbilly and Lee were go-fers for two separate teams. Their common objective for the night: blow up the jumping jacks the Japanese had strung out along the beach.

JJ's for short, each jumping jack consisted of three six-foot-long railroad tracks welded together at the center and placed on the bottom to discourage allied beach crafts from landing. Wedged into the sand their sharp points could rip open the soft underbelly of any Higgins boat careless enough to run one over. Over the past month the UDTs had become adept at blowing up these simple, yet effective devices. Good thing, because the Japs were just as adept at putting them back together again. More often than not, the very next day. That's why frogmen did their most productive work the night before a landing. Give the enemy another day and more than likely the JJs would be back in place, good as new.

Lee was checking out his UDT's Hagensen pack when Hillbilly strolled over. Inside the pack were eight wrapped sections of tetrytol, a frogman's explosive of choice. Forty pounds total, if attached at the critical point the payload could blow apart a couple dozen jumping jacks.

Looking like a block of clay, when fired off by an igniting string of primacord two pounds of *tet* could send a plume of water a hundred feet in the air. And give a serious headache to any living thing in the water within a thousand foot radius. Innocuous enough without its primer—primacord burned at a rate of three hundred feet per second—you didn't want to be anywhere near the stuff when the fuse was lit.

Hillbilly spit into his face plate. Cocked his head to one side. "You know... I've been thinking, Stump."

"Questionable pastime, considering you never finished high school."

"Very funny. All joking aside... You ever wonder why they didn't put us on the same team? What with our being such good friends."

Lee cinched his weight belt tighter. The damn thing had a tendency to slide to the left on his hip, up-setting his stroke. Then he too spit in his mask.

"*Good friends?* Is that what we are?"

"I'm serious. You, me, and Frenchie. We'd have made a good team."

"Maybe the Navy doesn't think along those lines. Remember what happened at Guadalcanal? When the JUNEAU was torpedoed all five of the Sullivan brothers lost their lives. I hear the death notification officer almost committed suicide after talking to their mother."

"But the Sullivans were brothers. We're just friends."

"Oh... so now we're *just* friends?"

"You know what I mean."

"More likely the Navy didn't want you two over-sized goons in the same boat."

"And what about you? At most you're a half pint, soaking wet."

"They probably wanted me to keep an eye on you two fat bags of mostly water from afar. So I could save your fat asses in a pinch. You slackers may have a couple of inches on me but we all know who's stronger in the water."

Hillbilly snorted a laugh.

"As if those scrawny arms of yours could ever save either one of us."

"You and the horse you rode in on."

Frenchie's swamp whistle cut their banter short. A man of few words when he was working—and more importantly the guy in charge of the explosives—he nodded towards the three rafts tethered to the fantail.

"If you ladies have finished raggin' on each other... It's time to get wet."

Both Hillbilly and Lee mocked simultaneous salutes. Hillbilly added a wet raspberry.

"Yes, sir! Mr. Boss Man!" crowed Lee as they jumped backwards over the side. As a departing punctuation mark he flipped a bird.

Shaking his head Frenchie followed them into the water. When he came up he had a grin on his face.

"We've got a hard swim ahead of us. I hope you two jerk-offs can keep up after all that gum flapping."

Using a short paddle Lee nudged his raft away from the stern. Hillbilly did the same.

"Let's make this interesting, Frenchie," said Lee. "A buck says we lowly go-fers make the beach before you do."

"Listen to the big-time gambler. A whole damn dollar! Make it a five spot and you're on."

TWENTY-NINE

TWELVE FROGMEN SET off from their mother ship minesweep in the middle of the night, hanging low off their rubber rafts to minimize their silhouettes. Another zero dark thirty evolution, it was when they did their best work. Late enough for the moon to fall behind the island so they wouldn't be back lit—but not so late their return trip could be profiled by a rising sun. To conceal their numbers from possible prying eyes they maintained a rigid single file. Using his thighs—rock hard from months of training—Lee propelled his blunt-nosed inflatable towards the beach at a steady, if not blinding pace.

The Japanese weren't stupid. They were well aware the Americans were out there, somewhere in the dark. They also knew they would attempt to scout out possible landing sights, chart the beaches, and blow up all the obstructions the Japanese had so carefully planted the day before. After having the crap shelled out of them for the better part of two days they knew an invasion of some kind was imminent. But they didn't know where it was coming, or exactly when. And it was the Navy's job to keep them guessing.

If all went well for the frogmen they would be in and out before the Japs knew they'd been there. If not, Lee and his buddies could count on the minesweeper to bail them out. And if—knock on wood—it turned out her big guns weren't enough, they'd just have to improvise.

Taking point, Frenchie and his crew were leading the way. As the senior UDT it was his prerogative to go first—actually his duty. A heavy and dangerous responsibility, it did however make him the obvious choice to win the wager. Lee was in the second boat and it didn't take him long to realize the big *race* he'd so unwisely asked for was lost before it began. Along with his five bucks.

Once again he'd been had. Frenchie knew what he was doing when he upped the stakes. The Swampman was already fifty feet ahead of Lee and—according to the planned and very rigid formation—he would stay there until they reached the rendezvous point. Game, set, and match. Then again, there was always tomorrow's poker game. As good as Frenchie was with his knife, he was lousy at anything that involved a deck of cards and a bit of luck. Even pinochle was beyond his comprehension.

Resolved to his loss—but confident it was only temporary— Lee reached into his boat to make sure his *tire iron* hadn't fallen overboard. Yep. Still there.

Ah, well. Easy come, easy go. Five bucks won't break me.

An important piece of equipment, the so-called tire iron was used to pry things apart underwater, dislodge objects from the bottom, and fend off curious sea critters. Shorter than a machete—but with more heft—it was a sturdy hunk of metal, bent at one end with a short flat blade at the other. Simple yet efficient, in a pinch it could even be used as a weapon.

Reassured, Lee resumed his two-handed grip on the raft. Lulled by the warm water and the steady cadence of his leg kicks, his mind began to drift. The water lapping along the length of his body was warm and inviting, almost soft. Not cold and hard like the surf at San Diego. It almost seemed less salty, not so tart as it trickled through his mouth. And the air seemed cleaner, somehow friendlier. Even easier to breathe.

Off to his right a rounded fin broke the surface. After a languid roll to the left it dropped out of sight. Glittering silver in the moonlight as it went, it was soon followed by another. Then another. Six fins in all, hopefully they were attached to a school of curious fish at play. And not large, hungry predators. Eying the last of the bubbles Lee nudged his partner.

"See that, Willie? I sure hope those weren't sharks."

"Willie" Williams was the team's chart maker, mainly because of his ability to draw. At five foot four he'd been the only one in the frogman class shorter than Lee. And one of the few who had a natural ability to swim a straight line at night underwater. Casting a wary eye where the fins had disappeared, he nodded in agreement.

"You and me both, Stump. Getting a leg bit off by a blue tip might slow us down a mite."

"Can the chatter," admonished their team leader. "The Japs might hear you. Besides, those were just dolphins. Sharks never surface like that."

Iowa born and bred, Norman "Biggles" Hammond was a string bean with an off-beat sense of humor who liked to play practical jokes on his friends. A half-way decent clarinet player whose tunes livened up the ship during the day—at night he was all business in the water. For all their sakes right now he was thinking more about maintaining strict silence than making music.

"Gotcha, boss," whispered Lee.

Below him at a depth of three fathoms or so, an ominous dark shadow glided by in the opposite direction. Six to eight feet long, hopefully whatever it was had satisfied its curiosity. Swallowing hard, this time Lee kept his comments to himself.

THIRTY

IT TOOK THE three rafts twenty more minutes to reach their dispersion point. As the middle boat Lee's team maintained their position while the other two teams moved off to the right and left at a distance of a hundred yards. The moon was bright enough so they didn't have to use their flashlights and after a few hand signals they got down to business.

As expected the Japs had secured their jumping jacks in eight feet of water. Deep enough to hide the sharpened prongs just below the surface, but shallow enough to rip the bottom out of any wayward LCVP. The frogmen's immediate objective was to blow apart as many of the nasty suckers as they could before dawn. A simple dive in relatively calm water, it entailed securing a one pound wedge of tertrytol to where the jacks had been welded together. Wrapped with primacord the explosives could then be detonated using the wires strung back to their rafts. After, of course, moving off to a safe distance. You didn't want to be anywhere near one of those wedges when it went off. The concussive effects on the human body could be deadly.

Halfway through the night the teams had already wired twenty JJs. Ahead of schedule, it looked as if they'd make it back to the minesweeper in plenty of time for breakfast. And maybe hoist a brew or two. Since frogmen weren't actually members of the crew, they were afforded a certain leeway. And that included an illicit stash of beer. Officially enlisted men weren't allowed to drink onboard a Navy ship, but knowing the hardships the froggies went through officers tended to look the other way.

As Lee surfaced for the twentieth time that night he was starting to feel good about the operation. So far things had gone off without a hitch, and—knock on wood—again they hadn't run into a single snag. They'd found the jumping jacks with no trouble and had rigged them in record time. Their wires trailed like strands of rubber spaghetti from the beach back to his raft. It seemed as if Lady Luck was shining down on him.

Looking forward to packing it in for the evening Lee could almost taste that first beer. Confident their work was just about done he permitted himself the luxury of a satisfied smile. Hanging on to the raft he let his feet dangle and drift with the current. Every muscle in his body ached and he was close to exhaustion, but it was a good tired. A tired that came from a job well done. That warm and fuzzy feeling lasted all of ten seconds.

Suddenly a round of gunfire from shore split the night calm. Dozens of bullets whizzed overhead, sounding like angry bees in flight. Followed by a line of waterspouts trailing off to Lee's right. A Jap sniper was spraying the area with bursts of machine gun fire. Luckily he hadn't pinpointed the frogmen's exact location. Not yet anyway.

As soon as the firing let up Lee snatched a pair of binoculars from inside the raft, then pulled the walkie-talkie close. Focusing on the beach he located the next muzzle flash. It came from a copse of decimated palm trees about fifty yards in from the shoreline. More angry bees flew his way. Followed by more waterspouts. This time a couple of yards closer. Thank goodness the sniper was a lousy shot. That or maybe he hadn't drawn a proper bead.

"Beach control, this is Team Alpha," Lee said into the talkie. "We're taking rapid fire from shore. Probably a single automatic weapon. Stand by for coordinates."

Even though this was his first time under actual fire—and his heart was pounding to beat the band—his reaction had been calm and concise. It had to be. The lives of three frogman teams depended on it. It was what he'd been trained for.

"Two-Nine-Zero degrees from my location. Range Three-Five-Zero yards"

More gunfire flashed from shore. Another waterspout. This time on Lee's port side. And closer. The sniper was finding the range.

"Make that Two-S*even*-Zero degrees. Three-*Two*-Zero yards. The bastard must be on the move."

"We've got you covered, Team Alpha," came from the radio.

His eyes glued to the binoculars, Lee thought he saw a shadow bolt from the trees—in its right hand the unmistakable outline of a sub-machine gun. He was about to relay the sniper's latest position when the minesweeper opened up with both fifty calibers. To hell with more coordinates, when in doubt strafe the whole damn beach.

Red hot tracers raked the shoreline, walking back and forth across the area of the copse of palm trees. From Lee's vantage point it looked like a Roman candle festival. But he saw no further sign of the sniper.

"I think he's gone to ground, Beach Control."

"Roger that, Team Alpha. Hold on to your hats. Here comes the big stuff."

THIRTY-ONE

TWO SECONDS LATER the ship opened up with their forty millimeter. Its thunderous POM...POM...POM drowned out the fifty chatter. On automatic fire the dual barreled cannon could spit out a hundred and sixty rounds a minute, propelling a five pound projectile up to five thousand yards. And the sniper was a lot closer than that.

In half a heartbeat the shore was lit up bright as day. That copse of trees was leveled in a series of fire-spewing mushrooms. Watching the conflagration Lee almost felt sorry for the sniper. *Jesus! Nobody could live through all that shit.*

But when he nudged his binoculars half a degree to the left he saw a dark figure emerging from a hidey-hole at the base of the lone palm tree still standing. Engulfed in flame and clearly shell shocked, the sniper staggered a few steps towards the nearest sand dune. He hadn't gone more than five yards when the fifties cut him in half. Dead before his upper torso slammed into a mound of sand ten yards away, his lower half crumpled to the ground. Where it would burn for the rest of the night. Designed to maximize the damage done to human flesh, the fifty caliber machine gun was one nasty weapon.

Lee watched in stunned silence as red flames began to dance around the sniper's already charred legs. A horribly gruesome way to die, at least the end had come quick. Stump had never witnessed a violent death before and its sheer abruptness left him dumbstruck. One second you were alive and kicking, trying to pick off an enemy in the water. The next you were a smoldering pile of ashes. Worm fodder. How frail the human body.

SOB never knew what hit him.

With a shake of his head Lee remembered to call in his final report.

"Good shooting, Beach control. That got him. Bastard's toast."

"Roger that, Team Alpha."

Over his earpiece he heard a *Cease fire* in the background. The rolling thunder from the minesweep ceased and an unnerving silence fanned out across the water. Lee's brain told him it was only his ears adjusting to the sudden lack of noise, but later he would swear on a stack of Bibles he could hear his own heartbeat echoing off the surf.

A few fires still flickered here and there on the beach. But in less time than it took Lee to realize he'd been holding his breath during the entire firefight, the beach went dark again. And except for one dead and halved Japanese sniper, things returned to normal. The minesweeper's barrage had lasted less than a minute, but for Lee it had seemed like an hour. For the first time that night a hint of emotion crept into his radio voice.

"Thanks for having our back, Beach Control."

"No problem, Team Alpha. We aim to please."

With the sniper eliminated Lee turned his attention to the explosive packs. In two hours the teams had rigged the row of JJs closest to the beach. Wired in series, they could be detonated from his raft by a single switch. Danger addressed and hard work over, it was time to begin the retraction process.

THIRTY-TWO

AS "BIGGLES" HAMMOND approached their rendezvous point he gave a thumbs up, then circled his forefinger. Another row of jumping jacks remained farther out but it could wait until tomorrow. After seeing their comrade blown to smithereens, the chances of the enemy trotting out another sniper were slim. The Nips were running out of men as fast as they were running out of ammo. But given the fanatical mind set of the average Japanese soldier—who'd throw sticks and stones at you if he had to—there was no need to take chances. Besides, the sun would soon be coming up and that would only complicate things. When Hammond finally reached the raft he shoved his mask to his forehead.

"Everyone here?"

"All three boats present and accounted for," said Lee.

"Then let's blow this pop stand. Wanna do the honors, Stump?"

"All yours, Biggles. You and Frenchie planted most of them." Hammond snorted a chuckle.

"And I suppose it's gonna be *my* fault if they don't go off?"

"Never crossed my mind," grinned Lee. "But now that you mention it..."

When Hammond grabbed the detonator all twelve frogmen hauled their torsos onto the sides of their rafts. To minimize the impending concussive wave.

"Well... Here goes nothing," he said as he twisted the switch to ignite the primacord.

Twenty explosions went off in rapid succession.

FOOM! FOOM! FOOM!

Twenty spouts erupted in a straight line, spraying hundreds of gallons of water into the night sky. In the moonlight the scattering droplets looked like a thousand twinkling stars.

"Music to my ears," said Hammond. "Time to pack it in and head for home."

On the way back to their *belligerent little yacht* Lee had time to contemplate what had happened. He had just completed his first combat mission. And survived a firefight, brief though it was. Huge doses of adrenaline were still pumping through his body—just as they had been on his way to the beach—but this time it felt different. They'd done well, faced all the challenges, and now they were on their way back, returning from harm's way. Gone was the goose-pimply excitement of setting out to face the unknown. In its stead was a warm, satisfied glow. Reflecting on the evening's festivities an odd stream of consciousness swam through his head.

Before the Navy shelled the crap out of it, I'll bet that was a beautiful beach at one time. Clear blue water, a gentle surf, palm fronds swaying in the warm sea breezes. It must have been idyllic. Now all that's left is a shredded stand of trees and one dead Jap soldier. What a waste.

But Lee also knew there was worse to come for Tacloban. When the landing finally came off it would tear up that beach even more. And probably devastate the entire island.

THIRTY-THREE

AFTER DEFLATING THE raft and hanging up his wet gear, Lee shuffled his way aft to flop onto his bedroll, exhausted and half in a daze. Dawn was less than two hours away and his eyes kept fluttering at half-mast. Beyond tired but too jazzed to fall asleep, for ten minutes he lay on his back contemplating the stars. Glad to be on a dry ship again—and just thankful to be alive—he took time to pick out Orion then the Big Dipper, the two brightest and therefore the easiest constellations in the southern sky. Reaching down to gingerly massage a throbbing calve he let out a slow grunt.

"I'm so tired I can't even muster up a respectable fart. My body's beat to shit and I ache all over."

Equally fatigued Hillbilly rubbed the bridge of his nose between a thumb and forefinger. Then scratched at his chin stubble.

"Everything below my bald spot hurts. And my body is speaking to me in a language I don't want to understand. Even my damn whiskers are in pain."

Groaning from the effort Frenchie tried to raise his swollen right knee. He'd banged it against the side of the ship climbing aboard. When an electric shock shot up through his brain stem he gave up and rolled back on his side. Wriggling his fingers he tried to make a fist. Couldn't do that either. It proved too painful.

"My hands are cramping so bad I can't even grab my dick to take a piss."

"As if they could ever find something that small," said Lee, forcing a grin.

"Look who's talking. We don't call you *Stump* just because you're short."

"Very funny. I think I may die laughing."

"Pretty weak, half pint. You call that a comeback?"

"Go fuck a duck."

Off his game tonight, Lee was too tired to come up with one of his normally witty retorts. It required too much damn effort. And he'd already blown his wad ducking sniper fire. He knew how lame he sounded but he was too mentally spent to come up with something better.

Over their many months together he'd perfected the art of ragging on his buddies. They'd even come to expect it. All three used the good natured jibing to ease the tension, bolster their confidence and pass the time. But as drained as they were tonight no one was up to it. So for several minutes silence reigned. The next time anyone spoke Orion and his belt had dipped below the horizon.

"Do you think tomorrow's gonna be any easier, Stump?" asked Hillbilly, tacking his question onto the tail end of a sigh.

Letting out another groan, Lee shifted slowly to one elbow. Propped his head in an open palm.

"Gotta be. There can't be many JJs left. So it shouldn't take us half as long this time. And without any Japs taking pot shots at us it should be a piece of cake."

"You think they hightailed it for the hills?"

"For sure. The way those fifties lit up that sniper I think the Japs will think twice about attacking us again. At least for the next day."

Scratching at his crotch Frenchie twisted his neck to the right until it cracked. Then back to the left.

"Talk about a human blow torch! Who in their right mind would be foolish enough to follow in that poor bastard's footsteps?"

"Whoever said the Japs were in their right mind?" countered Lee. "Hopped up on rice wine they're apt to try anything. I'm sure there's a few ricers left on this island willing to slither out of the sand for one last shot at a round-eye. They all want to get an American in their sights before dying for the emperor."

Frenchie patted the gun tub next to him. Five feet above his head a fifty caliber barrel jutted into the night sky, still cooling off.

"If they do, you can rest assured this baby will cut them in half. And give them one-way tickets to rejoin their ancestors. Just like it did tonight."

Hillbilly inhaled a soft whistle.

"Criminitely! Did you see the way it ripped that dink apart? Arms and legs were flying everywhere."

Lee looked up into the night sky.

"Nothing left of him but assholes and elbows." Big yawn and a stretch. "But I guess there's worse ways to die. If my number does come up over here... that's the way I'd like to go. Wham! Bam! Real quick like."

Hillbilly looked down at his hands. Swallowed hard as he turned them over.

"Five years ago I watched my grandpappy waste away to skin and bones. It took the stomach cancer a whole year to eat him up. In the end he was little more than a sunken shadow wrapped in a thin layer of skin—coughing up blood and shitting the bed. The way he died took a harsh toll on the entire family. My grandmother aged twenty years. Died a month later, in fact. My mother's hair even turned white."

A sudden shudder wracked Hillbilly's body as he fought off the image.

"No siree, Bob... You can bet the farm this ol' country boy ain't gonna be checkin' out like that. Just prop me up next to my shooting iron and I'll take care of business."

Interlacing his fingers behind his head Frenchie leaned back to contemplate the stars.

"When it comes to kicking the bucket... If I had my druthers I think I'd like to pass from this mortal coil in a nice warm bed. Flat on my back with my boots on and my britches off. Lying next to a tall blonde with big tits who'd just screwed my brains out."

"Always a blonde," chuckled Lee. "As if you could ever find one in this part of the world."

"When it comes to dying," said Frenchie, "I guess anyone with tits would do."

"At this stage of the game I'm surprised you have any standards left at all, Swampman," said Hillbilly. "But I like the way you think. I've changed my mind. Yours is definitely the better way to go."

"I can see it on both of your death certificates now," said Lee. *"Cause of death: Heart attack brought on by excessive fucking.* Given what horn dogs you two are, what more could you want for a eulogy? Come to think of it... There's something poetic about mustering out with a stiff dick pointing your way to heaven. If—by a stroke of pure luck—heaven's the direction either of you jackasses will be heading. And me and the Lord have some serious doubts about that."

Hillbilly wet his lips.

"If I had me a bottle of beer, or the strength to hoist one, I'd sure as hell drink to that."

Lee shot a cautious glance towards the bridge. Looked right and left. Then reached into the gun tub to pull out three bottles of San Miguel from his private stash.

"I think that can be arranged."

After a few toasts to this and that the three drifted off into a thankfully dreamless sleep. Properly numbed, their aches and pains soon faded into the early morning mist. And for a few hours at least, their worries about tomorrow were put on hold.

Unfortunately their peace would not last long.

THIRTY-FOUR

SHORTLY BEFORE DAWN the three were jarred awake by an ear-shattering rumble rolling over the horizon. The big boys were at it again. Fifteen miles off shore—out of sight and well out of the range of anything the Japanese could throw at them—the Navy's thundersticks had roared to life. All because one poor misguided sniper had taken a few pot shots at Team Alpha the night before.

Wanting to make sure there were no more surprises waiting for the troops the next morning—when the LCVPs were scheduled to drop their ramps en masse—the Navy was trying to eliminate every living creature anywhere near that beach. That included birds, lizards, and sand crabs. Most of which had the common sense to scurry for higher ground the moment the shooting started.

An American battleship sported nine gargantuan barbette guns. A single blast from one of those sixteen-inch monsters belched fire that could be seen ten miles away. Its twenty seven hundred pound shell could travel twenty miles beyond the horizon to rain terror on the unsuspecting enemy. Large enough to be seen with the naked eye as it screamed across the sky, it could reduce a good-sized hill to a pile of rubble in the blink of an eye. When that first salvo went off it sounded as if the gods of war had woken up angry. Lee was the first to sit bolt upright.

"What the hell was that? It sounded like a damn freight train going overhead!"

Then came the telltale distant thunder clap. Unfortunately for the sleepy trio their minesweeper had anchored between the USS Nevada and the beach, directly under the flight path of her big guns.

Hillbilly's jaw dropped. Sucking air in between his teeth he pointed at the dark object streaking across the heavens.

"God Almighty! It's as big as a damn bus!"

From shore came a conversation stopping KA-WHUMP! And what was left of last night's sniper disintegrated in a towering cloud of sand and debris. Along with the two dozen soldier crabs that had been nibbling on his charred innards. The fallen palm tree where his torso had been laying was turned into instant sawdust. The mound where it had been growing for half a century was flattened. God-like in its umbrage, the power of the explosion seemed to quiver the very ocean. Sensing the vibration through the deck plates beneath him Lee shook his head in disbelief.

"Damn! I felt that in my ass!"

Even though he was hunkered down next to the gun tub and several hundred yards off shore, wind from the explosion sent his cap flying over the side. When a third shell screamed overhead he forgot about the cap and dived into the tub for cover. Followed in short order by Hillbilly and Frenchie.

Huddled behind an inch and a half of solid metal—and feeling none too confident about it—Lee counted off four mores explosions, each one louder than the last. Several batteries of nine-inchers from the cruisers then joined in on the fun, adding their distinctive FEEE-SSSH screams to the battleship's deafening opus. Hillbilly thought he might have shouted an expletive or two but he wasn't sure since he couldn't hear them.

Clamping both hands over his ears Lee noticed that despite the ruckus, Frenchie wasn't moving. His first thought was that his buddy might have been injured, that he could have conked his head diving into the tub. But upon closer examination he saw that the son of a gun seemed to be sleeping. And that wonder of wonders, he was actually snoring. At a time like this? Lee couldn't believe his eyes.

"I'll! Be! Damned! Can you beat that? The Swampman's actually asleep!"

Chancing one eyeball Hillbilly verified it for himself.

"Frenchie always said he could sleep through a tornado... But that's just downright ridiculous."

"You're closer to him," nodded Lee. "Give Rip Van Winkle there a kick in the ass. He shouldn't be missing this."

"Not on your tin type. Let the man sleep. I ain't gonna chance getting my head bit off. You know what a grouch Frenchie is when he wakes up."

The next screamer was close enough to do the trick. Exploding in the nearby surf it bounced Frenchie two inches off the deck.

"Huh?" he wuffed, eyes wide as dinner plates. "Whazatt?"

"Good morning, sleepy head," said Lee. "Better hold on to your hat, my friend. It looks like it's gonna be a long day."

For the rest of the morning the Navy continued to fire its big guns, sending several thousand rounds of various shapes and sizes at the beleaguered beach. All of the teeth-rattling variety. By the time noon rolled around Lee and Hillbilly had resorted to using hand signals. The pragmatist of the group, Frenchie gave up trying to communicate entirely. Standing in the chow line a shell-shocked Lee yawned wide to pop his ears.

"Damn this infernal ringing. All this shelling is turning me deaf."

"What?" mouthed Hillbilly.

"I *said*—Oh, never mind."

Realizing the futility of trying to be heard, Frenchie simply shrugged his shoulders, grinned and reached for another helping of powdered mashed potatoes.

A few minutes before sundown a welcome cease-fire was called. And just like that the shelling stopped. One second the screaming fires of hell were reverberating all around. The next a dead calm fell over the entire ship like a giant velvet curtain, staggering everyone onboard. Plodding through the last of the din—hands firmly cupped over his ears—Lee was on his way to the fantail to see if anything was left of the beach when the bombast came to an abrupt halt. Walking next to him Hillbilly almost slipped and fell, scuffing his shin bone on a gunnel. Frenchie was so shaken he had to grab the nearest stanchion to keep from losing his balance.

"Thank God they've finally stopped!" said Lee.

"What?" said Hillbilly.

Popping his ears Frenchie merely nodded his relief.

THIRTY-FIVE

LATE THAT NIGHT Stump leaned on the fantail railing to ponder the destruction on shore. The sun had just dipped below the horizon and a gentle breeze was nudging a thin mist towards the minesweeper. Enough to fuzz-up his vision but not enough to hide the devastation wrought by the Navy's all-day barrage.

"Jesus Christ..." Reverence in his slow words. "They sure pounded the hell out of those poor Jap bastards on that island. The *Nevada* must have air mailed them a thousand tons of TNT today."

"And then some," nodded Hillbilly. "I bet there ain't a single tree left standing anywhere on that beach. Maybe just a few dazed sand fleas. It's sure gonna make our job a whole lot easier tonight. Leastwise we probably won't get shot at."

"Let's hope so," said Frenchie.

Their mission tonight would be the fifty or so jumping jacks they hadn't blown up the night before. Since they were imbedded in deeper water at least they wouldn't have to swim so far. That meant they would be closer to the protective guns of the minesweep. Consensus was it would be duck soup easy. And it was. At first.

The moon turned out to be in its full phase, with very little cloud cover. The resulting brightness would be a problem, but nothing the frogman teams couldn't handle. Besides, after the Navy spent all day battering the beach into even finer sand, the Japs were probably all hunkered down in their holes trying to patch their eardrums back together.

Lee had just finished his fourth round trip and was holding on to the side of his raft when something tore a hole in its hind quarter. In two seconds the back half of the raft deflated with a loud WHOOSH! He was sure it couldn't have been another sniper. No Jap with half a brain would have come anywhere near that shoreline after all those fireworks.

At first he thought he might have accidentally punctured an air-tight compartment with his prying tool. It was pretty sharp at one end. But when a bullet whizzed overhead he knew the Japs hadn't given up on them.

"Goddam it! They're back. Somebody's shooting at us again!"

Eyes to his binoculars he took a few seconds to zero in on the culprit. Illuminated by the full moon—and with no cover in any direction—the sniper wasn't trying to hide. A sitting duck, he hadn't even bothered to assume the prone position. He was just standing there. Not sure of what he was seeing, Lee rubbed his eyes. Nobody could be that stupid. When he looked again the guy seemed to be fussing with what appeared to be an old fashioned, long barrel rifle, yanking its bolt mechanism back and forth. Could his antique weapon have jammed? A distinct possibility considering the sand and high humidity.

What's this guy doing?

"Beach control, you aren't gonna believe this. But we've got ourselves another sniper. Thank God he brought a broken down rifle to the party and not another machine gun."

"That you, Stump? You gotta be kidding me."

Definitely unprofessional and not by the book, at least it was to the point.

"You froggies been hitting the booze again?"

"Ain't touched a drop all day. I'm telling you true. Some asshole on the beach is shooting at us. Just like last night. This time I got a hole in my raft to prove it."

"Damn... Hard to believe—considering all the shit we poured into that beach. OK. Give me the coordinates."

Back to the binoculars Lee watched the sniper give his piece-of-junk rifle one final tug. When it didn't respond he let it fall to the sand. Then surprisingly, he didn't make a run for it. He just continued to stand there, looking out to sea. Lee was shocked.

What's this son of a bitch gonna do now? Shoot at us with his side arm? As if he could hit anything from that distance with a peashooter pistol.

"Roger that, Beach Control," said Lee finally. "He's about where the other one was. You can't miss him. He's standing there like a statue—as if he's waiting for a train or something. *Two-seven-zero* degrees at about *four*... make that *three point five hundred—*Hold on. Something's happening."

Kneeling down, the sniper pulled a small object from a jacket pocket. After bowing his forehead twice in the sand he sat erect and took a deep breath. Raising his right hand in a Banzai salute, he slammed the object against his helmet with his left. Hard. Then stuck it underneath his chin.

What's with this chucklehead?

With a muffled *whump* the sniper's head burst from his shoulders, spewing a crimson mist as it tumbled through the air. Spurting blood from its severed neck his body shuddered, then collapsed face-less first in the sand. His right foot jerked back and forth a few times and for one brave but foolish Japanese soldier the war was over.

"Holy shit!" blurted Lee.

"Please repeat your coordinates, Team Alpha." More professional this time, but also to the point.

Stunned by what he'd just witnessed, Lee let the binoculars drop.

"We won't be needing your help after all, Beach Control. The problem seems to have taken care of itself. Looks like our sniper took one for the emperor."

"Say again your last, Team Alpha."

"The crazy bastard saved us a few bullets by committing hari-kari. Blew his head halfway back to Japan. Must have used a grenade."

"Roger that, Stump. Wish they were all so easy. If you run into another problem just give us a call."

THIRTY-SIX

LEE RAN A gloved hand across the weld at the center of the jumping jack. The tenth one in a row of a dozen or so, the jack was sitting at a strange angle on the bottom. Apparently the Japanese had been in a hurry when they were laying the thing and just dropped it overboard. Even though it wasn't properly secured it could still do some serious damage to a Higgins boat. So it had to go. From the roughness of the metal it was clear the pieces of railroad track had been reassembled more than once.

"How many of these suckers we got left, Bigs?"

"Three or four," answered Hammond. "One more load and we should be able to wrap this up."

"Good thing. My fingers are starting to cramp up. I'm getting sick and tired of the Japs putting these things back together. Maybe you should beef up the next charge. Make it more difficult for the industrious little bastards."

"Wish I could, but no can do. Too much *boom* in the mix and you might not be able to pass your next short-arm inspection."

"Spoil sport."

"I don't know about you, Stump... But when this war ends I plan on going home with my nuts intact and a working pecker. All ten inches of it. After all these years I wouldn't want to disappoint my blushing bride."

"You forget I've seen you in the shower, Bigs. Ten inches? In your dreams."

"What can I say? It's a poor workman who blames his tools."

Lee was on his way back to the delivery point to pick up his last load of tertrytol when he felt —more than saw—an explosion off to his right. Too far away to be personally dangerous but close enough to be heard, it came from the general direction of Hillbilly's team. He tilted his head to one side but all he could hear now was the gentle sound of waves slapping the beach. And other than the faint drone of the sweep's diesels an ominous silence fell flat across the water. It was almost as if Nature herself was holding her breath.

Swallowing hard he subconsciously crossed his fingers and concentrated on kicking harder. The sooner he delivered his charges the sooner they could head back. Something had gone terribly wrong over there in the dark but there was little he could do about it now. Despite a growing apprehension he still had a job to do.

When the final jack had been rigged Biggles surfaced first. Then tossed his pry bar into the raft. Lee was right behind him.

"That last one was a bitch," said Biggles. "Thank heaven there's no more left. I wonder what that explosion was all about. I was ten feet down when I felt it. I hope to hell it came from the beach."

Shaking his head Lee took the longest breath of his life.

"I don't think so. It sounded like all water to me. I pray to God no one got hurt."

Lost in his own fearful thoughts Biggles finally grabbed hold of the raft and started to kick.

"You and me both. But I guess we'll find out soon enough."

When they reached the rendezvous point Team Bravo was waiting for them. One, two, three, four... all present and accounted for. But from the looks on their faces they too were worried about the explosion.

"Team Charlie?" asked Lee.

"Not here yet," said Frenchie. "But I think I hear them coming."

Lee grabbed his binoculars. A gossamer mist had begun to rise from the surface and it took a few seconds for him to make out the shape of the third raft. It didn't look to be damaged but it wasn't making much progress. Not a good sign.

"They aren't moving as fast as they should," he said, a lump welling up in his throat.

"It's been a long night," offered Frenchie. "Could be they're just tired. I know I am. Or maybe Hillbilly's getting lazy in his old age." Trying unsuccessfully to lighten the moment.

Lee wiped salt water from his eyepieces. Refocused.

"I count only two heads." An even worse sign.

"Shit!" growled Frenchie. "We'd better give them a hand."

When the two reached the errant inflatable one look confirmed their worst fears. Bleeding from their eyes and ears, what was left of Team Charlie was in bad shape. Tom—the go-fer and the only one kicking—was seconds away from passing out. Hank, the chart maker, groaned from inside the raft.

THIRTY-SEVEN

MINDLESS OF ANY snipers on the beach Lee boosted Tom into the raft. With Frenchie kicking furiously at the stern he elevated Tom's feet then wedged an empty Hagensen behind his head. From the raft's canteen he trickled a few sips of water across both wounded men's lips. Then let them take a shallow swallow. It brought Hank around.

"What happened?" asked Lee.

Hank coughed twice, spitting up blood both times. His insides torn up, it took several tentative breaths before he could gather any words.

"P-Pack must have exploded prematurely." Another trickle breath. "The two of us were hanging on the side of the raft when it went off..."

A racking cough brought up more blood. Lots of it.

"M—Must have blacked out from the concussion. When I came to I found myself inside the raft."

Hank coughed two more times. Then threw up. Wiping his mouth he slowly turned his head to the side. Looked back towards the beach.

"Tom must have saved my life. Tried to help him kick at first, but I wasn't much help so he lifted me in here... Still can't feel my legs."

Lee laid a reassuring hand on the man's shoulder. "You did good, Hank. You both did. Save your strength, we've got it from here. You're gonna be fine."

His next question stuck in his throat. It was a one-worder when it finally came out.

"Hillbilly?"

Hank turned his head to the side as he hawked up more blood.

"I-I never saw him, after the last time he went down. As close as he was to that jack...he must have been blown to pieces. You know... what those charges can do."

Hank's torso twisted into a spasm. When he threw up again it was a dry heave. The explosion must have messed him up bad. It would be a long time before he dived again. If ever.

"After it exploded..." he forced himself to continue, "I started to swim down. B-but I couldn't breathe. My lungs were on fire... And I couldn't get my legs to work. At first I thought they'd been...blown off."

When he tried to sit up and look back at the beach again Lee pushed him back down with a gentle hand.

"You did all you could, Hank. You're lucky to be alive. Lie back and take it easy. Slow, gentle breaths. We'll have you back aboard ship in no time. You're gonna be all right."

But Lee wasn't so sure. Hank was bleeding from every orifice on his face, and even in the moonlight he could tell his color was several shades on the wrong side of pale. The explosion must have ruptured something deep inside, so his chances of surviving the night were fifty/fifty at best.

Sliding back into the water Lee glanced off to the right, where Team Charlie had been working. In his heart he knew there was no helping Hillbilly now. If he wasn't dead already he soon would be. A diver anywhere near an explosion that big would have been turned into instant chum.

No words were exchanged when he joined Frenchie at the stern. A single glance conveyed the hopelessness of it all. Adding his own legs to their wake Lee swallowed at the growing lump in his throat and concentrated on his kicking. They had to get this hunk of inflated rubber back to the minesweeper as quickly as possible. They'd probably lost a good friend that night and didn't want to lose another. Finding Hillbilly's body would have to wait until morning.

THIRTY-EIGHT

NO ONE SLEPT a wink that night. Eight frogmen kept a worried vigil on the fantail all night long. Around 0400 word was passed that the landing was going down early that morning so they didn't have much time. As soon as the sun's first rays sliced over the horizon eight pairs of fins hit the water simultaneously. Covered by every available gun on the minesweeper they paddled feverishly in two boats toward Team Charlie's last position. After several dives their worst fears were realized.

They found a shredded hand and half a foot wedged beneath some rocks two hundred yards from where the exploded jack had been. The remains had either drifted with the current or been dragged there by bottom feeders. That and a few shredded pieces of bone and flesh were all that remained of Hillbilly and his technician. Hardly enough to identify, much less bury. When the recall came over their walkie-talkie they couldn't hesitate.

"That's it," said Frenchie. "Time's up. We've been ordered back. The landing's a go."

As soon as they were back onboard, the minesweeper hauled anchor, turned and headed out to sea. Their part in the operation complete, it was time for small stuff to get out of the way and let the amphibs do their job. Standing next to the gun tub— watching their wake trail off in the distance—Lee passed out the last of his stash to his fellow frogmen. Still dripping water from their dive he raised his beer bottle toward the beach in tribute.

"To Hillbilly..." he toasted. "The best fucking friend a guy could ever want."

"Or need," added Frenchie.

In a prelude to what would later be called the Battle of Leyte Gulf, for the next day MacArthur's Navy threw everything they had onto the beach at Tacloban. By noon the largest amphibious assault ever launched in the Pacific had pushed the Japanese defenders far enough inland to establish a tenuous foothold.

Observing the last stages of the massive operation from the bridge of the cruiser *USS Nashville,* General MacArthur was chomping at the bit. In his mind's eye he was so close he could almost taste it. Ignoring the concerned pleas of his staff to wait until the beach was officially declared secure, he finally said to hell with it and ordered the launch of his private whaleboat. Never a patient man, he'd waited too long for this moment and wasn't going to let the possibility of a stray sniper or two keep him from his triumph.

"Hell, if I have to I'll shoot the bastard myself," he told his fretful aide de camp. But to prevent the poor man from having a conniption fit the general promised there'd be no flags flying, that he'd keep his head down, and most importantly that he'd leave his trademark corn cob pipe in his stateroom. No sense in making himself a bigger target than he already was.

Then, after one last look in the mirror—to make sure his bald spot wasn't showing—he donned his battered cap with the greenish scrambled eggs on the brim and set off to fulfill his destiny. And star in one of the most famous photo shoots of the entire war.

THIRTY-NINE

OBLIVIOUS TO THE gaggle of reporters headed his way, Lee was already on the beach when General MacArthur was preparing for his historic landing. After the initial assault Stump had been assigned to assist the beachmaster by interpreting the charts his team had made the night before. In charge of seeing wave after wave of supply vehicles charging ashore, the beachmaster's job would have turned an ordinary man into a blithering idiot.

An evolution in barely controlled chaos, large machines of every shape and size hurtled this way and that. In each was an over-worked driver who had a chip on his shoulder and was in no mood to stop for anyone or anything. During his first ten minutes on the beach Lee had been bumped by two jeeps and almost flattened by a Sherman tank with what appeared to be a huge plow blade attached to the front. When a hell-bent-for-leather Amtrac lurched out of the surf he jumped aside just in time.

"Hey! Watch where you're going, dickwad!" he yelled.

A stogie-smoking driver stuck his head out of the forward hatch. Clad in dirt-streaked goggles—and sporting a four-day stubble—after a quick shift of gears he flipped Lee the finger. He may have added an "Up yours!" to the roar of his exhaust as he sped away, but Lee wasn't sure. With the clatter of straining machinery at a bone-rattling pitch it was a miracle anyone could hear anything. After dusting himself off, he turned back to the beachmaster.

"Sweet Jesus, Lieutenant... With all these vehicles flying around every which way and that, it's a miracle we're still alive. How do you keep from losing your mind in all this bedlam?"

"You don't. I lost what was left of my sanity an hour ago."

Jerking his head to the right the lieutenant waved a red flag at a straggling line of geared-up soldiers heading in the wrong direction. Then bellowed into his bullhorn.

"No, assholes! Your *other* right!"

His eyes rolling, he turned back to Lee.

"You know the old saying, *When you're up to your ass in alligators it's hard to remember your objective was to drain the swamp.*"

Lee jumped to avoid another jeep, this one loaded down with four junior officers. Each shouting at the top of his lungs and pointing in a different direction.

"The Navy couldn't pay me enough to do your job, sir. I'd rather be up in the front lines. Where it's a whole lot safer. And not half as hectic."

When the lieutenant waved his flag to the left a deuce and a half cut sharply in front of him, its wheels showering sand and dirt into his face. Running a hand through his mud-caked hair he spit a wad of oil grit from his mouth.

"I can't remember the last time I was clean. You froggies got it made. You guys can go swimming anytime you want. Take a dip in the ocean whenever the spirit moves you."

Lee looked out to sea, in the general direction of Team Charlie's last position. Sucking a quick breath in through his nose he thinned his lips.

"And sometimes when the spirit DOESN'T move you. I lost one of my best friends two days ago. His last *dip in the ocean* blew him to pieces."

Feeling like he'd stepped into it big time, for a second the lieutenant didn't know what to say.

"Geez... I'm sorry. I meant no offense."

"None taken," said Lee, his attention drawn to another

Higgins boat floundering on the reef. "Every job in this damn war has its drawbacks. Need any more help with our charts?"

"No, I'm good. Now that I've got the lay of the land I can take it from here. No sense in both of us going crazy."

Lee picked up his gear and headed off towards the staging area.

"If you need me I'll be over there with my friends, where it's not so damn noisy. We're gonna hold a wake for our buddy and I've got some serious drinking ahead of me."

"Save a beer for me," said the beachmaster. "I'm gonna need one before this cluster fuck is over."

FORTY

IN THE HOT sun it didn't take long for the beers to take effect. A dozen toasts under his belt and Lee was feeling no pain. Normally able to handle Herculean amounts of booze, Frenchie wasn't far behind. His emotions raw, maybe the occasion was getting to him. Draining his fourth bottle of beer he let out a rousing burp.

"At least Hillbilly got his wish and went quick. Big guy probably never saw it coming. Didn't even have time to break a sweat. Just a quick *Aw, shit!* And that was it."

Lee reached for another beer. Draining half of it in one swig he wiped his mouth on a bare forearm.

"Brave man, that Hillbilly. Me? I'd have probably crapped my drawers."

Greased by the beers a wry grin inched onto Frenchie's face.

"Iff'n it was me, Stump, I'd have probably crapped your drawers, too."

Lee choked on his beer so hard he farted. When he exchanged glances with Frenchie both men lost control. In a split second the two were rolling on the ground, laughing their asses off. At a time like that maybe laughter was the only way to grieve.

They laughed from the belly, long and hard. They laughed for Hillbilly. They laughed at the war. And they laughed at the incomprehensible fact that they both were still alive. They laughed until their sides ached and tears were streaming down their cheeks.

Finally able to catch their breaths again they slowly stood to face the sea. Lee farted again. Frenchie hiccoughed twice. Wobbling at attention they both snapped off a sloppy salute.

"Here's to you, Hillbilly," said Lee. "I'm sure gonna miss you, buddy."

"Adieu, mon ami," said Frenchie.

For a minute the two wavered back and forth in silence, like the drunken sailors they were. Light-headed and queasy, finally Lee plopped into the sand ass first. After a healthy belch he tugged at his chin.

"Maybe we'd better head back. My head is swimming and I'm starting to see double. Worst of all I've gotta take a monster piss."

"I already did," grinned Frenchie, slurring his words. "And most of it's still dribbling down my leg."

FORTY-ONE

LEANING ON EACH other for support, the two frogmen staggered toward an abandoned LCVP beached ramp down fifty yards to their right. Despite the thin wisp of black smoke coming from the engine compartment it was the perfect place to empty Lee's hyper-extended bladder. After taking the world's longest piss he collapsed on the open ramp and let his bare feet dangle in the water. He had his head down contemplating the growing throb over his right eye when he spotted a flurry of activity around a distant cruiser. Closer in, another wave of small craft was headed their way. All circling what appeared to be an over-loaded whaleboat.

"Looks like something's going on out there," he managed between shallow breaths.

"Strange..." said Frenchie. "From the way they're riding high in the water, those LCVPs have to be three quarters empty. And they all seem to be clucking around that whaleboat."

"Whatever's in that whaleboat must be pretty damn important."

"You ain't just whistling Dixie, sailor," said a nearby voice. "The general's on his way in."

This coming from a tall thin man with a movie camera strapped to his shoulder. One of three dressed in khaki, but obviously not a soldier—at least not of the shooting kind—he sported a press insignia on his spotless helmet. Probably a combat photographer for one of the news services.

Twisting around, Frenchie popped an eyebrow.

"A general, you say. Which one?"

"The ONLY one," replied the photographer.

"MacArthur? Here? Are you sure?"

"You think I'd be wasting my time in this dung heap if I wasn't?"

When Lee gulped down a final breath of air it tasted like panther piss. Five beers in the hot sun had flip-flopped his stomach and for a few seconds he thought he was going to throw up. Forcing himself to sit up straight he pinched off his nose. Now was not the time to get sick. Especially not in front of the great general.

"How about that! General Douglas fucking MacArthur himself! Headed towards this very beach."

The photographer set his battered camera down. Then jammed a tripod in the sand.

"Yep. To be exact... about a hundred feet from where your two drunk asses are sitting."

"Then I guess I'd better not blow lunch on his shoes," chuckled Lee.

"Good thinking. Rumor has it, the last sailor to puke anywhere near Mac was transferred post haste to solitary duty on a laundry barge anchored to a submerged atoll in the middle of the Pacific. The only time he got to see another human face was once a week or so when a ship slowed down to throw their dirty laundry at him. It was him and a flock of seagulls in the middle of nowhere. I'm told the poor schnook went crackers in a month."

FORTY-TWO

THE LCVPS LANDED first. As soon as their ramps struck sand two dozen heavily armed Marines stormed the beach to take up defensive positions. Weapons at the ready, they immediately began to scan the far tree line for signs of activity. Woe be unto any Jap sniper foolish enough to upstage the general.

"Looks like they aren't taking any chances," said Frenchie.

"Would you, if it's really MacArthur in that whaleboat?" asked Lee.

"Seems like overkill to me. All that firepower to protect one man? He may be a fucking general but he still puts his pants on one leg at the time. Just like the rest of us poor slobs."

"Only difference... He's got a bigger set of balls. Hell, Frenchie, the man's in charge of the entire shebang. Damn straight they're gonna protect him. MacArthur's the man with the big picture, the only one who has the foggiest idea of what's really going on over here."

Frenchie shrugged a nod. "Yeah... I guess I see your point."

The whaleboat made it past the break line then circled for a minute while the driver picked out his spot. When he started to make his run to the beach Lee saw immediately there'd be a problem. Having charted the shoreline last night he knew the boat was headed for a submerged sand bar. He also knew what was required to pass over it. That sand bar was just under three feet deep in the water. The whaleboat had just over a three foot draft. Something had to give and it wasn't going to be the sandbar.

"They ain't gonna make it," said Lee.

So he wasn't surprised when the general's whaleboat ran aground thirty yards from the beach. The tall, thin photographer was impressed.

"How in blazes did you know that was going to happen?"

"A little fish told me."

Onshore people began to run around like chickens with their heads cut off. Someone yelled at the beachmaster to send out an LCVP to retrieve the general. Another idiot asked for a long rope—for God only knows what purpose. To his credit the lieutenant kept his cool and provided the only plausible solution.

"An LCVP's backwash might swamp the whaleboat. Have them wade ashore instead. The water's only a couple of feet deep. Nobody's going to drown. Especially not MacArthur. He's too damn tall."

A few feet away a gaggle of oak leaves gathered in a circle to come up with a more palatable alternative.

General Douglas MacArthur getting his feet wet? Preposterous! Maybe we should do this. Maybe we should try that. How about floating out a pontoon—or something?

The beachmaster finally made the decision for them. Despite being outranked, this was HIS beach and as such he had the last word. Besides, a hundred yards farther down the beach a mike boat had breached and all hell was breaking loose.

"Walk them on in!" he bellowed into his bullhorn. End of discussion. He turned his attention to his other, more pressing disaster.

The tall, thin photographer had been fiddling with his camera when he noticed the commotion offshore.

"Omigod! They're wading in! And they're headed right for us!"

"Better back it up a bit," offered Lee. "You wouldn't want to cramp their style."

"Chop, chop," smirked Frenchie. "Or you'll miss the shot. I ain't no whiz with a camera, but from where I'm sitting, the position of the sun seems all wrong. Won't it be shining in your lens?"

After a quick exchange of glances, three red-faced photographers hot-footed it across the beach to find a better angle. Botching up this once-in-a-lifetime shot would sidetrack their careers. Probably demote them to the mailroom. After replanting their tripods they barely had enough time to focus before the parade started.

Lights, camera, action... and the circus was underway.

FORTY-THREE

AS PLANNED, THE first one to hit the beach was MacArthur. Tall and stately, his four-star demeanor gave him away. As did the weathered hat laced with two rows of scrambled eggs. With his jaw jutting forward and his corn cob pipe hidden in his right hand—he'd lied to his aide—he rose from the sea at a manly pace, parting the knee-deep water like a warrior Moses.

Struggling to keep up—a few steps behind and almost a foot shorter—followed the swarthy Sergio Osmena, the Philippine president. With the rolling surf up past his crotch he was having a rough time of it. To MacArthur's left and farther to the rear straggled several high rankers the cameras were ignoring. If ever there was a one man show, this was it.

"Great press." Lee heard one of the other photographers murmur. "This'll make all the newsreels."

Destined to be knocked out of first place by five Marines raising Old Glory on Mt. Suribachi, for now this was shaping up to be the number one morale raiser of the Pacific war. A photographic icon that would stand the test of time. And the shot had to be perfect. With the cameras whirring at full speed the star-striking entourage made its way towards shore. All was going well until an unnamed colonel in the back row took a header into the surf. In less than two seconds a discombobulated junior grade rushed up to the stand of photographers. His voice several octaves higher than normal.

"Tell me your cameras didn't catch that!" His voice borderline frantic.

"Hard to miss it," said cameraman number two.

"Affirmative on Colonel Clod," agreed cameraman number three. "His pratfall was definitely in the frame."

A wounded look washed over the young officer's face. As if he'd been stabbed in the heart.

"Is there any way you can edit it out?"

"Not without blurring MacArthur's image," offered cameraman number two. "And I don't think you want us to do that."

"Aw... shit!" groaned the JG. "I'm totally screwed."

Removing his piss cutter to wipe his brow he glanced up towards the sun, hopefully, to the heavens beyond. No relief there, a man's shoulders couldn't have sagged any lower.

"This means a re-shoot," he said with a slow shake of his head.

"Which part?" asked cameraman number one.

"All of it. The general is unequivocal when it comes to releasing material to the press."

"Unequivocal?"

"The man's the world's biggest hard-ass. Everything has to be cross-the-t's-dot-the i's perfect. We'll have to restage the whole damn thing."

By the time the frazzled officer reached the general's party they were already thirty feet up the beach. When he told them about the mishap they weren't pleased. Especially MacArthur. Even at a distance Lee could make out most of their words. And none of them were complimentary.

When Lee walked over to the photographers the tall thin one had already set aside his gear and was sitting on his duff in the sand. A bent unfiltered Camel hanging from his lips, he had adopted the *hurry-up-and-wait* stare common to G.I.s everywhere.

"Problem, guys?" asked Lee.

"Just another bucket of worms," chuckled cameraman number three. "Situation normal all fucked up."

"SNAFU strikes again, eh? What the hell happened?"

"Some chubby colonel stepped on his dick and went swimming and we caught it on camera. Unfortunately."

The cameraman nodded towards the congregation of agitated colonels circling around the poor lieutenant junior grade—soon to be busted down to an ensign. As if on cue they all began to point this way and that, each trying to out yell the other. Except of course for MacArthur, who stood off to one side quietly seething to himself as he stared out to sea.

Although it wasn't his fault, the JG took his reaming like a man, nodding his apologies where appropriate. After extracting their pound of flesh the colonels finally tired of blustering and turned their attention elsewhere. Seizing the opportunity the JG popped off a salute, turned on his heels and double-timed it back to the safety of the photographers.

"You all right, Lieutenant?" asked cameraman number one. "Looked like they were chewing you a new one."

"My ass is a few pounds lighter but I'll live. All part of the job description, I guess. At least they didn't shit can my commission. Not yet anyway."

"What did they decide?"

The JG chin-nodded out to sea.

"They're returning to the ship. Sorry guys, but this first one was a mulligan. This time the general will be riding in on an LCVP. And go *around* the damn sand bar."

"If at first you don't succeed...?"

"That's why we're in the Navy."

Having overheard, Lee had to laugh along. Most times it was better than crying. Watching the JG head back to the landing spot he glanced down at the man's soaked pantlegs.

"Uh...sir?" he shouted. "I don't mean to eavesdrop, but I think you have another problem. One that may cause you even further grief down the line."

That stopped the young officer in his tracks.

"And what is that, sailor?"

"Well... You might want to make sure the general changes his pants?"

"His pants? What in God's name for?"

"Wouldn't it look strange if they were wet *before* he hits the water? Some poor slob sitting in a dark movie theater back home might even think he had an *accident*. If you know what I mean."

Looking once more to the heavens, the JG's sigh could be heard halfway up the beach. *Why me, Lord?*

"Damn it... you're right! Thanks for the heads-up. You saved what's left of my butt."

And with that he hustled off to make sure the star of the show was properly attired.

So... thanks to the keen eye and quick thinking of one Seaman Lee "Stump" Kelley, when take two finally went down, General Douglas—no middle name—MacArthur was wearing a pair of clean, pressed, and, most importantly, dry pants.

FORTY-FOUR

TAKE THREE TURNED out to be better than take two. The fourth better than the third. But when several high-ranking staffers suggested a fifth go-around—just to be on the "safe" side—the beachmaster almost popped a blood vessel. In the Navy two silver bars never talked back to four gold stripes. Careers came to a screeching halt for a lot less. But the lieutenant was teetering on the edge of his patience. The day had already turned to shit and even though the morning wasn't half over he'd put up with a year's worth of bureaucratic garbage. Biting his tongue he chose his first words carefully.

"Sirs... You see those thirty or so mike boats out there beyond the reef line? They've been circling for over an hour now, burning up petrol. All waiting for this photo shoot of yours to finish up. If they don't land soon they'll have to return to their mother ships for fuel. And that's gonna take at least another two hours."

The highest ranking colonel of the bunch cast a nervous eye towards the mike boats. Then shot an even more nervous glance in MacArthur's direction. Through all this the General had been waiting forty yards down the beach, getting ready to face the cameras one more time. Hopefully he was out of earshot.

"I hear what you're saying, Lieutenant, but this shouldn't

take much longer. It's a golden chance to send some badly needed good news to America. I don't know if you're aware of it, but up until this point the war hasn't exactly been going well for us. And this photo shoot could have widespread ramifications on morale back on the homefront."

That tore it. The lieutenant's gut reaction was to punch this time-wasting colonel right in his fat, self-righteous nose—but he fought back the impulse. Wiping his sweat-soaked brow with an equally sweat-soaked dirty rag, he tried counting to ten. When he got to five he lost control.

Ah,well, he thought. *I wouldn't look good in oak leaves anyway.*

"No disrespect, sir. But the only *front* I'm concerned about is the one five miles inland from where we're standing wasting precious time. The real front where men are fighting and dying while we cluck about some damn photo opportunity. I've never met General MacArthur but I think he would take a dim view of anything that would endanger those brave men. I'm sure at this point *their* morale is more important than anything those three shit-for-brains photographers could piece together in some fucking newsreel."

"Now see here," said the colonel, puffing out his chest. Raising his finger he was about to give this upstart officer a piece of his mind—along with a proper bracing—when he thought better of it. A bean counter for his entire career, the colonel was no dummy. The eagles on his collar hadn't come from sticking his neck out. If MacArthur ever found out the consequences of such a delay... he'd be back in Washington handing out No. 2 pencils. Even though the lieutenant's response bordered on insubordinations—and probably deserved a court martial—the colonel took a calming breath to reassess the situation. Bottom line: The man was right. Dead right. No sense in chewing out the messenger.

"Um...I think you've made your point, Lieutenant. You can signal your boats to land."

Thankful he still had his bars the lieutenant snapped off the sharpest salute he'd mustered in years.

"Thank you, sir! I'll get right to it."

After securing Tacloban the Allies launched what at the time would be the largest joint naval operation in history. The Battle of Leyte Gulf was actually four separate actions pushing ever northward. As expected the Japanese diverted seventy thousand troops—and most of their naval forces—from Luzon to Leyte to keep from being shoved out of the Philippines entirely. Their homeland supply pipeline and dwindling oil reserves depended on it.

In four days of intensive sea battles the US Navy won decisive victories in the Subuyan Sea, Surigao Straight, at Samar and Cape Engano. With those heady successes under his belt MacArthur then set his sights on retaking Manila, a daunting task that would require additional naval support. But to the west, Admiral Chester W. Nimitz had a different outlook. In charge of a large portion of the *additional support* MacArthur coveted, Nimitz had his eye on Formosa, hoping to use it as a forward air base to bomb mainland Japan into submission. When presented these conflicting plans President Roosevelt eventually gave the nod to the hard charging general who had guts enough to promise an earlier victory.

Given the executive go-ahead MacArthur landed his 6th Army at Mindoro Island. Bogged down by miserable weather and difficult terrain, the 6th finally overcame stubborn resistance and conquered the island's vital air bases. By then Mac's growing Navy had mastered an amphibious operation's four phases. In large part by trial and error.

First came the approach phase, where the proposed landing site was bombarded day and night—along with any enemy shore batteries and support facilities. Included in this stage were constant mine sweeps and the removal of underwater obstacles by teams of frogmen—who also made topographical charts to assist landing craft on their way to the beach.

The second phase was the actual landing itself, where forces were put ashore under the protective cover of both aircraft and the guns of the naval fleet off shore. As soon as a foothold was established on the beach this was followed by a third, support phase that provided continued air and artillery bombardment—some of it provided from the beach itself—until the enemy was driven out of range and the shore-based squadrons could take over.

The final phase involved guaranteeing the security of their supply lines—so vital to maintaining the ever-inward push of the troops. A matter of exacting coordination, on paper it was a sound plan and if all went well it would be just a matter of time before the enemy capitulated.

And at first things did go well. But as the 6th would soon learn, wars are never fought on paper. And taking back the Philippines turned out to be a can of worms.

FORTY-FIVE

AFTER A FEINT at South Luzon, on the ninth of January 1945, a landing was made at Lingayen Gulf. Facing little opposition a beachhead was quickly established and in less than a day later, Allied forces began to move inland. Caught by surprise this time, the Japanese had abandoned the shoreline and retreated farther inland to the more easily defended mountains. At first the strategy was much appreciated by Lee and his bodies, who couldn't find a single jumping jack.

"How'd it go last night?" asked Biggles Hammond—who'd missed last night's dive due to a bad ear infection.

"It was a walk in the park," said Lee. "We might as well have been skinny dipping in my neighbor's pond. The Japs didn't leave anything for us to blow up. No JJs, no blocks of concrete, no barbed wire, nothing. Hardly worth getting our dicks wet."

"Maybe next time," grinned Hammond. Bending closer he looked right, then left. "Mum's the word, but a friend of mine up in the radio shack said a second class overheard the XO talking to the skipper, something about heading for Manila Bay after we wrap up here. And according to the chatter he's been picking up over the wire, they're blowing the shit out of the place. So hold on to your hats, we should have tons of stuff to blow up when we get there. If, and when."

Frenchie snapped open his switch blade. Scraped dirt from underneath a thumbnail.

"Let's hope so. We've hop-scotched so many islands the past few months I've lost count. I'm itching to destroy something. Anything. Sometimes I wonder why the Navy even bothers to send us in for a look anymore. We never find anything. The Japs seem to be going out of their way to avoid us. Mind you, that's not all that bad... but—and I know you'll think I've gone stir crazy— they don't even try to make it interesting anymore."

"Are you kidding me, Frenchie?" said Lee, an incredulous look popping onto his face. "You've got your head wedged up your ass. *Interesting?* Is that what you call getting shot at?"

Fisting his right hand into the shape of a trumpet, Frenchie blew on his thumb and up popped his middle finger. Aware that Lee was a big Andrews Sisters fan, he began to hum the chorus to "Boogie Woogie Bugle Boy" for good measure.

"Right back at you, short stuff," he grinned. "This tune's for you. Don't twist my words. You know what I meant. All this easy living is getting to me."

Lee returned his grin.

"Says the man who spent most of his life ass deep in the swamps. Thank you very much, but I'll take easy living over getting shot at by a Jap sniper any day of the week. And twice on Sundays."

FORTY-SIX

EVEN AFTER TWO weeks of constant bombardment, taking Manila turned out to be both the rock and the hard place. MacArthur himself was flummoxed by the stubborn resistance his troops encountered. Having broken the enemy's radio codes earlier, intelligence officers had been well aware of the decree sent down by the Japanese high command to abandon the city and retreat to higher ground—a tactic that had served them well on other islands. What intelligence didn't count on however, was an overly zealous Rear Admiral who took it upon himself to disobey that decree and defend the city with the twenty thousand soldiers at his disposal. Who made life miserable for the 6th Army by fighting and dying virtually to the last man.

Manila eventually fell to the Allied forces on March 5, 1945, the same day the first crippled B-29 made an emergency landing on Iwo Jima. Both events signaled the beginning of the end for Japan. The fall of Manila effectively severed the island empire's last remaining supply route. And taking Iwo meant America's super-fortresses could now bomb Tokyo at will.

But in mid-February both issues were still very much in doubt. After six months of sporadic air bombardment, on the sixteenth of that same month the Navy began to shell Iwo Jima in earnest. For three days and nights they pummeled the nothing little island around the clock, devastating its landscape for years to come.

At the same time, the battle for Manila was still undecided in the Philippines. In an attempt to deliver the knock-out blow, two thousand paratroopers landed on the island of Corregidor— also on the sixteenth of February. Initially caught off guard, the Japanese shore forces quickly regrouped to inflict heavy losses. Further air drops had to be cancelled and with the element of surprise gone, a subsequent landing the next day was met with stiff resistance. With bodies piling up on the beach, the Allies had to dig in before moving inland. Slugging it out against a force that had vowed to fight to the death, in the end it would take the war-weary Americans eleven agonizing days to take Corregidor.

Soldiers had to mow down wave after wave of maniacal Banzai attacks, firing so fast that the barrels of their weapons often turned red hot. When the smoke finally cleared only twenty Japanese made it off the island, all of them badly wounded. Like everywhere else in the Pacific, Hirohito's minions believed dying for their emperor was the ultimate, and only honorable end—a philosophy the Allies found both confusing and disheartening.

To most Americans it made more sense to live for your county than die for it. In the end it made them better soldiers. As a pearl-handled pistol toting general would later say, "No poor fool ever saved his country by dying for it. He saved it by making some other poor fool die for his." Or something to that effect.

Even then, a large number of America's finest soldiers never made it off Corregidor's beaches. A depressing statistic that laid a gruesome task on Lee and his frogman buddies.

FORTY-SEVEN

AFTER SCOUTING THE beaches at Corregidor, for the last three days Frenchie and Lee had been biding their time on a transport ship anchored a mile offshore, awaiting further orders. Having lost interest in their card games they were bored silly. Even their illicit beer had gone flat.

Looking for something to pass the time, dusk on the fourth day found both of them gravitating toward the fantail—along with the rest of the frogmen teams— to watch the ground fighting taking place two miles inland. A line of 6th Army tanks had reached the foothills and were creeping forward using their flamethrowers to incinerate anything that moved—a spectacle both exhilarating and terrifying. Coming to the stern Lee leaned forward to grab a top railing with two hands. Setting a foot on the lower railing he nodded at the bursts of yellow snaking out of the jungle.

"Looks like they're trying to burn the Japs out of their tunnels."

"They say the island's laced with miles of them," said Frenchie. "Just like every other island we've had the misfortune to run across. And I hear tell some are over two hundred feet deep. Probably explains how the Nips can survive our shelling."

When a long tongue of flame flickered into the sky he let out a slow whistle.

"Like the fires of hell... Damn, but that napalm sure is nasty stuff. Gets you a'comin' and a'goin'. Shit burns off your 'air then sears out your lungs. Not my idea of a fun way to die."

Said Lee, "First thing the Japs do when they get to one of these islands is dig in."

"You got that right. Maybe that's why they all got buck teeth and slant eyes. They're turning into a bunch of moles."

Off to the right and higher up on a hill, several Shermans cranked up their *Zippos* a notch. And for a few blazing seconds the surrounding jungle lit up bright as day. Watching the inferno a heavy silence settled over the two frogmen. Both men hated the Japanese with a burning passion, but they wouldn't wish what they were witnessing on their worst enemy. Which, of course, is what the Japs were.

Lee was heavy into thoughts of his own frailty when the chief walked up, a crumbled piece of paper in his hand.

"Gather 'round, guys. The good news is we've finally got some orders. Bad news... you ain't gonna like them one damn bit."

"Another dirty job?" asked Lee.

"They don't come any dirtier."

Waiting for the rest of the men to circle up, the chief took off his cap. Rubbing a hand across his balding pate he looked off toward the battle still raging on shore. Then took a long, deep breath. This wasn't going to be easy. Bad news never was.

"As you all know, a few days ago our paratroopers took a pounding on the beach. And, sorry to say, many of them are still floating face down in the surf."

Looking down at the deck, Frenchie sucked air in through his nose. Shook his head.

"I know where this is going. And I hate it already."

"So do I," said the chief. "But somebody has to retrieve their bodies. And unfortunately that somebody is us."

A soft curse drifted from somewhere in the back. Followed by the sound of twelve choked up sailors swallowing hard.

"Listen up, all of you," continued the chief. "Because the fighting has been so intense they haven't been able to send in anyone until now. As it is, there still might be a few Jap stragglers lurking about so you'll have to keep your eyes peeled for snipers."

"What else is new?" said Lee. "And I suppose we'll be operating in broad daylight this time."

"No other way. But if a dink bobs his helmet so much as an inch out of the sand our guys will blow him to pieces. In addition the Army has detailed two platoons to patrol the beach while you're in the water."

"That's reassuring," said Frenchie. "Let's hope they can shoot straight."

"Our Army?" snickered Lee. "They couldn't hit the broadside of a barn. From the inside."

"If you two jokers are quite finished..." admonished the chief, "rafts in the water at 0700. A Higgins boat will be attached to each of your teams. It will act as your drop off point and provide further close in cover. When you find a body you'll secure it in your raft and swim it back to the boats. They'll transport him back to the troop ship and we'll take it from there. According to the numbers I've been given, this is going to be an all-day evolution. Probably longer. Finally, since explosives aren't involved, the UDTs are going to sit this one out."

Lee poked Frenchie in the ribs. Whispered, "Lucky dog."

"But don't think they're gonna skate," added the chief. "Operations has a separate evolution planned for them in Manila Bay. One last thing: If I were you I'd skip breakfast tomorrow morning. Some of those paratroopers have been in the water for over forty-eight hours now. So they're gonna be in pretty bad shape. Probably stink to high heaven." Shaking his head he rubbed the back of his neck. "Any questions?"

Dead silence on the fantail, the time for joking was over.

"That's it then. Better try and get a good night's sleep. You're gonna need it."

FORTY-EIGHT

DESPITE A COOLING breeze from the south, at midnight the temperature still hovered in the mid-nineties, and for the next few hours a bare-assed naked Lee Kelley would toss this way and that on top of his bedroll. With so much swimming through his brain he was destined for yet another restless night. Still front and center in his mind was Hillbilly's untimely death. Right behind that was what he and his frogman team would be facing come dawn. Around two dark-thirty he gave up on sleep entirely and gravitated back towards the fantail. Always the fantail.

Willie Williams—his partner for tomorrow's gruesome assignment—was already standing at the starboard railing. Propping his right foot on a lower wire, Lee looked off at the darkened hills above the bay. Through a fine mist in the distance he could barely make out several rows of Sherman tanks lined up like a herd of giant black beetles, waiting for tomorrow's barbecue to begin. Their flame throwers had closed up shop for the night, so other than a few scattered fires on the beach, *all was quiet on the western front.* A few minutes had to pass before either of them spoke.

"I see you couldn't sleep either," said Lee.

"Not a wink," replied Willie.

"Lot of that a going around."

"I guess it's to be expected. Considering..."

"I know what you mean. I'm sure as hell not looking forward to what tomorrow's gonna bring."

"I don't think anyone is. Least of all the chief."

Small talk finished, the two turned their attention back to the beach. Reflections of the few remaining fires flickered out across the calm water. Another time, another place the view might have been enchanting, peaceful even. From the fantail of a tired troop ship anchored off the battered shores of Corregidor, however, at best it was disheartening. Peace had nothing to do with the shimmering lights dancing up at them.

"Sight like that brings back memories," said Lee at last. "Kinda reminds me of the bonfires we used to have back home around Halloween, when the air started to get a bit nippy. And the frost was creeping on the pumpkins. Especially that one Saturday night after the big game with Jefferson. Me and Debbie Hooper made out beneath the bleachers. Jefferson may have beat the pants off us that afternoon, but that evening I got to second base with Debbie. Almost beat her pants off, in fact. So the night wasn't a total loss.

"I had a hell of a time with that bra of hers, though. Damn thing seemed to have a mind of its own. Took me forever to get the sucker unhitched. Infernal contraption that it was."

"You always were all thumbs, Stump."

"Yeah, but in the end love triumphed. Sorta. I guess where there's a will, there's a way."

Savoring the now all too distant memory, Lee looked out to sea as he expelled a slow sigh.

"Good times... I wonder if they'll ever come again."

Suddenly a high-pitched whine—almost a soft scream— trickled out from the beach to shatter Lee's warm feeling. Offensive to the ear—like long fingernails being dragged across a blackboard—the quasi-scream grew louder and louder, until it ended with a muffled explosion. Almost a pop. A few seconds later another whine rose from the beach, turned into a scream, then another mushy pop. Sounding like a watermelon splattering on a concrete floor.

"What the hell was that?" cringed Willie.

"Yesterday the chief told me they've been burning Jap bodies late at night on the beach. My guess is that when hot gases pass over the vocal cords they must generate something sounding like a scream."

"Good guess..." said Willie, his face looking like he'd been sucking on a lemon. "And those disgusting *pops?*"

"I'm not sure. Only thing I can think of is when the fire gets hot enough it starts to cook the brains. Eventually all the heat *pops* the skull."

"Yuck! Too much damn information. Remind me never to get creamated."

FORTY-NINE

FIRST IN LINE for breakfast that morning—and ignoring the chief's warning—Lee had already downed a hefty portion of scrambled eggs—powdered though they were—four sausage links, and a bowl of lumpy oatmeal. Even though he'd almost gagged on the coagulated milk it was floating in. And hard to believe, but he'd dished up a second helping across the board. He was munching on his third piece of toast when Frenchie strolled over scratching an armpit. Among other things. Probably the only frogman who caught any sleep, he cast a dubious eye at Lee's messy plate.

"I see you didn't take to heart the chief's advice about eating light this morning. Might not be a wise choice considering what's waiting for you out there. I sure hope you can keep all that down."

Lee swallowed the last of his toast. Reached for his coffee mug.

"Not to worry. I've got a cast iron stomach. Haven't puked in years."

"Oh, yeah? What about that last liberty in San Diego? If I recollect rightly, you blew lunch all over some chief's shoes. Or how about that beach blow-out in Hawaii? Tossed a ton of cookies if I'm not mistaken. And that was only a few months ago, my forgetful friend."

"Those don't count. They were both brought on by excessive amounts of alcohol. And I haven't touched a drop in days. So, I'm not sweating it.

"For your team's sake, I hope you're right, Stump."

"Wanna trade jobs?" asked Lee.

"Nope. Ain't gonna happen."

"Aw, come on, Swampman. I can lay charges almost as good as you. What's the big deal?"

"Dragging a bunch of dead bodies out of the surf? Not on your life. Mine either."

FIFTY

AT SIX FORTY-FIVE sharp the chief gathered his men on the starboard side of the ship. Tethered to the landing platform at the end of the ship's ladder, three LCVPs bobbed with the incoming tide—their engines idling, crews at the ready. As indicated by the bags under his eyes, the chief had also spent a rough night. He too had no stomach for what lay ahead. But unlike Lee, he had wisely avoided eating any solids for breakfast. Strictly coffee only.

After a quick head count he turned his attention to Team One—the go-fers. Although he wouldn't be going ashore with them to retrieve the bodies, he'd be standing by when the LCVPs returned with their grim cargo. Not something he was looking forward to.

"All right," he sighed, "let's get this over with. Kelley, I'm putting you in charge of the Corregidor detail."

"Me, Chief?"

"Yeah, you. You make the smallest target."

"Hey, wait a minute. Willie is shorter than me. By at least half an inch." Trying to lighten the moment—if that were even possible. "And... he used to play the tuba back home in his high school band. Shouldn't that count for something?"

Despite his foul mood, the chief couldn't help but crack

a grin. Leave it to Kelley to spice things up.

"The *tuba*? What the hell has that got to do with the price of eggs? Or anything else for that matter? Besides, Williams is too quiet. And he squeaks when he talks. In the water he sounds like a field mouse drowning at high tide. I need someone with a booming voice. Someone who can be heard over the pounding surf. And you're the one with the biggest mouth in this outfit, Stump. We all wish you would shut the fuck up at times, but at least no one complains about not being able to hear you. Like it or not, you're my man."

"Thanks a pantload."

"Okay, men..." continued the chief, anxious to get on with it. "This is a simple bag and tag operation. You bag them, send them back to the ship, and we'll tag them."

Shocked by what had just come out of his mouth, the chief blinked twice. Took way too deep a breath. It must have been the lack of sleep.

"Sorry, that didn't come out right. Those are our boys out there, and they should be treated with the utmost respect. It's gonna be hard on you—harder than you can possibly imagine—so if things start to weigh you down, or if you find yourself losing it... just call back to the ship and we'll rotate shifts. We don't want anyone going batshit on us."

Williams raised a tentative hand.

"Uh, Chief. How many can we expect? Bodies, I mean."

"I'm not sure of the exact number. More than a thousand troopers were dropped that second morning. And a good portion of them never made it to the beach. At least two hundred probably. Maybe even three. So you're in for a long, hard day."

"How much actual diving is this going to involve?" asked Lee.

"Not much. Since a lot of those guys have been in the water for over two days now. Well, as you'll soon find out, decomposition gases have popped most of their bodies back up to the surface. And according to our last coordinates the tide has concentrated three quarters of the floaters on the windward side of the island. What with them bobbing around like corks you shouldn't have any trouble finding them."

"Any special instructions?"

"Just be careful how and where you grab the bodies. They may have a tendency to come apart on you. Above all we want to bring our boys back in one piece if possible. One more thing... I know how you hate nose clamps. But you might want to keep them handy."

Rubbing the back of his neck the chief puffed out his cheeks, exhaling the weight of the morning.

"If there are no further questions let's hop to it. Stump, get your men into their boats."

With the chief watching their wakes, in less than five minutes two LCVPs were halfway to the beach. Thankful he wasn't in their shoes—or in this case, fins—he turned to his remaining charges.

"You're next, Team Two. UDTs and chart makers, front and center. That last LCVP will transfer you to a pier on the south shore of Manila Bay. Probably the only one left standing. There you'll meet up with a Seabee officer. Consider yourself lucky you're not on Stump's team, but for the next few days you're gonna be busier than a one-armed paper hanger with a hemorrhoid. I'm not sure what the Bee's have in mind for you— only that it involves a shit-pot load of explosives. So you can bet it'll be something right up your alley. Like blowing up everything in sight. You'll get your marching orders when you arrive."

Punching up a raffish eyebrow, Frenchie ticked a half grin onto the right corner of his mouth.

"At least we'll get to blow up something other than fucking railroad tracks. Any restrictions?"

"Not that I've heard. Grapevine has it, anything within ten feet of the surface is gonna be fair game."

"Tully" Sullivan, Frenchie's temporary diving buddy for the next few days, shot an exuberant two thumbs up.

"Hot damn! We're gonna have ourselves a hot time in the old town tonight!"

"Not so fast, Tully," cautioned the chief. "This ain't no knee-slappin' shindig you've been given a ticket to. What with all the mangled iron in that bay, no doubt you're gonna run into some hairy-ass problems. The kind of hairy-ass problems that could get you killed if you're not careful. From what I've heard, the bottom is piled so high with wreckage you can walk across the whole damn bay without getting your feet wet."

Narrowing his eyes the chief leveled his most potent stink-eye at the cocky frogman. Tully's mouth was always in gear before his brain.

"I'm warning all of you. Treat this evolution as a shits-and-giggles lark and I'll be sending what's left of your bony butts back to the states in a fucking bag. There'll be no grab-assin' on my watch. Do I make myself clear?"

Quick head nods all around. And one timid "Yes, sir," from somewhere in the rear. Having to work for a living the chief hated it when someone mistakenly addressed him as a lowly ensign. But this time he let it slide.

"OK. You know the drill. Let's get this show on the road."

FIFTY-ONE

WHEN THE FORWARD lookout circled his fist, Lee's LCVP slowed, settled in the water and started to come about. Directly ahead lay a curved sandbar the length of two football fields. Exposed by the receding tide it was flanked on three sides by a ridge of sharp coral reefs that could shred the bottom of any Higgins boat. Between the reefs and the sandbar stretched a calmer expanse of water. Protected there from the surf, several dozen bodies had collected in a macabre bobbing circle. Even from a distance the stench was overwhelming.

"Ready with your rafts, divers!" alerted the driver, shouting to be heard over the roar of his engine. "This is as far as I can take you! From here on you'll have to swim!"

A final twist on the wheel and the boat settled into its own wash, its bow pointing toward the beach and expertly shielded from the incoming waves. In a few seconds the ramp was lowered halfway down. Any farther and the LCVP would have taken on water.

"On the double! Everyone out! We don't want to swamp the boat!"

In two seconds flat both teams leaped overboard. As soon as they hit the water the ramp was on its way up. While he was backing away the driver shouted out his final instructions.

"We'll be circling farther out, where the reefs aren't so shallow! When you're loaded up give us a signal and we'll come back in for a pickup!"

When he was sure his prop wash had cleared the divers he turned and headed out to sea. The lookout had already resumed a position by his locked and loaded thirty caliber. Pointed at the beach, its barrel was a reassuring sight to the men in the water.

The day had broken bright and cloudless. The sun had barely edged free of the horizon and already the temperature had climbed into the mid-nineties. The humidity a zillion percent, Lee felt as if he was sucking air from an exhaust pipe as he fiddled with his mask strap. Sometimes the damn thing wouldn't catch right, making it difficult to get a proper seal.

"Looks like it's gonna be a sunny day at least," he said, trying for humor. "Just another day in paradise."

Considering the circumstances the joke fell flat.

Willie spat into his face plate. Spreading the spittle around with a forefinger he nodded toward the gaggle of dead troopers swaying gently face down on the surface fifty yards to his right.

"My idea of paradise isn't filled with rotting bodies. Besides, it's too damn hot for my druthers."

Lee cleared his snorkel. Checked to make sure his diving knife was secure.

"Point taken about the heat. At least we're in the water."

"Which is also too damn hot."

Scanning the surface, Lee took a quick head count.

"Twenty-two, twenty-three... I count twenty-four bodies over there. Twenty-six, counting those two drifting toward the beach."

Twenty-six bodies in such a small area. And who knew how many were floating on the other side of the sandbar. Or were still hovering on the bottom—snagged like rotting strands of flesh searching desperately for the surface. The figures were too staggering to contemplate and for several depressing seconds Lee and his crew tread water next to their rafts, hoping against hope that the scene played out before them was just a dream.

They all knew what had to be done, and done quickly—the rotting rays of the sun could not be denied—but to a man they nurtured the futile hope that any moment they'd wake up from this nightmare and they'd be back on the ship. On top of their bedrolls, hungry for breakfast and ready for another day of playing cards and swapping tall tales. That the ill-fated landing never happened. That the Japs never attacked Pearl Harbor. That Hitler and Tojo had never been born.

The *what if's* came to an abrupt halt when the wind shifted.

Enveloped in the stench of death revisited, Lee felt his innards twist to the right. The rancid stink of hot iron hung so thick in the air he could almost taste it. When his guts lurched back to the left he suddenly realized his stomach may not have been made out of cast iron after all. And that maybe he shouldn't have been so cavalier about eating a big breakfast. Gagging back two eggs and four sausages, for the first time since he'd been issued swim fins he snapped on the hated nose clamps. Breathing through his mouth had always been cumbersome—even when he was swimming races. Fearful of his breakfast backing up on him he gulped down a big breath. Then another.

"Team Bravo, you guys head for the sandbar," he managed finally. "As soon as Willie and I gather those two stragglers we'll join you. And remember what the chief said. Be careful how you handle these guys. Kid gloves at all times."

FIFTY-TWO

THE TWO WAYWARD paratroopers had drifted halfway to the beach so it was a struggle to reach their bodies through the pounding surf. It cost Lee valuable time and set his team behind schedule. Having first been riddled by bullets then tossed about by the waves, the corpses were in worse shape than their brethren—who had been protected by the sandbar's curve. Even from twenty yards away Lee could tell this was going to be the hardest thing he'd ever done in his life. Or probably would ever have to do.

"Sweet Mother of God..." he groaned. "These guys are nothing but bags of jelly."

Williams had to pinch off his nose to keep from gagging. His eyes were watering and even though he was up to his nose in salt water, he could feel his skin creep.

Thank heaven I listened to the chief and had the good sense to skip breakfast.

Unlike someone he knew.

"They've bloated up so much they've split their uniforms. And most of their faces are gone. They don't even look like human beings anymore. Just sacks of goo. How are we gonna handle that? Talk about shit's creek!"

"Thank God they drifted clear of their parachutes," said Lee.

"Or we'd have a hell of time trying to untangle arms and legs from the shrouds."

A few more strokes and the frogmen's feet touched bottom. The shallow water came as a welcome reassurance. At least now they'd have some leverage.

"Let's put the raft between the bodies and the shoreline," suggested Lee. "If the surf washes them onto the beach they'll break apart even more. And then we'll have to pick them up with a sponge."

Reaching out, he grabbed the first trooper by his harness belt—which was dragging several strands of seaweed. *When it rains, it pours.* Holding his breath—and subconsciously crossing every finger he had—he pulled ever so gently. But it was enough to tear skin. Propelled by expanding gases the poor man's lower regions exploded, splattering Lee in the face with rotting guts.

Startled by the mass of rancid slime at his throat, he gulped seawater down the wrong pipe. As he started to choke, up came breakfast through his mouth and nose. Before he could clear his mask a second burst of entrails hit him and he found himself entangled in a glob of fetid intestines. Writhing with small crabs and sea critters, the jumble seemed to be a living, breathing thing.

Grappling with several strands of shredded sinew, Lee felt a surge of panic rising from his gut. He'd been trained to control his emotions and gotten good at it, but this was above and beyond. It was as if some viscous sea creature had risen from the depths and was trying to drag him down. Twisting this way and that, when he was finally able to free himself from its clutches a convulsive shudder rippled up and down his entire body. Backstroking a few yards he forced himself to choke back his revulsion and take stock.

Get a grip, Kelley. There are no monsters here. You've still got a job to do. So get on with it.

"Jesus, Stump," said Willie, swimming over to help. "Are you all right?"

Still gulping air Lee raised his right hand in front of his face to make sure all his fingers were attached. They were still shaking. And his heart was pounding so hard it took him a few seconds to respond. Even though he was totally emerged in water, he could feel himself sweating. And for a moment he thought he might pass out.

"Lee? You okay?"

"I—I think so," he said finally.

"Damn," said Willie. "If that had been me I'd have shit a brick."

"I'm not so sure I didn't."

Breathing through his mouth had become tricky so Lee loosened his nose clamps. The wind had shifted and with it came a new odor.

"Christ," he groaned. "What now? That smells like burned hair."

Williams nodded his chin toward the smoldering pile of ash on the beach.

"Must be coming from all the Jap bodies they burned last night. Has to be hundreds of them."

Lee clamped his nose clips back in place. Burnt hair, rotting flesh, slimy sea creatures—it was all too much. Even for his hardened nose. Lowering his mask he pulled a small piece of intestine from his hair.

"After this I may swear off meat altogether. And I know damn well I'll never be able to face a plate of spaghetti again."

Puffing out his cheeks, Willie shook his head.

"You and me both, Stump."

FIFTY-THREE

THEY NEEDED ALL of thirty minutes to gather the exploded trooper's remains. At least what they could find of him. Some of him had drifted away with the current to become fish food. It then took several attempts to nudge what was left of his body into the raft. Since it was oozing so much fluid Lee decided they should transport him back to the LCVP immediately. Before he and Willie set out he gave instructions to the rest of the team.

"We won't be able to put that other body in the raft with him. He's in worse shape than this poor fellow so we're gonna swim him back solo. Telling what belongs to whom is hard enough without mingling body parts."

Mingling body parts! Did I really say those three words? Hell of a war you've gotten yourself into, Kelley.

"You guys stay here and make sure our second trooper doesn't drift away with the tide. We'll be back as soon as we can."

As the two of them set off Lee kept his head down, his shoulder to the raft. Concentrating on his kicking he tried to block out the images that had just been seared into his brain. Fat chance. And with those indelible images came a flood of inevitable questions. Questions that would plague him for the rest of his life.

How could a loving God allow something like this to happen?

And if He truly loves us... Why does He put up with all the shit we do?

Did He create us in His image only to kill one another?

Why doesn't He put a stop to this damn war?

How can He sit up there on His almighty throne and not do anything?

Is there any hope for us all?

Too many questions. Not enough answers.

Lee was just getting around to pondering his own mortality when Williams bumped into a large coconut drifting out on the tide. At least it looked like a coconut. When he pushed it aside with his free hand it rolled over to reveal an empty eye socket.

"Holy shit! What the hell is that?"

Lee twisted the coconut around to expose the rictus of death.

"I think it's a man's head. Or what's left of one. The eyes are gone and most of the flesh has been eaten away, but it's definitely human. American, I'd say, from the size of it."

"Probably got blown off one of our troopers by a mortar," said Williams, his composure returning.

Lee turned the severed head around to examine the neck.

"No, I don't think so. A mortar would have made a jagged tear. And this was a clean cut. My guess, this man had his head hacked off by a samurai sword."

"Slant-eyed bastards!"

"At least the end came quick. Better than a gut shot anyway. The Japs must be running out of ammo if they've taken to using swords."

Lee looked off toward the LCVP circling in the distance. Wallowing in the gentle swells outside the reef line, it was still a hundred yards away. Only halfway there, they'd have to quicken their pace if they wanted to catch the tide. Grabbing the rotting head by its hair he placed it in the raft with as much dignity he could afford. He apologized as he tucked it into a corner.

"Sorry, fella. But I promise we'll find the rest of you. And then we'll send you home."

That morning the frogman teams retrieved fifty more bodies. Several had severed arms or legs. Two were cut in half. And one was missing his head. At least Lee was able to keep his promise.

FIFTY-FOUR

TO GET A better view Frenchie had taken up a position in the rear of the Higgins boat, right next to the driver. So when they rounded the break wall he was the only one on his team who could see where they were going. And he couldn't believe his eyes.

There must be some mistake.

The battered wooden structure dead ahead had taken several direct hits during the battle for Manila Bay. Bullet-ridden and tilting to the right, it looked like it couldn't support a well-fed barnacle—much less three teams of frogmen. Raising a skeptical eyebrow Frenchie tapped the driver on the knee. Then pointed at what might have been a pier at one time.

"I know I'm not in charge of this here boat... and that I have no say-so in the matter. But don't you think the beach might be a better place to drop us off? A healthy sneeze and that piece of kindling's history."

"Sorry, friend, but I've got my orders. The Seabees checked it out yesterday afternoon and said it was probably safe. Even though it does look like a pile of shit."

"Probably safe?"

"What can I say? I'm only the boat driver. I go where I'm told."

With a shrug of his shoulders the driver reversed his engine to sidle up to the only stretch of pier still intact. But when a chance wave caught the LCVP amidships the bow nudged into a splintered stanchion with a loud crunch. Two seconds later two hundred pounds of bullet-pocked planking toppled into the ocean. Leaving a gaping hole where he had intended to tie up.

"Oops, my bad."

Putting the boat in forward gear again he tried to edge ahead a few yards. Without much success.

"This ain't gonna be easy," he said after his second try. "Good thing you fellas can swim."

Clicking his tongue Frenchie scratched his head.

"Can't do much swimming if what's left of that damn pier falls on top of us."

After another fruitless try the driver gave up and backed off a few feet. He couldn't chance sinking the boat.

"I'd have better luck trying to thread a needle with a sausage link. Sorry, guys, but this is as close as I can get. Looks like you're going to have to jump for it. And I'd make it quick. No way of telling which way that hunk of junk is going to lean."

Against their better judgment twelve frogmen promptly heaved their gear onto the pier, setting the thing to wobbling back and forth. After waiting for the bucking bronco to calm down, Frenchie looked to the heavens, crossed himself and took a flying leap of faith—half expecting to break a bone or two in the process. As their leader he felt obligated to go first.

Here goes nothing!

After a nimble tuck and roll on landing, he could feel the whole pier shaking beneath him. And for a split second he thought he'd have to ride the eyesore into the drink. When he didn't, he signaled the rest of the frogmen to follow suit. Immediately the driver jammed it into reverse and backed off to a safer distance.

"Good luck to you guys!" he yelled, his words almost drowned out by his laboring engine. "Don't get caught by the short and curlies!"

"Thanks a bunch!" Frenchie hollered back. "It's easy to give advice when you're the one cutting bait and heading for the hills! Wish we could be so lucky!"

A quick head count revealed the frogman teams had landed safe, if not exactly sound. And that—thank God—the pier was still standing. Sort of. Normally his wise-cracking partner would have come up with a smart ass remark by now, but Tully looked a little green around the gills. In his woozy state he wasn't able to come up with anything witty. Like Lee, maybe his breakfast wasn't sitting so well. In addition—being the least coordinated of the bunch—he'd taken a blow to the solar plexus upon landing. Apparently he was as clumsy as he was obnoxious. Head down, hands on his thighs, he looked like he was this close to ralphing up his breakfast. More embarrassed than hurt, he tried to wave it off.

"Okay, we're here. So to speak." His face a dark shade of red now. "So what's next on the friggin' agenda?"

Thinking the day was getting longer by the minute, Frenchie straddled a gaping hole in the pier to retrieve his duffel bag.

"First thing we do is gather our gear and make sure nothing is broken. Then as soon as we find out who's in charge of this boondoggle, we get to work."

His bag was caught on a jagged sliver of wood a foot above the water. Reaching down to grab it his heart skipped a beat when he spotted a huge hammerhead shark two feet below the surface. A twelve footer at least, as the monster glided by it rolled on its side to reveal a large obsidian eye. Covered with a layer of film it looked like a doll's glass eye. Lifeless and without pity. Definitely a bad omen—and coming from a voodoo background Frenchie was more than a little bit superstitious—he followed the tail fin until it disappeared under the pier.

"That's great! Just what we need. I sure hope that damn shark ain't of the nosy kind."

"Or more importantly," smirked Tully, "of the *hungry* kind."

If a nosy, hungry, and exceptionally large fish with sharp teeth wasn't bad enough news already, after Frenchie secured his gear he was met with an even more disturbing sight.

Arrayed before him was a vast graveyard of sunken ships. Manila Bay had to be the world's largest underwater junkyard. A scene right out of Dante's Inferno—somewhere near the seventh circle of Hell—it looked as if a demented sculptor had run amok across the entire harbor. As far as the eye could see twisted steel jutted from the surface at every angle imaginable.

In places the mangled iron was so thick a baby jellyfish couldn't have squeezed through. Not to mention a full grown frogman. For only the second time in his life Frenchie was totally speechless—the first being when his father was bitten in half by Big Jake. Back then his response had been to blow the damn alligator's brains out with his 'aught six. Today's problem, however, couldn't be resolved by a bullet. Unfortunately Tully was the first to regain his tongue. Along with some of his color.

"Christ Almighty! That chief wasn't bullshitting us. This damn harbor is one damn mess. Looks like the entire Jap fleet bought the big one out there."

Always complaining about something, the guy never shut up. Thank goodness this pairing was only temporary. After one short boat ride with the man, Frenchie could already see why Stump had called him a colossal waste of human skin. *A patch of crabgrass in the lawn of life*—his very words.

Too annoying to be a friend, but too loud to be ignored, Sullivan was as skinny as a rail. In the middle of his ferret face a hooked nose barely separated a pair of beady eyes. To top it off he had the world's worst case of B.O. The man always smelled like garlic. Even when he came out of the shower.

How anyone can stink underwater is beyond me, thought Frenchie.

"You gotta be shitting me," Tully continued to whine. "It's gonna take us fucking forever to clean up this damn bay."

"And then some," mumbled Frenchie.

"You won't have to, lads," boomed a voice from behind them. "Not this week at least."

FIFTY-FIVE

NO ONE HAD noticed the broad shouldered warrant officer reclining against the far bollard on the other side of the pier. With his back to them he had blended into the woodwork. His voice was so commanding even the seagulls stopped their squabbling. For sure it caught Frenchie's attention. Hands behind his head, the warrant gave the teams a quick once over.

"'Bout time you froggies got here."

Casting his cigarette butt into the water he rolled over and began to unfold himself. Cracking his knuckles as he rose, he almost blotted out the sun. Closer to seven feet tall than six, the man was beyond large. After an eye-popping yawn he tugged at his crotch. Then scratched an armpit. Finished with adjusting himself he crossed a pair of muscular forearms that would have put Popeye to shame.

"For now your orders are to clear out a narrow channel in the middle of the bay. Wide enough so's our boats can make it to the beach and back without running aground."

Stepping in front of Tully Frenchie extended his right hand. Engulfed in the warrant's ham hock of a fist, his fingers couldn't span the man's palm. The vise-like grip didn't make it any easier.

"You sound like the man with the know. Name's Frenchie. And this here sorry sack of shit is Tully."

"Pleased to make your acquaintance, Frenchie. I'm CWO3 Melvin Ott," said the giant. "Fresh out of Mobile Construction Battalion 62. But my friends all call me Mel. That is if they know what's good for them."

"Duly noted, Mel," grinned Frenchie. "I take it then that we're attached to you."

"Roger that. Me and my crew of 'Bees have been assigned to clean up this *damn mess*, as your observant friend there so aptly called it. We've already scoped out the bay and charted a possible path of least resistance. But the final choice will depend on what you guys find underwater."

"Glad to hear you've got an open mind," said Frenchie. "Lot of officers don't."

"*My way or the highway* don't cut it with us construction types. Most of us were riding bulldozers or pounding nails a few months ago back in the states. So this *yes-sir-no-sir* crap is new to us. And about as useful as a spare dick at a wedding. Help us get the job done as fast and safely as possible and we'll get along just fine."

Frenchie liked the man already.

"We can live with that. Got any idea what's waiting for us out there?"

"Just shit and more shit. The wrecks are recent and therefore mostly unstable. We've watched a few shift when the tide goes out, so I'm guessing you'll want to steer clear of those suckers."

"Passably smart advice."

"I'm probably preaching to the choir, but if I were you I wouldn't stray too far from the pack. Lots of things out there can mess you up real bad. And I see you've already met one of them. His name is Henry, by the way. And I can assure you his personality matches his looks."

"Henry?"

"The bag-of-teeth hammerhead you were staring at. That motherfucker is one bad, ugly fish. With an appetite that won't quit. Nosier than my mother-in-law, he'll eat anything that moves and most things that don't. Two days ago the son of a bitch snatched my tool box off this very pier. Swallowed the damn thing whole. Turned my back for a second and it was gone."

"Don't tell me…" chuckled Frenchie. "Inside was a hammer."

"My favorite. Had it for years. I hate that fucking shark." Ott patted the holster at his side. "I've got a special bullet in the chamber with his name on it. Every day about this time he comes sniffing around, looking for something else to gobble down. But he's a smart one. Always stays deep enough so's I can't reach him with my '45. One of these days though, he's gonna get careless and POW! I'll have me some shark fin soup."

As if on cue Henry's dorsal fin broke the surface a hundred yards away. Well beyond the range of Ott's pistol. After a languid circle the shark straightened up and headed back out to sea, raising a taunting fin as he went. Almost as if he were waving.

"That's right! Run away, you bastard! Your time will come!"

Turning back to Frenchie:

"Not to tell you guys your business, but with all the crap swimming around I wouldn't take any chances. Water's clear and the visibility is great, but I'd still play it safe. Keep your buddy within an arm's distance and have your head on a swivel at all times. You never know what's gonna pop out of those wrecks. A lot of bodies are still trapped down there and that makes good eating for all kinds of fishes."

"How's the bottom?" asked Frenchie.

"Torn up in most places. The big boys shelled the hell out of this bay for a week so it's still settling. Loaded down an LCVP can navigate in a yard of water. Two feet if her skipper doesn't mind mud on his keel. Adding another twenty feet or so for good measure… you shouldn't need to dive any deeper than twenty five. With any luck you'll never have to touch bottom."

"Any special critters we should worry about, other than Henry?"

"Just the usual nasties. Barracudas, moray eels, a few sea snakes. Maybe a curious grouper or two, although they're more annoying than dangerous. One good thing… those that survived the barrage have to be shell shocked so they shouldn't give you much trouble. To be on the safe side however, I'd wear leather gloves anytime you come close to the bottom. That's where the stonefish like to hide."

"Thanks for the heads-up. We'll keep our eyes peeled."

Ott looked west toward the last vestiges of a lazy sun dipping slowly into the horizon. Then down at his watch.

"It's getting late. Today's pretty much shot. Light's fading fast so there's no sense in trying to lay any charges now. Our detachment is camped out beneath that scrawny clump of palms over there. Probably the only trees left standing in the bay. After you stow your gear we can see about rustling up some chow for you and your men."

"Sounds great," said Frenchie with a smile. At the mention of food suddenly he was hungry. "What's on the menu?"

"Fresh crabs?"

"Fresh?"

"Sweetest meat to ever tease butter. From the biggest crab legs you'll ever find on this planet. About the size of my arm, in fact. Cipaye, the locals call them. Coconut crabs to us. The shelling drove them out of their burrows and we've been pigging out ever since. Slow as molasses above ground so they're a snap to catch. Gotta watch out for their giant claws, though. Two of my men lost fingertips when they got too close. Crabs clipped them clean through the bone."

Frenchie let out a slow whistle.

"I know crabs can pinch the hell out of you, but I never heard of any that strong."

"And then some. The suckers can shred a coconut in less than ten seconds. Hence the name."

"In that case I think me and my team will concentrate on the eating. And leave the catching to you."

"Good thinking."

FIFTY-SIX

THEIR BELLIES FULL of succulent coconut crab, the following morning Frenchie and his men were once again standing on that rickety pier. With the thermometer already past ninety a gentle rain was falling, raising a thin mist across the bay. Most places in the world the rain would have cooled things down. Here it only made the air thicker.

"Another day, another dollar," smirked Tully. "Looks like it's going to be another hot one. Just like yesterday was, and tomorrow's gonna be. One thing you can say about this fucking country... at least the weather's consistent. Consistently bad, that is. Yuk, yuk, yuk."

Jesus, thought Frenchie. *Can anyone use more words to say less? And I've got to spend the whole day with this gasbag. Ah, well... at least when we're underwater I won't have to listen to his infernal jabbering.*

"Gather around, guys. You all heard what the warrant said yesterday. These are treacherous waters so stick with your buddy. Never lose sight of him. And no long dives. Minute at the max, I don't want any blackouts. We aren't here to break records so anything below twenty five feet is out of bounds."

"How long are we gonna be stuck in this fucking shit hole." Tully with another interruption. The man could never keep his thoughts to himself.

"As long as it takes, Sullivan, and not a minute more. Give it a rest, will ya? You think you're the only one who doesn't care for this assignment?"

Turning to the rest of his men:

"We'll start with the wreck closest to shore and work our way out. Bravo Team, you take that fishing boat over there. It shouldn't take you more than an hour to blow her apart. Charlie, that rusty tramp steamer is all yours. And tread lightly, she looks as if she could tip over any second. When you're both done you can join up with Alpha and me. We'll be working on that Jap patrol boat lying on her side. Any questions?"

A well-timed stink-eye in Tully's direction for once brought a welcome silence.

"OK, then. Let's get to it."

FIFTY-SEVEN

IN THE SOUTH Seas a frogman's first dive of the day was always exhilarating, an underwater feast for the eyes that took even an experienced diver's breath away. Left even Tully Sullivan speechless. And today was no exception. Snorkeling over to the patrol boat, the first thing to fill Frenchie's face mask was a gathering of Jap tanks imbedded on the bottom thirty feet below him. Clearly from a nearby sunken cargo transport ship, the tanks had landed tread down, dooming their now impotent gun barrels to rust for eternity in the shallow depths. From that distance they almost looked like a herd of brown cows grazing peacefully in an underwater meadow.

When Frenchie looked closer however, he could make out the torso of a dead Japanese soldier dangling from one of the tanks, his arms waving with the current as if he were making a final Banzai salute. A gunner probably, the poor bastard had tried to escape from a hatch and drowned in the process. There'd been a lot of that going around. On both sides. No longer a threat to anyone, his eyes and most of his face were gone, nibbled away by the schools of small fish darting about. Standard funeral arrangements when you were buried at sea.

Hmm... Nothing peaceful about that, thought Frenchie as he continued on.

When he finally reached the patrol boat he realized the wreck presented a handful of unseen headaches. First, the damn thing was a lot larger than it appeared to be from the pier. More like a small destroyer than a patrol boat. Second, the superstructure was jutting forty five degrees upward, the perfect angle to inflict maximum damage to a passing ship, large or small. Third and worst of all, the bridge had taken a direct hit head on. Jagged metal from the overhead fanned out in all directions, like a giant blossom of razor sharp flower petals. Left untouched it was more dangerous than a hundred jumping jacks.

"Damn, this ain't gonna be easy," said Frenchie, more to himself than his crew. "Looks like we'll have to blow her apart at the deckline. Given her size, it'll probably take over a dozen dives just to plant the charges."

"Great, just fucking great!" grumbled Tully, always the pessimist. "It's gonna take us all damn day to blow up just one damn ship."

"If it does, it does. But this sucker has to go. First things first, let's check her out."

FIFTY-EIGHT

FRENCHIE HAD A shocker waiting for him on the bottom. Due to the patrol boat's awkward tilt—and the way half of its bridge had been blown apart—he didn't see the apparition until he was pulling himself through a shattered port window.

Lashed to the ship's bent wheel were the head, half torso, and right arm of a Japanese naval officer. No doubt the captain. As all good captains are supposed to do, he had chosen the honorable path and attempted to go down with his ship by committing *hari kari* with his ceremonial sword—now lying at where his feet should have been. But a five incher from an American destroyer must have beaten him to the punch, tearing him limb from limb in an instant. At least it was quicker than gutting yourself with a dull sword.

Since you never knew what you'd find in a wreck, Frenchie had braced himself for anything. But the grisly sight took his breath away. Jerking backwards in a reflex action, he banged his head into the overhead. Hard enough to draw a thin trickle of blood, it also cost him the last of his tidal capacity. Not a good combination when you are underwater, twenty feet away from your nearest air supply, and have to swim back up through shark infested waters. Lungs afire, he headed up, stars already bursting in front of his eyes. Back on the surface again he was still gulping down air when Tully swam over.

"Jesus, Frenchie. Your eyes are wide as saucers and you're pale as a sheet. What did you see down there? A ghost?"

Yanking off his mask, Frenchie shuddered a final deep breath in through his nose. Of all the people in the world. Damn, this was embarrassing.

"Half of one anyway. There's a fucking Jap body tied to the ship's wheel. His guts are splattered all over the bridge. It startled me, that's all."

"Not to question your words, my friend... especially considering how handy you are with that pig stabber of yours, but I'd say you were more than startled. *Scared shitless* comes to mind. 'Course had it been me to run across that stiff—"

"But it wasn't you. Now was it, Tully?"

"Geez, take it easy, willya? No need to go hostile on me. I was just trying to show a little concern." Scratching his head, Sullivan looked back toward the pier. "So, what's next?"

A final deep breath and Frenchie glanced up at the sky. At least the clouds had parted and the sun was now shining.

"The ship's in a tricky position so we'll have to blow the starboard side first. If we can split the bridge in two maybe it will collapse on itself and tumble to the bottom."

"Sounds good to me." Tully's shortest conversation in years.

FIFTY-NINE

IT TOOK ALPHA team thirty dives to lay their string of charges along the deck line of the bridge. Placed opposite of each other in and outside the bulkheads, if the tetrytol was detonated in the proper sequence it would sever the support plating and separate the bridge from the rest of the ship. If they were lucky—and gravity took its proper course—it would then slide down the deck, over the side and sink to the bottom where it would no longer be a hazard to navigation. The plan was a bit iffy at best—and not without a modicum of risk—but at least it was workable. After planting the last charge the team was treading water at a safe distance. After counting heads to make sure everyone was safe, Frenchie gave a thumbs up.

"Well... Cross your fingers, guys. Here goes nothing."

When he twisted the detonator switch a mound of water the size of a small house heaved from the surface with a thunderous FAH-WHUMP! A thin shiny silver object shot into the sky. Glinting in the sun, it slowly arched over to complete a graceful curve and then splashed down a few feet in front of Frenchie. The dead Jap captain's sword swash-buckled once, then plummeted hilt first as it began to spiral out of sight. All of Team Alpha was flabbergasted, speechless. Including, at first, Tully.

"Wow," he mumbled finally. "What are the odds of something

like that happening? Gotta be a million to one. Maybe a billion. It was almost as if the damn thing had a mind of its own. As if the ghost of that dead Nip captain was coming for you, Frenchie. Rising from the grave to hurl his fucking sword at you. Lucky thing the bastard's aim was a bit off."

"Nothing to concern yourself about, Tully. There's no such thing as ghosts."

This guy is REALLY getting on my nerves.

"Listen up, team. As soon as the dust settles we'll lay our next charges amidships. If we can break what's left of the ship in half it should settle deeper in the water. First thing we do is search for cracks or weak points. Tully and I will take the starboard side. John, you and Bill take port. You come across a good spot to lay a charge, mark it with a flag. Any questions?"

But before Sullivan could open his mouth, Frenchie cut him short.

"Except from you, Tully. All right, let's get to it. The blast made the ship even more unstable so be extra careful. If you feel even the slightest vibration hightail it back to the surface. And whatever you do, don't get stuck in a confined space. You don't want to snag yourself on something down there."

Being deeper, the starboard side was the more dangerous. It was the main reason Frenchie had chosen it for himself. On his third dive he discovered a hatch eight feet below the gunnel that had been blown open when the ship sank. It was hanging by a single bolt in a downward position, opening up a large passageway. A hairline crack extended from one corner of the hatch all the way to the deck. On the surface again, Frenchie related his find to his partner, who for once had the good sense just to listen.

"That crack's a perfect breaking point, Tully. If we can set opposing charges deep enough inside, she should break apart like an egg. Next time down I'll check out the rest of the compartment. The hatch is wide enough for one but that shouldn't be much of a problem. You can station yourself above the opening as my backup. I'll signal you if I need you."

Tully mocked a salute.

"Got you covered, boss. I'll be on the lookout for any more ghosts. Yuk, yuk."

Asshole.

The downward angle of the hatch forced Frenchie to dive deeper than he intended. Twenty five feet instead of twenty. No big deal, he gave Tully the high sign when he reached the opening. Lungs still comfortable, he made a mental note to limit his first look-see to thirty seconds. Plenty of time to get back to the surface. Glancing over his shoulder he saw that Tully was treading water where he should be. Reassured, Frenchie ducked his head and pulled himself through the hatch.

The crack turned out to be even wider on the inside. It split at the overhead and ran amidships as far as he could see. Both good signs. Even better, hovering in the far corner was a substantial bubble of air. At least a dozen lungs full, it was an excellent backup in case of an emergency. If he got into trouble breath-wise, he knew where to go.

Grabbing a wing latch he pulled himself forward until his head stuck in the first passageway. Thankfully daylight from the surface was penetrating deep into the compartment, enabling him to see that a few feet down the crack widened into a full-fledged gap. So wide he could stick his small finger into it. Perfect. Now all he had to do was...

SIXTY

FRENCHIE FELT THE sudden shift first. Then heard the ship groan as it began to slide further over on its side. Time to vacate the premises, he reversed his position to plant his feet on the tilted bulkhead. Shoving off hard he headed back toward the hatch, now five feet deeper than it had been. Halfway across the compartment his right leg rammed into something sharp. A small pink cloud billowed from his knee. Damned if a shredded strip of metal hadn't snagged him. The thing had hooked itself into the fleshy part of his lower thigh and wouldn't let go. And it burned like hell.

Way to go, Frenchie! Now you've gone and got yourself stuck. Just what you told your team not to do. Practice what you preach, dumbass!

A closer examination revealed the strip was buried deep into the meaty portion of his leg just above the knee. Bad news, the tip of the thing was shaped like a fish hook so when he tried to pull back it took an even bigger bite. And tripled his pain in the process.

Damn! That hurts like hell!

Flashes of light filled his face mask and he almost screamed. His lungs burning, he fought off a chest spasm. The first of many to come if he didn't find air soon. A quick glance upward revealed the shift had allowed his back-up bubble of air to escape into the passageway. Where he could no longer reach it. Just one bad thing after another.

Now's not the time to panic, Frenchie boy. Just calm down and think things through. Sure, your tit may be in the wringer, but there's got to be a way out. There always is. Remember your training.

Gritting his teeth he probed the metal strip with the tip of his diving knife. An immediate mind-numbing electric bolt shot straight to his brain. The wound was deeper than he thought. And somehow the damn thing had hooked itself around his kneecap.

Okay, you're between a rock and a hard place here. But you've been in worse shit than this before.

But for the life of him he couldn't remember when.

When he closed his eyes to calm himself a childhood memory of his father came flashing back. Standing in that rough-hewn pirogue of his—silhouetted by a full moon—his father had his feet spread wide apart, his trusty trident spear in his right hand. A quick throw, a sudden splash and he bagged two frogs. In the dead of night.

Way to go, Pops!

His dad had been the best gigger in four states. Always brought in the biggest hauls. Proud of his father, Frenchie could have used his keen eye and steady hand right about now.

Using the butt end of his knife Frenchie banged on the bulkhead. When up shit creek without a paddle, four hands were always better than two.

Damn it, Tully! Where the hell are you?

But when he looked toward the hatch his partner was nowhere in sight. Unbeknownst to Frenchie, Henry the shark had showed up right on schedule and driven Tully away. If there was one thing motor-mouth Sullivan never joked about, it was sharks. Especially large, hungry, hammerheads.

Past burning now, Frenchie's lungs had begun to spasm, trying to hiccough down air that wasn't there. His heart thumping out of his chest, his hands began to shake. With precious seconds ticking away he realized help would not be coming anytime soon. And that if it came at all it would be too late.

What did pappy always say? Oh yeah. The helping hand

you're looking for is at the end of your own arm... Good words to live by. Or in this case, maybe die by.

To survive this mess Frenchie would have to cut himself free. He'd probably lose part of his leg but what other choice did he have? Setting his jaw he reached for his knife. But as he was pulling it out of his sheath again a sudden contraction in his right forearm sent it spiraling away. He watched helplessly as it hit the deck then slowly slid across the tilted surface until it finally came to stop against the far bulkhead. Ten feet away and well beyond his reach.

Well, now you've gone and done it, Frenchie. You're totally screwed so I guess it's time to panic.

With no hope of being rescued he mustered the last of his strength for one all-or-nothing pull. Down to his final option, he'd have to tear himself free. He may never walk again—might even lose a leg, but what else could he do?

Planting his free foot against the bulkhead, Frenchie took half a second to steady himself. Then gave a mighty shove. Tendons snapped, muscles ripped. And somewhere deep inside his knee a bone splintered as the metal sliver ripped through his inner thigh. A wave of white hot pain washed over him and for an instant he passed out.

When he came to a few seconds later he found himself floating near the overhead, enshrouded in a reddish cloud. Good news, he'd torn himself free. Bad news, he'd severed his femoral artery in the process and was bleeding out. Light-headed and spent, he extended his right arm in a feeble attempt to pull himself toward the open hatch. He stroked once, twice, but he was too weak from the loss of blood and lack of oxygen. He didn't have the strength to swim ten inches, much less the ten feet required to make it to the hatch. To Frenchie at that point, it seemed like ten miles.

A circle of warm, inviting light filled his mask. At the center floated another image of his father standing tall in his boat, his right arm outstretched. And this time the sun was shining and he had a loving smile on his face.

"Don't fight it, son," his father said, clear as a bell. "It's your time, that's all. No big deal, it's all good. I've been waiting for you. All you have to do is take my hand."

And just like that the pain drifted away. The burning in Frenchie's lungs cooled. The spasms stopped and he felt his body becoming one with the sea. With an eternal smile whetting his lips he closed his eyes, relaxed, and let it happen.

Hell, dyin' ain't so bad after all. Sorta like lyin' down in a soft field of sun-warmed cotton.

And ever so slowly that warm circle of light gently faded into a never-ending darkness.

SIXTY-ONE

THE BLOODTHIRSTY DOGS of war have no guilt. And certainly no worldly masters. As mere mortals all we can do is cry havoc and mourn our losses. All consuming, war stops for nothing. And certainly not for the death of one man. Mired in his own living hell, Lee did not learn of Frenchie's death until three days later. Exhausted from a long day of pulling bloated bodies out of the bay, when the chief told him the bad news it was too much for him to handle. He felt like he'd been hit between the eyes with a two by four. Devastated, Lee staggered forward two steps before collapsing to his knees.

Frenchie drowned? There must be some mistake! Not Frenchie!

But when the chief held out Frenchie's diving knife he knew it was true. No mistaking those initials carved into the handle, Frenchie never left that knife out of his sight. Lee couldn't breathe. He felt dizzy, clammy all over. Disbelief sliding inexorably into despair, he fought back the tears.

"Why...? How...?" The two words rasped out of his throat. Taking with them a large portion of his heart.

"He got caught on a piece of twisted metal in the hold of a Jap patrol boat. It must have shifted with him inside," said the chief. "Frenchie hooked himself real bad. Tore half his leg off trying to get free and probably bled to death. His diving buddy found his body floating near the overhead."

Crushed by the agonizing weight pressing on his chest, Lee reached out to steady himself. He gasped air in through his nose. Twice, three times.

"He really must have been stuck bad if his partner couldn't cut him loose." Then it hit him. "Wait a minute! You said *found* him?"

The chief scratched the back of his neck. Took a deep breath of his own. He knew his next words wouldn't set well with Lee.

"Um... Tully says he was chased away by a giant shark. By the time he got back and swam down... Frenchie was already dead."

"What!"

"Others saw the shark too. It was a twelve-footer at least."

"Son of a bitch! I don't care how big the fucker was! You never leave your buddy! *Never! No matter what!*"

"Now calm down, Stump. It happened so fast there was really nothing Tully could have done. Even if he'd been there, given the severity of his wound Frenchie probably would have bled to death anyway. He's all broke up about it."

His despair instantly morphing into anger, Lee jumped to his feet. Grabbed his *tire iron* and headed for the hatch.

"PROBABLY? Where is the gutless bastard? Broke up? I'll show him broke up. I'm gonna cave his fucking head in!"

Stepping in front of him the chief placed both hands on Lee's shoulders. Looked him square in the eye.

"You can't, Lee. Sullivan's already gone."

"Gone? What do you mean *gone?*"

"A shrink transferred him back to Pearl for mental evaluation. Something about suicidal tendencies. Or some such shit. I know how close you and Frenchie were, but there's nothing you can do for him now. He's gone. You bash in Tully's head and you'd only get yourself in a world of trouble. And it wouldn't bring Frenchie back."

Lee hurled the iron against the bulkhead, smashing a first aid box in the process. Never before had he felt so frustrated, so useless. For several seconds all he could do was stand there seething, clutching his fists, sucking air. He wanted to hit someone, anyone. Break something, anything.

"If only I'd been there..."

"I know how you must feel, Stump. I lost a good friend of mine a few months back myself. War generates a million *what-ifs*. But we all have to get past them. In times like these we have to learn to live with our losses. There's no other way. If we don't... we'll all go stark raving mad."

Words. Just so many words. And words could never make the pain go away. First Hillbilly. Now Frenchie. The big galoots were like family to Lee. Better, actually.

In their brief time together Lee had grown closer to them than either of his parents. He knew he must have loved his parents—at least as a child back then—but now that he was an adult he was no longer confident in that love. In reality they had been little more than two passing spendthrifts who had given him life. Two human beings who by the chance consequences of an act of procreation had shared living space with him for a limited amount of time.

For sure he'd shared more with Hillbilly and Frenchie. They were the big brothers he'd never had. The perfect friends who were always there for him, no matter what he did, or failed to do. They had protected him, accepted him, loved him for who he was. Not for anything they wanted him to be. And now both of them were gone. Gone forever. Never before had Lee Kelley felt so alone.

SIXTY-TWO

"YOU'RE ASKING ME to forget about it?" said Lee at last.

Setting his jaw, once more the chief looked him square in the eyes.

"No, I'm telling you to get on with your life. You don't have a choice in the matter, Stump. Nobody in this fucking war does. As for the forgetting part... that'll never happen. A day doesn't go by that I don't think of my dead friend."

"What about Frenchie's body?"

"They buried him two days ago. Had to, in this heat."

Crushed by this final blow, Lee sagged against a stanchion. It just kept getting worse.

"I didn't even get a chance to pay my respects... say a proper goodbye."

The chief took off his cap. Wiped the sweat from his brow. Today was turning out to be a hot one. And more heartless than most.

"You'll get a chance to pay your respects later, when this is all over. We've been ordered to join up with the Third Marines under Nimitz for an amphibious landing on Okinawa. They say it's part of a *big push* to bring Japan to its knees. As if we haven't heard those two words before."

"I don't give a shit about any orders. Okinawa's just another fucking island on a long list of fucking islands. They said the same goddamn thing about Iwo Jima."

Lee could have understood if Hillbilly and Frenchie had died in combat, taking a few Japs with them. But both of their deaths had been accidents, something they'd almost done to themselves. No brave acts of heroism had been involved. No glorious deeds done.

In the grand scheme of things nothing had been gained. Granted, they had been sent thousands of miles from home to perform a dangerous job and their past efforts had definitely contributed to the war effort. But when it came to the great tote sheet in the sky... what had their deaths accomplished? No great army had been destroyed. No mighty navy sunk. Not even a single enemy bullet had been wasted. Hell, at this point in the war the Japs were killing themselves faster than the Allies could.

Bad luck? The breaks? Wrong place at the wrong time? Or maybe it was simply a case of God's Will. Another painful message from an indifferent almighty.

Oops... Sorry about that down on earth. Just a little reminder of your mortality.

By two capricious twists of fate two more sailors were dead. Drops in the bucket really, considering what America had lost so far. Worst of all, the only thing Frenchie's and Hillbilly's parents would be getting were letters of condolence a few weeks from now, when some admiral sitting safely behind a desk somewhere in Washington found the time to sign them. Since they hadn't officially died at the hands of the enemy their families wouldn't even be getting a posthumous Purple Heart. If that could even begin to ease their grief. Mulling this string of depressing facts over, it didn't take long for the inevitable question to pop into Lee's head.

Why them and not me, Lord?

If bad things actually happened in threes, that meant that Lee was next. His only consolation: At this point in time he was ready to meet his fate. Actually yearned for it. At least then he'd be able to rejoin his friends. His mind still swimming in death's wake, he turned back to the chief.

"What's so goddamn important about Okinawa anyway?"

Searching for a positive thread in all this, the chief chose his next words carefully. The last thing he wanted to do was nudge Lee closer to the edge.

"Scuttlebutt has it, if we take Okinawa our bombers can hit Tokyo at will. Being hundreds of miles closer to the Japanese mainland, we can reach them with our super-fortresses. Maybe deliver that knock-out punch everyone has been praying for."

As the tears began to roll silently down his cheeks, Lee looked out to sea.

"When do we leave?"

"Tonight," said the chief.

On March 2, 1945, in an emotional ceremony General MacArthur oversaw the raising of the American flag on the war-torn island of Corregidor. By that time Lee Kelley's ship was already three days out of the San Bernadino Straights. And well on its way to Okinawa. It took every ounce of strength he had left not to jump overboard in the middle of the night and end it all.

SIXTY-THREE

A SEMI-TROPICAL island seventy miles long and seven miles wide, Okinawa lies three hundred miles to the southeast of Japan—about halfway between Kyushu and Taiwan. Formed from three mountain columns rising up from the ocean floor, for centuries the island has been prone to earthquakes as well as seasonal typhoons. Ever since it became a prefecture in 1879, Okinawans were looked down on by mainland Japanese as the *bastard cousins* who were dumb enough to live on land that never stopped shaking. And was under six feet of water every other year. But in early 1945—as the island became more and more important to their defense—all eyes in Japan turned toward Okinawa. And suddenly those same bastard cousins became their best friends.

By late March most of Tokyo lay in smoldering ruins, with over three quarters of its wooden buildings fire bombed into ashes. After the Americans overran Iwo Jima the nightly high altitude air raids had increased four-fold. As Japan ran out of both planes and pilots Allied bombers were able to fly their missions in broad daylight—at lower levels, and in most cases, unopposed. A day didn't go by when the skies weren't filled with B-29s dropping their deadly incendiaries. Through it all Japan's short-sighted military put on a brave front, promising to fight to the last man—praising their exalted emperor with their final breath when they did. But even Hirohito knew that if his armies couldn't make a stand on Okinawa, it wouldn't be long before the sun would set on his dwindling empire.

Made out of coral, over the years filtering rains had laced Okinawa with a vast network of caves. A fact that would cause American soldiers untold hardships. And cost the US Navy more casualties than any other battle in World War II. Code name Operation Iceberg—definitely an odd tag for a tropical island—Okinawa would be the site of the largest amphibious assault in the Pacific, as well as the last major campaign of the war.

From the beginning of April 1945 until the end of May, seven major kamikaze attacks were directed at Okinawa, involving over fifteen hundred suicide bombers from Kyushu, Japan's southernmost island. On land Japanese soldiers fought like demons to defend Okinawa. Launching wave after wave of attacks from over ninety-six miles of interconnecting tunnels—for two solid months they died in droves, determined to go out in a blaze of glory. On the twenty-first of June—after eighty days of the most bitter fighting of the war—Japan finally gave up. For the Tenth Army Okinawa turned out to be a living hell on earth. American personnel losses were the highest of the war. Over seventy-two thousand casualties with 6,139 dead.

A costly victory to say the least, the conquest of Okinawa proved vital to the Allied effort. A short three months later—on the main deck of the American battleship *USS Missouri*—an armistice would be signed in Tokyo Bay. And the war declared officially over.

SIXTY-FOUR

ON MARCH 29, 1945 however, what was left of Lee's San Diego frogman class reunited on the forecastle of an APA anchored off the eastern coast of Okinawa. A quick head count by the officer in charge revealed an attrition rate of over fifty percent. A staggering figure considering the relatively short passage of time. Looking for some of his long lost buddies—most of whom were not there—Lee had to shake his head.

I guess they had it just as rough as we did. This fucking war better end soon or there won't be any of us left.

When a fuzz-faced ensign emerged from a hatchway with an official-looking folder in his hand, "Willie" Williams nudged Lee in the ribs. Then rolled his eyes.

"Would you look at this joker, Stump? Talk about wet behind the ears, he doesn't look old enough to shave. Junior there is probably a fucking supply officer. Only action he's seen has been counting beans. And *he's* going to tell us what the hell we're doing here?"

"Orders are orders, my friend. No matter where they come from. That's a gold bar on his collar so I guess we gotta listen to the man."

"Doesn't mean I gotta like it none."

Opening the folder the ensign cleared his throat. After

checking off a few details he began to speak in a deep, no nonsense voice that surprised both frogmen.

"Listen up, men. For the next few nights you'll be laying charges a few miles north of here at Minatogwa Beach. Recon tells us there isn't much up there, maybe a jumping jack or two, but we want you to blow up anything you can find. A rock, a sandbar, a pile of seaweed... anything. It doesn't really matter what. And make as much noise as you can. Flash your lights, raise a ruckus."

Not liking what he was hearing, Lee raised his hand.

"I may not be the sharpest crayon in the box, sir, and I mean no offense, but it sounds like a ruse to me. Something to attract the enemy's attention."

"You got it, sailor. Most of the Japs have already retreated to higher ground at the southern end of the island. And just like they did at Iwo, they've dug in up there. Built pill boxes and blockhouses to catch our troops in murderous crossfires. Our soldiers will be facing caves protected by double-apron barbed wire, minefields, trap-door machine gun emplacements, the whole nine yards. Unlike Iwo however, the Japs don't know where we'll be landing. And we'd like to keep them guessing."

Sounded logical to Lee, but that still left one major concern. One that was nagging every frogman on deck.

"We must be putting on this show for someone, sir. So there's gotta be at least one or two snipers hiding in the bushes, just itching to get a big fat frogman in his sights. With all the flashing lights and noise, won't we be sitting ducks?"

"Good question. But there's nothing to worry about. Three minesweepers will be making dummy runs close to the beach the whole time you're in the water. With their fifties trained on the shoreline. If a slant-eye so much as farts in your general direction they'll turn him into instant hamburger. In addition the *Tennessee* has been stationed off shore, with her big guns locked and loaded. I'm sure a few two-thousand-pounders will discourage any target practice by the Japanese."

"That's reassuring," nodded Lee. "So... when do we go at it for real?"

"Two nights from now, on the evening of March 31. You'll be dropped off by an unlighted minesweep on the western side of the island. At some place called Hagushi Beach on the mouth of the Bishi River. If all goes well the Third Marines will storm ashore the following morning."

Willie Williams inhaled a soft whistle.

"Um... isn't that April Fools, sir? I don't believe in omens—knock on wood—but couldn't the top brass have picked a luckier day? An operation this big... we may need all the help we can get."

"It's also Easter Sunday," grinned the ensign. "And even if your aren't the God fearing type—or even a Christian—you can't ask for more help than that."

As it turned out, the frogmen didn't need much help at all. The bogus detail up north went off without a hitch. Despite making enough noise to wake the dead, the Japanese didn't fire off a single shot. And other than a few sporadic mortar rounds, the actual landing on the other side of the island was relatively simple. Preceded by a ground-shaking barrage from the *Tennessee*, fifty thousand troops in eight waves hit the beaches virtually unopposed. This came as no surprise to Lee, whose recon the night before had been little more than a midnight swim.

Their part in the operation done, he and Williams found themselves standing on the fantail of a large personnel carrier, coffee cups in hand as they watched the big show unfold. At five-thirty the *Tennessee* was finishing up her final volley. Then after circling half a mile off shore, the first wave of landing craft was about to hit the beach. Consisting of twenty-eight LVTs—Amtracs equipped with seventy-five millimeter guns—they picked up where the battleship left off, raking the shoreline with close-in withering fire. Right behind them were sixteen more Amtracs loaded down with assault troops. And there were more lined up in their wakes.

SIXTY-FIVE

THE DAY HAD broken clear and surprisingly crisp, warm as usual but not as hot as the day before. A perfect day to wage war. Unfortunately the wind was picking up. To the east a phalanx of angry looking clouds had gathered on the horizon. Not unusual for the start of monsoon season. Leaning on a railing Lee drained the last of his coffee cup. Then took a futile swipe at the permanent stain in the bottom. On a scale of one to ten the coffee graded out at a seven. Not the best he'd ever had, but far from the worst.

"Wow! What a sight! Have you ever seen so many ships in one place, Willie? There has to be a couple hundred out there."

"At least. Maybe even a thousand. Looks like they're having an easy time of it though. Not much resistance. All those Higgins boats headed for them, probably scared the Japanese shitless."

"Not like Pelilieu or Tarawa." Even though Lee was no longer religious he crossed himself. "Thank God."

"Maybe the Navy has finally learned how to pull one of these things off, Stump."

"About damn time. They've had enough practice screwing them up. Of course it helps that the Japs aren't putting up much of a fight. Probably skedaddled inland, south into the hills. Just like that ensign said yesterday."

"I'm sure glad I'm not a grunt," said Willie. "Seventy thousand Nips holed up in all those damn caves? Our guys are gonna have a hell of a time burning them out."

Williams had no idea how prophetic his statement would eventually be. The *burning out* would last all the way into June and completely destroy over ninety percent of the buildings on Okinawa. In the process the entire island would be turned into a vast quagmire of mud, mangled equipment and rotting bodies. But compared to what lay ahead for the troops further inland, coming ashore was turning out to be apple pie easy.

"Did you know I was almost a jarhead?" asked Lee. "Way back when."

"Lee Kelley? A friggin' Marine? That doesn't sound like the guy I've come to know and sometimes love."

"No lie. If it hadn't been for a fast talking recruiter in downtown Cleveland, I'd probably be puking my guts out in one of those Higgins boats right now."

"Talk about a twist of fate."

"More like dumb luck."

Dumb luck? Could it have been that simple? Until now Lee had never given his so called career path much thought. But he had to admit luck had played a large part in his joining the Navy. And his becoming a frogman. Then again, Hillbilly and Frenchie had also been blessed with the same *dumb luck*. And both of them were now dead. And he was still here. Able to drink coffee on the fantail of a large ship safely at sea, miles from the action, while other men fought and died. Good men, like his two best friends.

Why them and not me?

He still had no answer for that one.

Willie pointed toward a cluster of threatening clouds hanging low on the horizon. Dark and pregnant looking, they seemed to be getting bigger.

"Looks like a gulley-whumper is headed our way. The barometer readers say we're in for some nasty weather the next few days. Means we're probably gonna get hit with a ton of rain. Maybe we should dig out our slickers."

"Aw, they've been forecasting a storm for a week now. And those damn clouds have been forming up every morning for the last three days. But so far not a drop. By noon they're gone. Rain? I'll believe it when I see it. A buck says those thunder bumpers are gone by the time we finish lunch."

"You got yourself a bet."

SIXTY-SIX

LEE HIT THE rack a dollar richer that night. But Willie would have the last laugh. An hour after reveille on the fourth of April the seas picked up and the ships in the bay began to pitch and roll. Then the sky darkened and the rains came down in buckets. Buffeted by high winds, by 0900 Lee's ship began to drag anchor. Noticing that every LST in the area was already on the beach, the captain decided to head for open waters to ride out the fledgling typhoon.

After weighing anchor his first order of business was to avoid a collision with the destroyer floundering off his starboard quarter—no easy task in twenty-five foot seas. Broadsided by ninety knot gusts, within ten minutes anything not lashed down topside was washed overboard. When two lifeboats snapped free from their berthing stanchions the captain ordered all non-essential personnel below. And that included frogmen.

Heading aft down the nearest passageway, Lee bounced two feet up the starboard bulkhead when the ship suddenly lurched to port. Losing his balance he banged his funny bone into a metal wiring tube.

"Damn! That stings like hell! The seas get any rougher and we'll be walking on the ceiling."

Turning into the wind the ship pounded through a huge

swell, vibrating every nut, bolt, and metal plate on board. And two scrambling frogmen. Thrown to the deck by the shock wave, Lee and Willie had to crab their way on all fours. Not wanting to pinball the length of the ship they sought refuge through the first open hatch they could glom onto. Luckily for them it turned out to be the mess deck, the largest space on board. And for the time being, the safest. Struggling to gain their feet as they came through the hatch they were greeted by a dozen metal mess trays careening toward them.

"Incoming!" yelled Willie, ducking the first one.

Twisting to his right Lee was able to dodge the first three, but the fourth caught him flush on the shine bone. Frying pan into the fire, from the galley came two loud crashes. Followed by an even louder metal-on-metal scratching.

"Son of a bitch!" yelled an unseen cook in the galley. "Watch yourselves in there! Some serious shit's headed your way!"

Lee barely had time to duck and cover before several squadrons' worth of eating utensils flew through an open bay. Hunkering down to protect his head, knives, forks, and spoons began bouncing off the metal mess tables in staccato fashion—as if they'd been fired from a machine gun. From the galley came another loud crash. Followed by more cursing from the cook.

"Fuck it! I'm outta here!"

Venturing one eye only, Lee peeked around a table support to see the cook vault through the open bay head first. Nimble for such a short, fat man, after a quick tuck and roll he scrambled on his hands and knees to take cover behind the table next to Lee. Despite the morning he was having, the man was actually grinning. His flaming red hair and beard were powdered with flour, giving him a Santa-like aura. Still wearing his food-stained apron, he smelled like newly baked bread. Among other things. Even though he was huffing and puffing like a runaway steam engine he managed a playful wink.

"Hell of a morning we're having here, my friend. I guess we all shoulda stayed in bed."

SIXTY-SEVEN

FROM THE GALLEY came another loud crash. A second later a dozen loaves of bread—still warm from the oven—shot from the bay. Followed by several strings of sizzling sausages. Together the procession looked like a gaggle of chicks following mother hens.

"So much for breakfast," laughed the cook, who seemed to be having the time of his life. "I see you guys are frogmen."

"How can you tell?" asked Lee, dodging an errant loaf.

"Your shorts are a dead giveaway. And you don't stink half as bad as the rest of the crew."

"I'm Lee Kelley. And that wide-eyed waste of semen cowering behind the table next to you is my lilly-livered buddy, Willie Williams."

"Up yours, Stump," said Willie, flipping the finger. "Look who's talking. You're the one who dived for cover first."

"Yeah, but you're the one who screamed like a girl while he was doing it."

The cook brushed a cloud of flour from his crimson locks. Extended a flour-covered hand.

"Pleased to make your acquaintance, Lee. Name's Ralph Pepper. But my friends call me *Red*. For obvious reasons."

"Red Pepper? Sounds like the stage name for a stripper."

"I heard that one before. But with these bowed legs of mine I doubt I'd make much money stripping."

"Not to mention your hairy arms."

"There is that. Where you two from?"

"Cleveland, Ohio," said Lee.

"Chicago," said Willie, still nervously eyeing the open bay.

For the moment the galley had gone quiet. But with the ship still rocking and rolling, who knew what would be headed their way. Then a drain erupted. It sounded like a gigantic, bubbly fart and smelled even worse. Within a few seconds a hundred or so gallons of raw sewage sloshed onto the mess deck, forcing all three sailors to pinch off their noses.

"I come from Olathe, Kansas," said Pepper, despite the stink. "It's a small, one-horse town just west of the Missouri border. I wanted to be a frogman too when I joined up, but the Navy in their infinite wisdom told me I was too fat. Said I'd get my ass shot off when I bobbed to the surface like a cork. Some cross-eyed classifier said I looked more like a cook. So here I am, slinging hash on the other side of the world, on this puke-making bucket of rust."

Just then a heavy skillet caromed out of the galley. It bounced off the table to Lee's immediate right, then took out an overhead light with a resounding *Pop!*

"And now I'm chasing pots and pans around what's left of my poor galley."

"At least it's better than spending your days and nights in a leaky foxhole in the middle of the jungle. Getting your ass shot at," said Lee.

"Just what I need. Another fucking optimist. But you do have a point there, mate. Maybe I should count my blessings."

Something snapped in the galley and a heavy piece of equipment began to slide across the deck. Soon an ominous thud was followed by the sound of shattering porcelain.

"There goes the coffee urn and all our mugs," said Pepper. "Without their cup of Joe in the morning, there's gonna be a lot of pissed-off chiefs."

"Not only the chiefs!" groaned Lee. "Without coffee we might as well pack it in."

On the bridge, whoever had the conn ordered a hard right

rudder and the ship lurched to starboard. Down below, a large stainless steel mixing bowl shot from the galley. Missing Lee's head by a few inches, it bounced off the far bulkhead. When the ship snapped back to port, the bowl made a bee-line for the open hatch as if it had eyes. Ping-ponging down the passageway it sounded like church bells fading in the distance.

"Now there's something you don't see every day," said Willie.

Caught in a thirty-five foot swell, the ship began to shimmy into what seemed like a bottomless trough. The resulting slow deep roll put the mess decks at an untenable thirty degree angle. Holding on for dear life, Lee, Willie, and the red-headed cook had to spread-eagle to keep from suffering the same fate as the mixing bowl. Adding insult to injury, as soon as they hit the deck a three foot tsunami of warm coffee grounds, bread crumbs, coagulated sausage fat—and whatever else the galley drain had managed to regurgitate—surged forward to wash over them. Instantly all three were submerged in filth. Toes to nose in slop, they had to hold their breath.

Out-fucking-standing... thought Lee from underwater. *This'll look great on my tombstone. Here lies Lee Kelley. Served his country by drowning his sorry ass in a sea of garbage.*

When the ship finally righted itself the trio came up gasping for air.

"I hope you guys like C-rats," said Red. "'Cause that's all we'll be serving until this shit blows over."

Lee spit half a pound of coffee grounds out of his mouth. Wiped soggy bread crumbs from his eyes.

"No problem. I've kinda gotten used to canned crap."

Willie spat out half a sausage link. Almost gagged when a water-logged cockroach wriggled out of his ear. After wiping a glob of muck off his chin he chanced his first deep breath.

"I think I just lost my appetite."

SIXTY-EIGHT

THE HOWLING WINDS began to subside a few minutes past midnight, but with gusts still pegging out at over fifty knots the seas continued to roll. When it became clear they weren't going anywhere, around two in the morning Lee and Willie were forced to jury-rig hammocks in one corner of the mess deck, tying them off to a protruding air duct. Swaying back and forth as the ship pitched this way and that around them, every few minutes they bounced off a bulkhead.

At the apex of one particularly violent roll Lee banged his forehead into a pipe hard enough to rattle his teeth. So hard he spit out blood.

"Damn!" he grunted. "I think I bit off half my tongue on that last one. How in blazes are we supposed to sleep through this shit?"

"At this point, Stump," said Willie, "I think it's more a matter of survival than sleep."

Williams was having his own problems. In the middle of the roll his right foot had poked through the hammock webbing and he was now dangling precariously to one side. In danger of losing his balance completely, he was a twitch away from tumbling to the deck head first.

"Shit," he mumbled, trying to retrieve his prodigal foot,

"I never could get the hang of these damn hammocks. Whoever designed these pieces of shit must have been a fucking sadist."

Lee ran his tongue around the inside of his mouth, checking for damage. No missing teeth, but a back molar was loose.

"I hate them too. Every time I open my eyes I'm hanging in a different position. One second I'm halfway up the starboard bulkhead, the next I'm kissing port. All this swinging around is getting on my nerves."

Spreading his arms wide to regain his balance, Willie tried wedging his arms into the hammock's webbing. Still uncomfortable, he felt as if he'd been hung out to dry on his momma's washline.

"Try telling yourself it's all in your mind, Lee. That you're not moving, the ship is. If that doesn't work out just keep your eyes closed. What you can't see can't hurt you. Maybe."

"That's no help whatsoever. It just gives me vertigo."

Willie tried to pull himself up higher in the hammock. Failed.

"What bothers me most is all the fluids sloshing around in my belly. My poor stomach feels like a damn butter churn. Half the time I'm this close to puking."

"I told you not to drink all that water before we turned in."

"Well excuse me for being thirsty."

"What I'm gonna *really* mind," laughed Lee—at this point laughing was the only thing he could do— "is if you puke anywhere near my direction. Get one drop on me and I'll kick your skinny behind all the way back to Chicago."

"Oh yeah? You and who else's army?'

And so it went, back and forth to pass the time for most of the night.

SIXTY-NINE

THE STORM FINALLY blew itself further out to sea three hours later. Only then were the two frogmen able to fall asleep. For all of two fitful hours. A few minutes after nodding off for the third time, Lee was jarred awake by the clamor of the galley crew reporting for duty. And, as promised by Red Pepper, to the not-so-tantalizing aroma of newly opened C-rats. In this case something approximating over-cooked noodles wallowing in cold tomato sauce. Or maybe not tomato sauce. At least it was red. Rubbing his eyes Lee spied Willie straddling a nearby bench. Still in his skivvies, he was already chowing down.

"Omigosh," said Lee. "You're eating spaghetti? For breakfast?"

"I'm so hungry I'd even eat those pecker-track-encrusted shorts you've been wearing for the last week."

Lee swung out of his hammock to land barefooted on the cold, hard deck. Scratching his right buttocks he let out his first fart of the day. It was a doozy. He ached all over. His back was out of joint and even his teeth hurt.

"You'd have to be a couple years beyond starving to come anywhere near these skivvies of mine. Especially after that bodacious fart I just laid on you."

Willie raised his spoon to let a glob of the red stuff dribble onto his plate."

"It was either this or that green eggs and ham crap the Navy tries to foist on us. On the plus side, Red says the coffee machine should be back on line in a few minutes."

"Good thing. Without their morning transfusion of coffee the crew would string him up to the nearest yardarm. And I'd be first in line to hold the rope."

"Thank God the damn pitching finally stopped," said Willie. "I don't think this poor battered body of mine could have stood much more. As it is, I'm black and blue all over."

On the bridge a second class on watch obeyed the orders of the lieutenant who had the conn—and rang up All Ahead Full on the engine order telegraph. When the engine room responded Lee could feel the increased vibration through the soles of his bare feet. A few seconds later the helmsman swung his wheel thirty degrees to the right and the ship began a slow turn to starboard. A matter of having his sea legs, Lee leaned to the left automatically.

"Looks like we're headed back in."

"I guess it's time to check out the damage and pay the piper," said Willie, pulling on his pants. "Something tells me we're going to have a long day in front of us."

SEVENTY

BY THE TIME the two stowed their gear, finished breakfast—what there was of it—and downed their second cup of thankfully passable coffee, the ship was rounding the southernmost tip of the harbor. When they emerged from a port ladder Lee and Willie were greeted by clear skies, a warm breeze, and—Hallelujah!—a tamed sea. Smooth as a tabletop.

"Now this is more like it!" said a relieved Lee.

"As I've said many times before," added Willie, "just another day in paradise."

But their good mood evaporated when they caught their first look at the devastation on the beach. It looked as if some ancient malevolent god had played a game of pick-up-sticks with the landing fleet. Long and slow—with flat bottoms and frightful sail effects—the LSTs had had an even rougher night than the troop ship. At the mercy of the high winds, they'd been strewn this way and that, tossed about like so many bath toys.

"Holy crap!" marveled Lee. "What a fucking mess!"

In preparation for the storm the T's had attempted to beach themselves in a straight line, far enough apart so they wouldn't bang into each other. After dropping their huge shovel-like stern anchors—so they could later extract themselves from the beach—they had criss-crossed heavy lines forward, playing them fifty yards up the shore to secure their bows. Standard operating procedure for riding out rough weather. This time, however, it had all been for naught.

More powerful than forecast, the storm had yanked three LSTs off the beach and grounded them onto a reef to the right. Tilting at unnatural angles—their bottoms gashed open by the sharp coral—all three were leaking fuel. Oily slicks snaked from their hulls, gleaming in the sun like rivers of darkened rainbows.

Four LSTs had been washed three hundred feet inland and now lay high and dry behind a ridge of sand dunes. Two of those were resting on their sides in the sand, their barnacle-clad bottoms exposed like a pair of wounded whales. One had snapped apart amidships and was almost in two pieces. With its cargo fanned out across the beach it looked like the start of a giant omelet.

A sea of fetid garbage lapped against the ravaged ships still on the beach, wafting a stink so bad it could be smelled a mile away. Smashed vehicles and mangled equipment—most no longer recognizable—dotted the shoreline. Splintered wooden shipping crates and pallets, soggy boxes of rotting foodstuffs, dead birds, fish, crabs, rats and even a few dogs added to the flotsam. Standing guard over the whole mess was a Sherman tank that had been flipped on top of a shredded palm tree. With its gun barrel buried in the sand and its treads pointing skyward, from a distance it looked like a giant metal turtle unable to right itself.

Insult to injury, two days prior to the typhoon's arrival the harbor had come under attack from a squadron of kamikazes. Unbeknownst to the Japanese, however, the Americans had broken their radio codes and had stationed picket ships seventy miles off the coast of Okinawa. When the kamikazes took off from Kyushu their position was relayed via wireless traffic and most of them were shot down before they came anywhere near the island. The three that did were blasted out of the sky by Hellcats from the carrier *USS Hornet* before they could hone in on their targets. The scattered wreckage of one was still smoldering on the beach when Lee's ship hauled anchor to avoid the storm. Now it was nowhere in sight.

"What the hell happened to that Jap kamikaze?" asked Lee.

"It used to be over there, buried in the sand behind a ridge of palm trees."

Now the palm trees were gone too.

"The storm must have washed the son of a bitch out to sea," said Willie. "Along with half the damn island."

Lee scratched at his chin stubble. Sucked air in through both nostrils.

"From the looks of it that typhoon laid waste to most of our T's too. It's gonna be a long time before any of them are seaworthy again. If ever."

"Damn..." said Willie. "Look at that poor T on the far left. It broke completely in two."

Lee inhaled another deep breath. Then let it out slowly. He'd been doing a lot of that lately.

"I'm sure glad I wasn't on that sucker when the winds hit."

"I wonder why they didn't head out to sea like the rest of us."

"Ever been on an LST in rough seas, Willie?"

"Never been on a T. Period."

"Worst riding ship in the Navy. Bar none. If they'd have followed us out, every last one of them would be sitting on the bottom now."

"Rock and a hard place, I guess," said Willie.

Lee scratched the side of his head.

"I hitched a ride on the Hampshire County about a year ago. They had a balky rudder and wanted me to help loosen it up during one of their cargo runs. We had just cleared the southern tip of Leyte when a monsoon hit us. For half a day we took forty-five degree rolls. Got so bad I thought the damn ship was going to capsize."

"Forty five degrees!" Willie stuck out his arm to approximate the angle. "You gotta be shitting me!"

"Cross my heart and hope to die. You think our little dance down on the mess deck was bad? We had to lash ourselves down to keep from getting washed overboard."

"What about the cargo?"

"Everything below on the tank deck was pretty much mangled and had to be scrapped. Topside on the main deck we also had six deuce-and-a-half's gripped down. Couple hundred cartons of C-rats stacked in the back of each truck. When we hit that first thirty degree roll every last one of those puppies snapped their chains and hopped over board."

"No shit!"

"I watched the whole thing holding on for dear life in a starboard passageway. The Marines had used turnbuckles to squash their trucks down on their springs to keep them from swaying too much. But when those chains started to part those trucks jumped up like scalded cats on a hot tin roof. Bing, bang, boom they slammed into each other as they pin-balled across the deck. Quite a sight it was too. Raised a hell of a ruckus as one by one they dropped over the side. I made five bucks betting on number three. Two minutes and they were all gone."

"Wow!" laughed Willie. "Deuce-and-a-half's are damn big trucks. They must have trashed everything on deck."

"Took every pole, stanchion and railing in sight with them. It happened in deep water so they're still lying on the bottom."

"What about the cartons of C-rats?"

"Most floated free. But in the rough weather we couldn't come about to salvage any. Last I saw of them they were drifting toward Siargao Island. Some lucky natives must have feasted for a whole year."

SEVENTY-ONE

LATE IN THE evening two exhausted frogmen lay flat on their backs on the upper ramp of that broken LST. Steel beach to 'gator sailors everywhere, the ramp's incline provided the perfect surface to elevate their aching calves. A few hours earlier and it would have been too hot to touch. Salvage operations were on hold until daylight returned, and the two were taking a breather to watch the *show* taking place five miles inland. Warmed by the sun for twelve straight hours, the ramp's deck tread soothed their sore aching muscles. And almost made up for the stench coming from the beach.

Remnants of the Japanese army were now taking a pounding further inland. Sherman M-4's equipped with Mark I flame throwers had reached the foothills and were beginning the tedious process of torching the dozens of caves that dotted the island. Looking like an angry herd of fire-breathing dragons, they spat forth a solid stream of flaming petroleum thickened into a gelatinous ooze by napalm additives. A fearful weapon that struck terror into the heart of friend and foe alike, facing such an onslaught the Japanese often formed up into suicide squads to charge the tanks head on. Not the most practical of tactics—most of them died in vain, burned to a crisp where they stood. Those quick enough to avoid the flames and take cover underground suffocated when a pursuing fireball consumed all their oxygen.

"I see the zippos are out in full force again tonight," said Lee, a hint of reverence creeping into his voice. Beneath the reverence was a tinge of pity. Well aware of what was happening in the hills, he gave inward thanks he was nowhere near the business end of those flamethrowers.

"Yep," said Willie. "There might be some barbecued critters come morning." Trying to lighten the mood.

But his joke fell flat the minute it left his mouth. He too knew what the zippos did to human flesh. And like Lee, he was grateful his skinny ass was stationed on a ship, anchored safely in the harbor.

With the sun long gone, darkness began to overtake the island—enveloping it in an ever thickening mist. Every few seconds a snake-like tongue of flame from a tank flickered through the smoke-enhanced pall to light up the night. If one discounted its gruesome purpose, from a distance the spectacle could almost have been deemed beautiful. Almost. Sixty years later such a stunning display of power would be loosely categorized as *Shock and Awe.*

"I almost feel sorry for those poor bastards," said Willie. "I know they sucker punched us good at Pearl... but that ain't no way to die."

"As if there's any good way to die," said Lee. "Dead's dead in my book. Still... it does make you wonder how one human being can do that to another. No matter how much you hate them."

Kelley had come a long way since the start of the war. When he enlisted—a few lifetimes ago—the Japanese had been portrayed as bloodthirsty monsters bent on conquering the world for a mindless emperor. Hordes of yellow-skinned vermin to be exterminated without a second thought. According to most of the stateside papers, they still were.

But Lee had seen enough to realize the enemy was not a race of sub-humans. They too bled when shot. They too had families back home who grieved for them when they died. And they had died in appalling droves. At this point in the war they were dying in numbers ten, maybe twenty times greater than the Allies.

A succession of small explosions erupted in a line along a distant ridge. Followed by a towering fireball that seemed to shake the beach.

"Satchel charge?" asked Willie.

"That last one felt more like an earthquake," said Lee. "It must have been an underground ammo dump going off."

"Probably wiped out an entire Jap company."

"An explosion that big? Probably five or six companies."

For the next few minutes the sky blazed with fire. Rockets streamed this way and that. Grenades popped, smaller ammunition zinged off, forcing the frogmen to duck down and cover their ears. When the noise subsided to a mild roar, Lee raised his head a few inches.

"Yep. Definitely an ammo dump."

"Well... I think I've seen enough fireworks for one night," said Willie heading for the shoreline. "I'm gonna turn in. We've got another long day ahead of us tomorrow and I need my beauty rest."

"Right behind you," said Lee.

SEVENTY-TWO

EARLY DAWN, THE sixth of April, 1945, an hour before actual sunrise four hundred young kamikaze pilots gathered on a cold, mist-enshrouded macadam runway on the southern tip of Kyushu. To a man they had a faraway look on their face—for some it was fear, for others it was something approximating dedication—for all it imbued an aura no longer of this world. No doubt about it, they were going to die. No regrets allowed, it was what they'd been trained for.

After drinking their ceremonial cup of rice wine—and pledging their dying honor to the emperor with a deep bow—they boarded their waiting planes and took off to the cap-waving cheers of their loyal mechanics. After circling overhead for a few minutes they formed up and headed south. Their destination: Okinawa.

At the stick of a B5N *Kate* torpedo bomber—the same type of plane his older brother had flown in the attack on Pearl Harbor four long years ago—was twenty-three-year-old Sinsaku Fujida. Instead of a normal three man crew however, he was the only one in the cockpit. The sixth plane on the right in the formation, he didn't need a navigator because all he had to do was follow the plane in front of him. Nor did he need a bombardier to sight his weapon. There was no torpedo to drop. And the five hundred pound bomb he was carrying wouldn't be going anywhere since it was welded to the bottom of his fuselage. The last hope of a desperate country, this divine wind would not be returning home.

Lost in thoughts of his impending immortality, a sudden cough from his engine brought Sinsaku back to reality.

Damn! That third cylinder is missing badly. And the controls are pulling to the right. This piece of junk should have been scrapped months ago.

But this was all that was left of Japan's once mighty air force. Not a decorated officer like his brother had been, Sinsaku knew what he was talking about. Two short months ago he'd been a lowly mechanic. But when the war continued to go badly he'd been recruited into the kamikaze ranks, Japan's last best hope. A one month crash course—literally—on the basics of flying... and here he was.

Stupid rudder's been patched so many times it's miracle we got off the ground. Talk about sluggish, it looks as if I'll have to fight this hunk of tin all the way. Good thing this is a one way trip. This old bird would never make it back.

When he looked off to his left he caught a glimpse of the rising sun and his thoughts turned to his brother, shot down three years ago over Midway. In a plane much like this one.

How his chest must have swelled when he sank the Arizona. And how proud our parents were. Almost as proud as me... And now they're gone too. Burned to death in the fire bomb raids that leveled Tokyo.

It had all started out so well. So many high hopes. So many victories...Where did it all go so wrong?

A radio call broke into his reverie. It came from the battered Zero on his right. Once the terror of the skies, the now out-dated fighter had been knocked off its lofty perch by the faster, more heavily gunned American Hellcat. Now all that was left in her tanks was a death wish.

"Praise our emperor, it's going to be a glorious day," said Kazuko Izikawa, all of eighteen. "We will drive the Yankee dogs back into the sea. And strike a death blow to the heart of America."

All bravado, Isikawa's words were laced with doubt. And the

hitch in his voice gave away his terror. Little more than a kid, he was whistling in the dark.

Sinsaku opened his mouth to say something, but quickly closed it again.

Let the boy have his dreams. It will all be over soon enough. For us the war will come to a fiery end in a few hours. No sense in telling him how hopeless this all is. It would only dampen his spirits...

Then again maybe it's just as well we're going to our deaths. At least none of us will have to bear witness to our beloved homeland being brought to her knees... As if she hasn't been already.

The Zero's engine coughed twice and a thin trail of black smoke began to spew from its port exhaust. Chances were it wouldn't even make it to Okinawa.

"Are you as thrilled as I am, Sinsaku?" The kid again, looking for any kind of encouragement.

Before replying Sinsaku looked off to the sunrise one more time. Then took a deep breath.

"As you said, Kazuko... It's going to be glorious."

SEVENTY-THREE

MANY MILES AWAY and four hours later the Yamato—the largest battleship of the war—would also set sail for Okinawa. Without an escort fleet or any covering aircraft—and only enough fuel in her cavernous tanks for a one-way trip—it would be her final voyage. Intending to beach the mighty ship on the beleaguered island's southern shore and fight until she ran out of ammunition, her officers also made a death pact before she left port. It would be the final act of a country's last-ditch effort in a war that was already lost.

Japan's military leaders thought the Yamato's sudden appearance would both confuse and dishearten the American forces. Maybe foil their invasion plans by splitting their army in two. At the very least they hoped to give President Roosevelt second thoughts about invading mainland Japan. Make him think twice about what it would cost the US in men and material.

Born of desperation, the plan was doomed from the start. The minute the Yamato cast off her mooring lines the Americans knew where she was heading and were ready for her. Vulnerable from the air as she was, the Yamato would be destroyed by American dive-bombers before coming anywhere near Okinawa.

When both suicide missions failed the only thing remaining in the immediate future of a once great island empire would be two devastating bombs, a hundred thousand agonizing deaths, and unconditional surrender. Although the push to defend Okinawa would ultimately end in bitter defeat, for six days the Japanese kamikazes were able to inflict serious damage to the American fleet harbored there.

Hoping to catch the enemy unaware, a hundred miles north of Okinawa they massed into their standard kikusui formation. Named after the imperial symbol of Japan and known as the *floating chrysanthemum*, it was intended to strike a "typhoon of steel" into the heart of the invaders. Three hundred of the four hundred kamikazes would be shot down, but not before sinking twenty-five Allied ships and damaging a hundred and sixty-five others. Their fanatical efforts would kill more American sailors than any other engagement of the war.

Alerted by a wireless intercept, the fleet anchored at Okinawa knew an air strike had been launched, they just didn't know where the kamikazes would attack, or when.

SEVENTY-FOUR

ON THE MORNING of April 6 an early reveille roused Lee's ship to general quarters. Before the first gray mist of dawn snaked over the horizon all guns were manned, loaded, and pointed north.

But an hour before that call was sounded, Lee and Willie met on the mess deck to raid the midrats table. A normal routine of theirs when they couldn't sleep, they were hoping for their favorite, the makings for a peanut butter and jelly sandwich—maybe a left over cookie or two. This morning, however, the cupboard was almost bare.

"Three slices of stale bread and half a bowl of corn flakes?" grumbled a disappointed Lee Kelley. "Slim pickings tonight. The mid-watch must have been hungry."

"I can't really blame them," offered Willie, "considering what might be coming our way. You can't fight kamikazes on an empty stomach. And I here there's a whole flock of them out and about."

"The least the watch could have done was to leave us a few crumbs. I had my taste buds set on a cookie."

"I guess the crew needs the nourishment more than we do. Remember, we're only passengers on this here cruise ship. They're the ones who'll do most of the fighting."

"I know, I know. Beggars can't be choosers."

Resolved to the meager fare, Willie reached for a pitcher of warm powdered milk. Tilting it cautiously, a chalky white fluid poured over his half-a-bowl of cornflakes in a thin trickle. Followed by two solid glops that splashed soggy cereal all over the table.

"I think I've been at sea too long, Stump. I'm actually getting used to these damn lumps in my milk."

"You call that stuff milk? I call it white water."

Lee banged a brick-hard slice of toast on the table. When he did two little critters scampered away.

"The lumps are the only part of the milk that has any taste. And I've come to accept the disgusting fact that these black things in the bread aren't raisins."

"Weevils," chuckled Willie. "Just another source of protein according to our favorite red-headed cook."

"Remind me never to eat at Red's place back home."

"Another game of pinochle?" asked Willie.

"Don't mind if I do."

While Willie shuffled the cards Lee poured himself a cup of coffee. At least the watch hadn't drained the urn—a keel-hauling offense on every ship in the Navy.

A first sip brought a grimace from Lee.

"Ugh... This stuff's thicker than diesel fuel."

"Bottom of the pot, what did you expect?"

After arranging the board on the table Willie straddled a seat.

"How many of these pinochle games do you think we've played over the past two years, Stump?"

"Conservative guess, about a million and a half."

Lee took a second sip of coffee. Even bigger grimace.

"Yow! This actually tastes worse than diesel fuel." Sniffing the cup. "More like... unwashed feet. And it's not even halfway warm. Cold coffee in the morning? That's downright sacrilegious!"

"As I said before, beggars can't be choosey."

"Shut up and deal."

Thirty minutes and Willie found himself hopelessly behind. As usual. At least he was lucky in love—or so he liked to tell people. Resolved to losing again he let his mind wander as he watched Lee reshuffle.

"How many beaches do you think we've scouted so far, Lee?"

"I dunno. After ten or so I lost count. Fifteen, maybe twenty?"

"Sounds about right. So far—other than that damn typhoon—this one is turning out to be the easiest of them all. Knock on wood. Not counting the ones we skipped over, of course."

"After a while they all seem to blend together. Sand, beach, beach, sand... what's the difference?"

Slouching back, Willie stretched his arms wide. Let out a world-class yawn.

"I guess if you see one tropical island, you've seen them all. Kinda makes you wonder what's next after Okinawa though."

"Not hard to figure that one out. The only thing left is Japan itself."

Willie shook his head. Sucked a lungful of air in so hard it whistled through his teeth.

"That's what I was afraid of."

"You and me both, my friend. The Nips fought like cornered rats defending all these diddle-squat islands. What do you think they'll do when the first American tries to set foot on their sacred homeland? It ain't gonna be pretty, that's for sure. Every man, woman, and child in Japan will be hopped up on saki and out for blood. Our blood. If you thought Iwo was bad, Katie, bar the door."

"The Japanese can't have much left in the way of weapons," countered Willie. "We've bombed all their munitions factories into rubble. And most of their navy is sitting on the bottom of the ocean."

"Then they'll meet us on the beaches with knives and spears. Hell, they might even throw rocks at us."

Lee pushed himself away from the table. Sighed. With the outcome of their card game no longer in doubt, he'd lost interest in pinochle.

"For their sake—and especially ours—I wish there was some other way. If only someone could make them listen to reason. Maybe if we—"

But before Lee could finish that thought, an over-head speaker crackled to life:

BATTLE STATIONS!

SEVENTY-FIVE

A PICKET SHIP had spotted a huge swarm of kamikazes heading Okinawa's way. And sitting in the cockpit of each was a pilot harboring a death wish. On his lips—a sacred vow to take at least ten of the hated Americans with him.

Through the starboard hatch and down the passageway, before Lee reached that first ladder the ship's huge anti-aircraft batteries opened up on full automatic. Even three decks down their thunderous recoil rattled the overhead. With Willie hot on his heels Lee took the ladder two steps at a time, his ears stinging from the pressure.

Although not official crew members, the two had been assigned battle stations as spotters and back up ammunition handlers on a twin forty. Their duty was to point out enemy planes and pass ammo in case—Heaven forbid—any of the gun crew was injured. Four days prior a gunnersmate third class had given them a ten minute rundown on how to grab the bulky shell clips and even fire the big guns. Truth be told, however, neither was anywhere confident in their ability to handle the heavy shells. Much less fire a hot, smoking forty. Ducking to avoid a low hanging pipe, Lee offered up a silent prayer.

Lord... I'd sure appreciate it if they didn't have to call my number to fill in. If they happen to, however, please don't let me drop anything. Especially not on my own damn foot.

Before he could add the required *Amen* he burst from the hatchway into a staggering spectacle. Every gun in the vast American fleet was already blasting away, filling the heavens with ack-ack fire that spread from horizon to horizon. Hundreds of thick black smoke clusters polka-dotted the sky, turning it into a canopy of destruction. Sounding like angry rattlers, thousands of red tracers snaked their way upwards toward the attacking kamikazes. Adding to the deafening chaos, dozens of US Hellcat fighters swooped and dived helter-skelter, spitting out their own streams of fire and death.

Dumbfounded by the sight and weak in the knees, Lee grabbed a stanchion for support. Overwhelmed for a second, he had trouble catching his breath.

"Oh! My! God!" His only words.

Straight ahead of him a Japanese plane plummeted nose over tail towards the sea engulfed in flames. It came so close Lee was able to catch a glimpse of the pilot just before it exploded into a gigantic fireball. Death wish fulfilled, his goal of ten Americans would forever be a pipe dream.

"Sweet Mother of Jesus..." stammered Willie, his mouth agape as he scanned the horizon. "How could anyone live through all that shit?"

"For all our sakes," said Lee, "let's hope they can't."

SEVENTY-SIX

THE BATTLE IN the air raged for an hour. Maybe two. Given the bedlam on deck time quickly became irrelevant, heavy, and without apparent purpose. For two dazed frogmen it seemed to stretch into a year. In the all-encompassing din no one gave the concept of time a second thought. Officers screamed out their orders and the crew shouted back frantic demands for more ammo. Always more ammo. In the midst of the pandemonium here and there the faint trace of a prayer trickled through. Only to be drowned out by an immediate wave of louder curses.

Suddenly Lee's voice-powered radio came to life. He'd forgotten he'd put it on and in the midst of the clamor it sounded like a raspy growl.

"Say again your last!" he yelled into the mike. SOP when you didn't understand.

Willie tapped him on the shoulder. Pointed at a kamikaze making a run at the LST anchored to their left.

"I think the gunner is asking for a bearing!"

Shielding his eyes from the sun, Lee gauged the distance and the angle. Then spoke into the mike.

"Three o'clock! At seven hundred yards!"

Guns still blasting, the tub crew madly cranked away and the platform edged to the right.

POM! POM! POM! POM! POM!

Two, four, six, eight, ten shells shrieked off towards the streaking kamikaze. Along with dozens of fifty caliber streams from a whole host of nearby ships. Smoke burst from the kamikaze's tail. Flames shot out of its cowling. Punched full of holes and on fire, the plane kept on coming.

Mortally wounded and eager to join his ancestors, inside the burning cockpit the pilot tightened his grip on the stick and zeroed in on his target.

"Fuck!" shouted Lee. "The son of a bitch ain't going down! How in hell can he still be in the air?"

Then a stroke of luck. A forty millimeter shell scored a direct hit on the cowling and the kamikaze's engine blew, shredding the fuselage into a thousand shards of streaming white hot metal. Like feathers from a dying bird, jagged sections of the wings fluttered from the sky. Chunks of the pilot spiraled into the sea. Here an arm. There a leg.

Wiping cold sweat from his brow, Lee breathed a sigh of relief.

"Whew! That was too damn close."

"I thought that T was a goner for sure," said Willie.

"So did I. That sucker had her dead to rights. Thank God his divine wind finally petered out."

Willie crossed himself. Kissed his thumb.

"Amen to that."

"Ten o'clock high!" shouted Lee. "We got ourselves another customer!"

SEVENTY-SEVEN

THE NEXT TEN minutes shot by in a blur. Set ablaze by bullets from who knows where, six more kamikazes plunged into the sea around Lee's ship, now strewn with wreckage. To the right a flaming Zero spiraled to carom off the deck of a beached LST. Another stroke of luck, its bomb didn't detonate until it impaled itself propeller first into the sand a hundred yards up the beach. Instead of taking any Americans with him, the pilot had given his life to flambé ten sand crabs. Not exactly the tribute his emperor had been hoping for.

Finally a lull in the action and a tenuous cease-fire came down from the bridge. The roar of the guns stopped and a fragile bubble of silence enveloped the exhausted crew. Farther out to sea the battle raged on, but for now the attack seemed to have passed Lee by.

"Is that it?" he shouted, unable to hear his own words.

"I don't think so!" Willie shouted back. "A second wave's probably on the way. The Japs never give up this easily."

Inside the gun tub an ammo loader loosened his helmet strap. Looking up at the hot sun he coughed twice. Then hawked up a cordite-blackened glob of spit. Wiping his grime-covered forehead with a sweaty sleeve he looked toward shore. Then back out to sea. Sure enough, there they were.

"Here they come again!"

Puffing out his cheeks the loader glanced down at his hands. Even though he'd been wearing thick gloves both of his palms had been burned raw. For a second he couldn't fathom what he was looking at. A second ago he'd had two good hands. Now they were scorched to the bone and he hadn't felt a thing. Shaking his head he looked toward the beach again. Then over at Lee.

"Hot as hell today..." he sighed. "I think I've had enough of this shit."

His final thoughts on the subject, he removed his helmet and set it on the deck. One foot on the railing he turned to give Lee a wink and a nod.

"Good luck to you, mate. I hope you make it through this."

And then he jumped overboard. In the ensuing melee his body would never be found. Watching his limp body disappear beneath the waves, Lee was thunderstruck.

"What the hell! Why the fuck did he do that?"

Still smoking from their first go-around, the forties barked back to life.

"Kelley!" yelled the crew chief, not missing a beat. "Forget him! He's gone! Get your ass up here and take his place! You know the drill!"

In half a second Lee's limited training kicked in and he was madly loading shells as if he'd done it all his life. Soon he was up to his knees in hot shell casings. He would lose all his leg hair that day and suffer second degree burns on both calves, but in the heat of the battle he also didn't feel a thing.

For the next twenty minutes all he could hear above the roar of the guns was the chief's single minded orders

"Keep 'em coming! Faster! Faster!"

The shell clips were cumbersome. And so damn heavy. A mere five minutes and Lee felt as if his arms were being torn out of their sockets. His lungs on fire, his heart exploding out of his chest, stars began to flash across the insides of his eyeballs. His mouth a wad of blackened cotton, he felt woozy, sick to his stomach. Gulping back a wave of nausea, he was on the verge of passing out.

Not today, Kelley! You can't afford to pass out! Too much is riding on you now!

Arms aquiver, when he reached down to grab the next clip his back began to cramp up. Fighting through the spasms he slammed the clip into the breach and reached for another. Grab! Slam! Grab! Slam! At a dizzying pace. Finally a respite.

"Cease fire!" bellowed the chief. "That's got 'em!"

Totally spent, Lee sagged to the railing and retched over the side. Many in the dog-tired crew did the same.

"Thank God," he rasped, tasting his own bile.

His stomach drained, he wilted back onto his haunches to wipe his mouth. He loosened his chin strap to tilt his head back. Damn thing kept falling forward. Every muscle in his body burned, every bone ached. Twice he had to pop his ears before he could hear again. The only thing he wanted to do was collapse on that very spot and sleep for a year. Maybe two.

Then in the distance he saw it. The silhouette of a lone kamikaze. And this time it was headed directly for his ship. Low on the horizon—hiding in a smoke bank—it was hugging the surface a few feet above the waves. Almost impossible to spot, it was little more than a black dot in a dark gray cloud. And it had drawn a bead on them dead on, a difficult shot for even the most experienced gunners. Which Lee and his crew were not.

"Heads up!" he shouted as he struggled to his feet." We've got ourselves another live one! And he's headed right at us!"

SEVENTY-EIGHT

THE CHIEF NEARLY swallowed his cigarette. Cupping his eyes he scanned the horizon.

"Another kamikaze! Where? I can't see a fucking thing!"

"Twelve o'clock low!" shouted Lee. "Just above the surface! Maybe twenty feet!"

Snapping back into action two crew members began to ratchet the gun platform to the right. Two others cranked madly away at a separate set of wheels, trying to lower the still smoking barrels. From his position to the rear Lee could tell they would be hard pressed to zero in on the fast moving target. And even if they had enough time it would be a chancy shot at best.

"Commence firing!" yelled the chief. And once more the forties exploded into action.

And for Lee at least, the next few seconds seemed to pass in slow motion as one after another their shells sailed high, and sometimes wide.

"Son of a bitch! We're shooting over his head!"

But the guns had been lowered as far as they would go. The tub's railings wouldn't allow the barrels to drop any lower. The kamikaze was now flying safely beneath their angle of fire. And not a single shell had a snowball's chance in hell of hitting the target. Brought on by his exhausting stint as an ammo handler,

Lee's back had locked up. To make matters worse his fingers were cramping so bad he couldn't pick up a pencil. Much less a heavy clip of forty millimeter shells. So for the time being he could only watch. And maybe pray.

A helpless observer now, the scene transpiring before him seemed to play out in a series of stop action stills. Light-headed and approaching delirium, he visualized each shell screaming towards the elusive target—subconsciously willing it to strike home. But no matter how hard he concentrated—or prayed—he wasn't able to alter a single trajectory. The shells continued to sail high.

"Three thousand yards!" he barked. "And the bastard's still coming!"

When the kamikaze finally cleared the smoke bank it drew the attention of every fifty caliber on board. As well as from three ships in the area. Tracers from the fifties hissed through the enemy plane—sending rows of small water spouts shooting up when they came out. But it was far from enough. Even though the Jap trailed smoke now, it wouldn't go down.

Looking like a giant bird of prey swarmed by red hot bees, the kamikaze began to wobble back and forth—as if the pilot was flapping his wings in an attempt to get a few more precious yards from his dying plane. Just over a mile away now, it looked as if the flaming apparition was coming specifically for Lee. As if somehow this had all been pre-ordained.

"Two thousand yards!" he yelled.

Time slowed to a snail's pace. And so did the action in front of Lee. He swore he could see the propeller, even count its spinning blades. And for a split second he could make out the pilot's eyes, blazing maniacally, almost taunting him.

Hillbilly, Frenchie... and now me. Looks like you're gonna get your wish at last, Kelley. Your number's finally up.

Resolved to—and almost grateful for his now inevitable fate—a calming surge washed over Lee. Slowly closing his eyes he took a final deep breath. Like Frenchie before him, he was ready to let it happen.

"So be it," he sighed.

SEVENTY-NINE

FROM ABOVE FLASHED another stream of fifty caliber tracers. More intense, more accurate than those coming from any of the ships. Suddenly a Hellcat roared out of the clouds in a vertical dive, its guns spitting fire as it plunged headlong toward the kamikaze. The pilot's aim was uncanny. His fifties tore through the enemy cockpit as if it were tissue paper.

The Japanese Zero was a remarkable machine, one of the best fighter planes in the war. Early on it was superior to anything the Allies could put in the air. One major drawback was its lack of armor. Sacrificing safety for speed its designers surrounded the pilot with only thin aluminum sheets that provided little or no protection from a Hellcat's big guns. Torn to pieces in a flash, the Jap pilot didn't know what hit him.

More smoke billowed out of the kamikaze cowling. Then its engine exploded to gird the fuselage in flames. Amazingly still in the air, momentum continued to carry the burning wreck forward. And still on track to crash into Lee's gun tub dead center.

"Take cover!" he shouted. "It's gonna hit us!"

Trained to fire until an enemy plummets into the sea, the Hellcat pilot didn't let up. Maintaining his dive he switched to his twenty millimeter canons and kept on firing. Larger caliber bullets riddled the doomed kamikaze. Finally two shells penetrated the cockpit to detonate the bomb hanging below the fuselage. A larger explosion, and the kamikaze disintegrated amidst a brilliant red-orange cloud. Jagged chunks of the demolished plane cartwheeled everywhere. Smoking shards of hot metal clanged off the side of the ship. One small piece ricocheted harmlessly off Lee's gun tub, a foot from where he was standing. Apparently his time wasn't up after all.

The American pilot let off his trigger and pulled back on the stick. At the last second possible the Hellcat shuddered and pulled out of the dive. To Lee it looked as if its right wing tip skimmed the surface. The pilot applied full power and missed the gun tub by a mere ten feet. As the Hellcat passed overhead its roar was deafening. The throb of its straining engine rattled the teeth of every sailor on deck. Lee felt its bone-numbing power through the soles of his feet as he flashed a grateful two thumbs up. The entire gun crew cheered at the top of their lungs.

Too stunned to cheer, Lee caught a glimpse of the pilot as the Hellcat banked to the left. Was that a quick salute he saw? From a familiar face? Probably not. Things like that only happen in the movies. And only when John Wayne plays the lead.

Must be my damn imagination, imagined Lee.

What he didn't imagine, however, were the four rows of meatballs painted on the Hellcat's cockpit. Japanese flags signifying kills. If his avenging angel wasn't one already, he was well on his way to becoming an ace. For sure he'd have Lee's vote.

Even though the kamikaze was now headed for the bottom of the bay the crew stayed alert. They were not about to be burned again. Several minutes passed as all eyes scanned the sky for more enemy planes. None were sighted. Their grand scheme shattered, the Japanese had run out of divine wind. At least for today. The chief ordered an *all clear* and the gun crew collapsed where they stood.

Japan would muster other kamikaze attacks in the near future, but none as large as the one on the sixth of April. They put all their eggs in this one basket only to fail miserably. Back home the debacle would have a devastating effect on morale. Although the kamikazes inflicted serious damage to the fleet at Okinawa they didn't come close to *breaking the American Navy's back* as their leaders had promised.

Short on planes—and more importantly, experienced pilots—Japan's air force would no longer be a threat. Defenseless from the air, their once vast empire was now doomed.

EIGHTY

FOR SEVERAL MINUTES no one in the gun tub left his post. A few stray shells exploded in the distance, but they were afterthoughts, needless punctuations to a battle already won. Angry and relieved gunners getting off a last round, as if to say "Is that all you got?"

The only planes in the sky now were Hellcats searching for stragglers. But they couldn't find any. Eventually they turned and headed back to their carriers. Like the final curtain to the last act of a play, silence descended on the embattled bay. Oddly, the quiet was even more unnerving than the prior hue and cry of battle. Staggered by the surreal calm, for a few seconds Lee had to struggle for his bearings.

What time is it anyway?

As if the answer to that question could have any possible relevance. When he looked down at his watch he discovered it was still only morning.

Damn thing must have stopped. Probably while loading shells.

"Less than two hours have passed?" he mumbled out loud, mystified.

"Seems like two days," said Willie, equally stunned. Still gasping for breath, he leaned forward to prop his hands on his knees. "I can't believe we're still alive, Stump. That fucking dink had us in his crosshairs. Sure as eggs is eggs, I thought we were goners. If it hadn't been for that Hellcat pilot..."

"Saved both of our keisters, that's for sure," said Lee. "He must have brass balls to put his plane into a steep dive like that. I don't know how he kept from crashing into the drink. Brave fool almost bought the big one bringing that Jap down. I pray to God he makes it back to his carrier in one piece."

Far to their right—and miles out to sea—the silhouettes of two aircraft carriers dotted the horizon. Looking like wasps circling their nests, several Hellcats jockeyed into landing position. As they did, Lee watched the fighter on the far left turn on final. With bated breath he followed the plane's approach to the USS Hornet.

"For all we know that could be him landing now," said Willie.

"Let's hope so."

Only then did Willie note the gaping holes in Lee's singed pants.

"Whoa, those are some pretty nasty looking burns on your legs, Stump. We'd better get you to sick bay."

As soon as the order was passed down to secure from battle stations, mop up operations began. Hundreds of spent shell casings had to be removed and secured below. Brass was still a valuable commodity, even at this late stage of the war. After the gun barrels cooled to the touch they had to be cleaned out, swabbed with oil and made ready for the next attack. It was anyone's guess when the Japs would make their next appearance, but everyone knew they'd be back. Hopefully just not today. As exhausted as the gun crew was, they would have been hard pressed to even spit at another kamikaze.

The clean-up was back-breaking work—taxing their already drained bodies—but to a man everyone onboard was grateful. First for the break in the action, and second for having survived the ordeal.

Walking stiffly on his burned legs Lee was helped below by Willie. By the time he reached sick bay his calves were throbbing so badly he was on the verge of passing out. Seeing his dehydrated state a corpsman gave him an immediate IV laced with morphine. The last thing Lee remembered was the image of that big beautiful blue Navy Hellcat screaming down from the heavens.

EIGHTY-ONE

WHEN LEE CAME to an hour later his legs below the knee had been slathered with ointment and wrapped in a thick layer of gauze. Swaddled in a warm and fuzzy feeling, he felt no pain. Quite the contrary. Never before had he felt so at peace, so deliciously comfortable. And safe. It was almost as if he was living in a wide, forgiving smile. His eyes couldn't stop rolling and he had to blink several times to focus. When he did, the first thing he recognized was Willie William's smiling face.

"Welcome back, Stump. Enjoy your little snooze?"

Lee ran a gentle tongue across his teeth. At least that's what he thought he was trying to do. His mouth felt like cotton candy and he couldn't tell where his tongue ended and his teeth began. The sensation was definitely strange, but oh, so pleasant.

"More than you can ever imagine, Willie." His words came out slow and deliberate, almost as if he were chewing on them. "Um, how long was I out?"

"A little over an hour maybe, but you looked like you were enjoying every minute of it."

"I still am, now that you mention it," smiled Lee, the words tumbling off his lips like marshmallow marbles. "You should try this stuff sometime. It's great for what ails you. Better'n beer, and a whole lot quicker."

"So I've heard. Not so great on the memory, though."

Lee had trouble keeping his eyes open. No matter where he looked the room seemed to be rolling back and forth to a soothing cadence. And his head kept nodding this way and that. He felt so, so drowsy. But so damn good. So good he didn't want to waste the cuddly feeling by falling asleep again.

"Memory ain't what it's cracked up to be, my friend. And after what I saw today... I think some things are meant to be forgotten."

"So, you remember the attack?"

"Every second of it. Especially when that Hellcat roared over us at the end."

Willie clicked his tongue. Then scratched his head.

"That sure was something, wasn't it? The way he blew that Jap to pieces."

Lee propped his chin on the back of his right hand. Hissing air in through his nose, he forced at least one eye to focus.

"As long as I live I'll never forget that pilot's face."

"It happened so fast how could you have seen what he looked like?"

"I know it sounds crazy, but I swear to God he was the spitting image of Frenchie. Shit, for all I know it could have been his ghost."

"Morphine's powerful stuff, Stump. I'm no doctor, but it seems to me it might be messing with your brain. Make you see things that weren't there."

"Maybe. I know Frenchie's been dead for a couple of months now, but for half a heartbeat there I had a gut feeling that he—or at least his spirit—was in the cockpit of that Hellcat. Watching over me. Like he always did."

Running a slow hand through his hair, Willie raised both eyebrows.

"Man alive... that's spooky. Now, I'm not questioning what you saw... or what you thought you saw, but if I were you I wouldn't tell that to another living soul."

"I don't intend to. And if you ever breathe a word of it..."

Willie made a zipping motion across his mouth.

"My lips are sealed."

By April 22, 1945, the Americans had overcome all organized

resistance in northern Okinawa. Other than a few mopping up skirmishes two thirds of the island saw policing activities only. The southern peninsula, however, was a different story. With a can-of-worms ending tacked onto it. Having massed their decimated forces for one last stand, the Japanese would fight hand to hand for every inch of ground, dying in wave after wave of suicidal charges.

By May 26, eight weeks after the initial landing, the Marines had advanced a disappointing four miles. In the end it would take them another four frustrating weeks to push their way to the island's southern tip. The battle for Okinawa would officially end there on June 21, 1945, but small pockets of isolated Japanese soldiers would fight on to the end of the month. Often saving their last bullet for themselves.

By the time Okinawa fell, Lee and his team of frogmen were on their way to Guam to prepare for another operation. Their next landing would be the big one. The final one they'd all been dreading.

The invasion of Japan itself.

EIGHTY-TWO

ANOTHER HOT AND humid, bug-infested island in the middle of the Pacific Ocean, Guam had fallen to the Japanese three days after Pearl Harbor. Before a reeling America had a chance to catch its collective breath. Emboldened by their sneak attack victory, an invading force of over five thousand soldiers easily overran the small garrison of Marines stationed there. Two hundred against five thousand was hardly a fair fight. Especially on two hundred and twenty-eight square miles of jungle crawling with giant spiders and poisonous snakes. It would be three long years before the Americans were able to return.

Following a hard fought victory on Saipan the Marines retook Guam on August 10, 1944, providing America with a much needed base to launch her B-29 bombers and strike mainland Japan. Albeit unprotected. When Iwo Jima fell in late February, fighter air cover became feasible and the noose began to tighten on a now setting sun. Guam in turn became a vital supply center and strategic hub for the *Big Push* to Tokyo. An event every GI in the Pacific had been dreading for months. Expecting to ship out any day for the invasion of Japan, what was left of the remaining frogmen teams landed on Guam during the first week of June. Lee had a big surprise waiting for him when he walked down the gangplank of his transport ship—his third in as many years.

Flabbergasted at the mountains of C-rats stacked on the pier, he let his duffel bag slide from his shoulder.

"Holy Toledo, Willie! Would you look at all the pallets of food! They gotta be piled at least ten high."

"Them's sure a lot of beans," whistled Willie. "Enough to feed my hometown for a month. And I come from a little place called Chicago. Tons of mouths to feed there."

"Something's up, that's for sure. I just wish they'd give us a hint what it was."

"Yeah," snorted Willie. "What's with our orders anyway? *Report to the harbormaster for further assignment*? Ain't that just like the damn Navy. Never tell nobody nothing."

"I suppose they're just being careful. We got the Japs on the run but this war isn't over yet. Not by a long shot. And loose lips still sink ships."

"So they keep telling us."

Lee took off his cap to wipe his brow. Then re-shouldered his bag. Barely past sunrise and the temperature was already in the upper eighties. Humidity in the upper nineties—another hot, sticky one was in store.

"If we play our cards right maybe we can finagle a bunk on the beach tonight."

"Now you're talking," agreed Willie. "Palm trees swaying to a gentle breeze, soft white sands, maybe a wahini or two to spice up the night... I can see it all now."

"Wahinis?" laughed Lee. "I don't think so. Have you seen all the Marines lined up on the pier? And that's just from our ship. There's no telling how many have already landed. The ratio of men to women on Guam is probably a hundred to one by now. Maybe even a thousand to one. In my book those are lousy odds. I hate to burst your bubble, pal, but the chances of either of us getting laid on this island are zip, squat, diddley."

"I can dream, can't I."

"Yeah, you and your right hand."

His dream deflated, Willie shifted his bag to his other shoulder. Hitched up his pants.

"I wonder where this so-called *harbor master* is located."

"My first guess would be somewhere in the harbor. Hence the name *harbor* master."

Willie flipped Lee a good natured finger. Something he'd been doing a lot lately.

"Very funny. Everybody's a comedian these days."

"Does that finger represent your IQ or number of legal parents? Where ever he is I just hope this harbor master has an interesting assignment for us. Ever since Okinawa we've been sitting on our duffs, twiddling our thumbs. A man can play just so many card games."

A large native, about as wide as he was tall, nodded as he waddled by.

"Haf Adai, sailors. Welcome to Guam."

"What'd he say?" asked Willie.

"I'm pretty sure he said *good morning*," said Lee.

"He seemed to be a friendly cuss. And from the size of his belly it looks like he hasn't missed many meals."

"Guamanians do love to eat."

"How do you know that?"

"I read a lot," grinned Lee. "Wonderful inventions, books. You should try one sometime."

EIGHTY-THREE

IT TOOK THEM all morning to run down Guam's "harbor master," a harried looking mustang lieutenant whose threadbare khaki shirt was rotting off his back. When Lee and Willie handed him their orders he wasn't exactly pleased. Shaking his head he spat out the gooey end of a half-chewed cigar.

"What the fuck!" he growled. "No one told me you guys were coming. What the hell am I supposed to do with you two? I've got enough trouble with the shitbirds I already have."

Not quite a "Haf Adai," Lee could only offer up an apologetic shrug. So did Willie. No way were they going to contradict the man. Tan as last year's saddle—with biceps the size of full grown pythons—the lieutenant looked like he ate bricks for breakfast. And washed it down with kerosene. Taking Lee's cue, Willie mustered up a friendly smile.

"Just doing what we were told, sir."

The lieutenant snatched both sets of orders. Grumbled as he gave them a quick once over.

"Those no-account pricks up in admin! They don't know their assholes from a hole in the ground. Why'd they assign you two jokers to me?"

"We're frogmen, uh, divers, sir," offered Lee. "Since you're near the water all the time maybe they figured we might come in handy."

"Shit in a bucket! I got my hands full as it is. What I don't need is more fucking problems. I've got half a mind to—"

The lieutenant sucked wind. Looked out across the bay. Lee could almost hear his teeth grinding.

"Look, I know it isn't your guys' fault. You're only following orders. But I've got a hundred things twisting in the wind that needed to be done yesterday. And all of them have turned to crap. For the time being check in with the quartermaster. He'll tell you where you can bunk down. Tomorrow after I give it some thought, maybe I'll send along an assignment for you. Day after tomorrow at the latest."

Lee didn't like the sound of that. It meant more thumb twiddling. But he kept his disappointment to himself.

"Sounds like a workable plan to me, sir."

"The quartermaster's office—if you can call it that—is a small shack tucked in next to the mail hut. Two piers down at the end of the beach. If he's not inside he's probably out back tending to those fucking chickens of his. You can't miss him. He's probably the tallest, skinniest chief this side of Pearl. With the foulest mouth in the Navy. Puts me to shame when it comes to swearing."

Lee shot an *are you kidding me* glance Willie's way.

"Er, thanks for the heads up, sir. We'll try to keep on his good side."

"He doesn't have one," added the lieutenant. "The chief's older than the hills and smells worse than an outhouse on a hot summer day. Probably from all that chicken shit. Just follow your nose and you'll find him."

EIGHTY-FOUR

IT TOOK THE two frogmen the better part of an hour to weave their way down the beach, past this stack and that pile, before they found the quartermaster's shack. A ramshackle affair of cast-off tin sheets and mis-matched planks, it looked as if a gentle breeze could bring it down. Or a healthy fart. Even from a distance they could tell the chief was out front, smoking what appeared to be a long-stemmed pipe.

"I don't know what the lieutenant was talking about," said Willie, shading his eyes from the sun. "That there chief isn't much bigger than you or me."

"Look again, my friend. He's sitting down. In a broken down rocker if I'm not mistaken. Jesus, he has to be ten feet tall."

When they got within a hundred feet of the porch their eyes began to water.

"Good Lord," whispered Willie. "What is that god-awful stench?"

Lee pinched off his nose. Blinked rapidly a few times to fight off a sudden gag reflex.

"Man, what a stink! It smells like ten day old cat piss."

"I can hear you, dickwads!" snarled the chief. "I may be old but I ain't fuckin' deaf. And yes, that stink's coming from me. Ain't neither of you two cocksuckers been anywhere near a farm before? You can't raise fucking chickens without smelling like fucking chicken shit. Better get used to it if you're gonna bunk in my barracks. And if you don't like it, you pussies can kiss my ass."

The lieutenant had been right. On all three counts. Taking shallow breaths in through their mouths the two listened quietly to another string of colorful expletives while they checked in. Anything to minimize the conversation. Having spent the last three years on a string of ships— elbow to elbow with sweaty, sailors in hot, confined spaces—they were well accustomed to foul odors. But they'd never run across a stink like this. With their nose hairs shriveling up, the last thing they wanted to do was spend another second in the presence of a foul-mouthed, walking compost pile.

"You fuckers cause me any fucking trouble and I'll fuck you seven ways to Sunday. You can abso-fucking-lutely count on it."

The chief's parting words.

Around the corner and halfway to the barracks, Lee chanced breathing through his nose again.

"That beachmaster wasn't kidding. I never heard the word *fuck* in so many forms before. And in two short sentences. Noun, adjective, verb... the chief ran through them all."

"A true master," nodded Willie. "Way out of our league when it comes to the manly art of cussing."

"Thank God the barracks are a goodly distance from him and his chickens."

Willie wet a finger. Held it up.

"Let's just hope they're not downwind."

EIGHTY-FIVE

TOMORROW CAME AND went. Then the day after that. A week passed and still no word from the harbormaster lieutenant. During that time the only assignment given Lee and Willie came as an after-thought from Chief Smells-Like-Chicken-Shit. It consisted of a scribbled note to check on the mail. A mindless task that took a whopping ten minutes every other day.

Bored out of his skull from sitting around the barracks all day, Lee finally went looking for the forgetful lieutenant. Only to find out he'd been transferred somewhere up north. Probably to a psychiatric ward of the island hospital. His replacement—an even angrier and more overwhelmed JG—was in no mood to deal with a pair of "pain in the ass frogmen."

"You'll get your fucking orders when I'm fucking good and ready to give them to you. And not a fucking minute sooner!"

Same school of elocution as the chicken-raising chief.

Willie could tell things hadn't gone well the moment Lee stepped through the barracks door.

"They got anything for us to do yet?"

"Nope."

"More sitting around on our duffs?"

"Yep."

"Screw that shit," said Willie. "You did all you could. I say we check out the rest of the island. Sample some of the local flavor. If they need us they know where to find us. Not our fault somebody upstairs dropped the ball. Their loss, not ours."

Lee had to agree.

Out of sight, out of mind—for the next three weeks nobody came looking for Willie and Lee. So with a clear conscience and nothing on their hands but time, the two were free to act like tourists. Since Guam had been secure for over a year now they pretty much had the whole island to explore. And explore they did.

They started off by snorkeling their way up one side of Guam, then down the other. They dived the shark pits off Aghana Bay. They climbed the cliffs of a lovers' leap that overlooked the inlet to the harbor. They hacked their way through the jungle to traipse a field of burned out Japanese Chi ha tanks. They even survived the two day termite mating season. An annual event that left the entire island blanketed with a hundred billion bodies of dead or exhausted insects. That in turn set off an interesting set of events. Attracted by all that food, millions of frogs clogged every road to enjoy the bounty set before them. They in turn got squashed by any passing vehicle—it was impossible to avoid them. Fried up nicely by the sun, these *flat* frogs became a barbecued treat for every bird on the island. During this cycle most Guamanians played it safe and stayed indoors.

During it all they were befriended by a local Chamorro who taught them how to fish the Guamanian way. Lee and Willie got drunk on dark Guamanian beer—infinitely more palatable than San Miguel. They ate Guamanian food until it was coming out their ears. Kelaguen—a broiled chicken dish sprinkled with lemon juice, grated coconut and dried hot peppers—turned out to be Lee's favorite. Willie was more partial to pancit—a traditional noodle dish made with any kind of meat available.

Every few days someone in the village threw a party for this or that—the Guamanians never needed an excuse to have fun. A party that every man, woman, child, dog and cat attended. Their only objective: To eat and drink more than their neighbors. In less than a month the two Americans had fallen in love with the island and the Guamanians' easy going life style.

But after twenty-six days of living the high life, the beachmaster finally came looking for them. By that time Lee and Willie had put on at least ten pounds each. All of it around their middles.

"I see you two have been cavorting with the locals," said the JG. "Well... your goldbricking days are over. You're to report to the operations hut at 0600 sharp tomorrow morning. And for God's sake wear a uniform that fits. You're busting out of those fucking pants."

Sucking in his gut Lee popped off a salute.

"Any idea what they want with us, sir?"

"An admiral and a flock of full birds are going to ask you a bunch of questions."

"Questions? About what?"

"I haven't the foggiest. Probably something to do with the upcoming invasion."

Crammed into their best—and only clean—set of whites, bright and early the next morning Lee and Willie found themselves standing in front of the operations hut a few minutes early. You never wanted to keep an admiral waiting. No matter how many stripes you had on your sleeve. Nervous about what was waiting for them on the inside, both were already sweating through their jerseys. Pissed off at himself for gaining all that weight, Lee glanced down at his expanded gut. Let out a sigh.

"I shouldn't have eaten so damn much these past few weeks. I look like twenty pounds of shit crammed into a ten pound bag. Feel like it too."

"You and me both, Stump. If they ask me to go anywhere near the water I'm going to sink like a rock."

With a slow shake of his head Lee took a deep breath. Then mounted the first step.

"Well... no sense in putting it off. Let's get this over with."

"Are you sure you want to do this?" countered Willie. "I say we run for the hills. We know the jungle better than anyone now. They'll never find us."

"Yeah... but my conscience will."

EIGHTY-SIX

INSIDE THE HUT it took them a few seconds to adjust to the dim light. On a table at the far end stood a huge relief map, fifteen feet long, six feet deep and two feet high. Several four stripers were huddled at one end of the table, engaged in an animated conversation, each trying to shout down the others. Hidden in their midst—and the only one not talking—was a short man in starched khakis. With three stars on his collar. Arms crossed and nodding slowly, the admiral appeared to be digesting what was being thrown around.

"I wonder what they're arguing about," whispered Lee.

Willie nodded at the eager lieutenant in the rear of the pack who was motioning them forward.

"I don't know. But something tells me we're about to find out."

Noting their approach Vice Admiral Grover C. Heffner peered around the nearest captain and raised his hand. Instant silence from his staff.

"Ah, our experts are finally here. Maybe they'll be able to shed some much needed light on the subject."

Lee and Willie snapped to ramrod attention. And even though the Navy didn't require it indoors, they both saluted. After all, it was the first time they'd come within spitting distance of a real, live admiral.

"Petty Officer Second Class Lee Kelley, reporting as ordered, sir!"

For good measure he saluted again. Already shaking in his boots, Willie followed suit.

"I take it you two are frogmen?" asked the admiral.

"Yes, sir!" Simultaneously.

"And that you've got a few amphibious landings under your belt?"

"Yes, sir!"

"Good, good. Then you're just the men we've been looking for." Turning to his captains the admiral waved a hand. "Make a hole, gentlemen. Let's give these two a front row seat so they can see what we've been stewing about."

When the sea of full birds parted Lee and Willie found themselves at the table's edge.

"What do you think of our topographical representation, Petty Officer Kelley?" asked Admiral Heffner.

"Impressive, sir. It's very... detailed. Someone's gone to a lot of trouble. Um...what is it?"

"This is an accurate, three dimensional representation of the Japanese industrial port of Yokosuka."

"Yokosuka, sir?"

"It's a projected landing site. If and when we have to invade Japan."

Like every other American serviceman, Lee had heard rumors of the impending invasion. Up until this very moment however, they'd been just that. Rumors. Something you didn't talk about, hoping that by not talking about it, it would go away. But hearing the words from a three star made it official.

"As usual you frogmen will have to scope out the site in preparation for the actual landing so I'd like your opinion on what we can expect to encounter."

One quick glance told Lee that Yokosuka would be nothing but trouble. With a capital "T." Struggling with the enormity of it all, he couldn't find the proper words. The only two he could think of were *Oh shit!* A totally inappropriate response to the admiral's request. Lee opened his mouth to say something, then quickly closed it again.

"I know it's a lot to fathom, hitting you broadside like this," said the admiral. "So take your time, Kelley. No one's pushing you here."

Clearing his throat, Lee leaned forward.

"I don't need much time, sir." He pointed to the right side of the table. "I take it you've decided to land here, at this inlet."

A slow smile inched onto the admiral's face.

"That seems to be the consensus. I'm curious, though. My staff took two whole days coming to the exact same conclusion. Almost came to blows on more than one occasion. And here you waltz in—neat as you please—and take all of five seconds."

Lee gave his jersey a nervous tug.

"Well, sir, given the drop off from the shoreline, the protective break wall and the slope of the beach... in my humble opinion it's the only logical choice."

"I sense a big *but* coming, Kelley."

"Bigger than *big*, sir." Lee pointed to the sheer rock cliffs surrounding the inlet. "These cliffs look to be over two hundred feet high. And from what little I know of their history, the Japanese have had centuries to dig tunnels into them. Something they're good at. Who knows what kind of fortifications they've constructed up there."

"A salient point," nodded the admiral. "But we plan to soften them up with the heaviest naval bombardment the world has ever seen. Raining two thousand pounders down on them for a solid week should dislodge any defenders."

"No offense, Admiral, but I hear it didn't work on Iwo, Guam, or Saipan. And I know it didn't work on Okinawa. I was there. After the Navy leveled the entire island it still took the Marines a month and a half to dig the Japs out of their holes. Those they couldn't dig out, they burned out. In the end we won, but we lost many good men in the process."

Lee tapped the top of the cliffs with a forefinger. Ran it slowly down the incline.

"And if these are any indication...Yokosuka's going to be ten times worse."

EIGHTY-SEVEN

"WE KNOW THERE probably will be considerable losses," countered the admiral.

"Not *probably*, Admiral," said Lee. "*Definitely*. And our losses will be way beyond *considerable*. More like *staggering*. For starters, if we have to lay charges to remove any obstructions, not a single frogman will return from that beach alive. Even under the cover of darkness. No matter how many ships you send in to protect us. And that's before the actual battle even starts."

The admiral pulled at his neck. Looked at the cliffs again.

"How so?"

"I count at least twenty indentations where the Japs could launch explosive devices similar to the British hedgehogs. And I'd hate to be anywhere near those babies when they go off. Not with the extended underwater killing radius they pack. And there's probably ten times as many hidden nooks and crannies where they can position snipers with high powered automatic weapons. Angles like that, we'd be sitting ducks."

Another furrow appeared on the admiral's already worried brow. Pursing his lips he scratched an ear.

"And you don't think a concerted bombardment would dislodge these fortifications?"

"It didn't at Normandy. And we threw everything we had at the Germans—including the kitchen sink. But bombs and battleships alone couldn't do the job. The Nazis were still there when we came ashore. And these cliffs above Yokosuka are a whole lot steeper and higher. All the Japs have to do is hunker down, wait us out then trot out their big stuff. Bottom line, they aren't stupid. They know we can't continue to shell the area with men on the beach."

Big sigh from the admiral.

"I see."

"And that's not the half of it, sir," added Lee, far from finished. "See how open that stretch of beach is? Nothing but sand and pebbles all the way to the base of the cliffs. And even then there's no cover to speak of. The enemy will use that to their advantage. They'll have removed any rock larger than a baseball. The minute our guys hit the sand they'll be caught in a murderous crossfire. Just like at Omaha Beach. Only worse. The Germans were hard enough to push back in France and they were fighting on soil foreign to them. This is the Japanese homeland and they'll fight like demons to protect it."

"Relevant points all, Petty Officer Kelley. Ones that have given every swinging dick in this room a fucking case of heartburn. Excuse my French."

"Do we really have to invade Japan, Admiral? It seems to me their leaders know by now there's no way they can win this war."

Massaging his temples the admiral let out another weighted sigh.

"The Japanese are a proud and stubborn people. I'm sure you've learned they live by a code different from ours. A code of honor that drives them to die for that damn emperor of theirs. Consensus is they'll never give up without a show of force."

Taking a deep breath, Lee decided to speak his mind and tell it like it is—even though he was only a second class petty officer who'd never even seen an admiral before. After all, what could they do? Bust him back to seaman? At this late state that seemed kind of pointless.

"But can we allow them to take a million of us with them? 'Cause that's how many American lives it will cost us to march into Tokyo. And you can bet your bottom dollar one of those lives is gonna be mine."

Feeling like he'd overstepped his station, Lee shifted his eyes back to the cliffs.

"I'm no great military mind... but surely there has to be another way."

"You may be right, sailor. And, yes, to set your mind at ease, there are people in higher places—smarter than you and I put together—who are working on an alternative to what you see before you. Unfortunately I'm not at liberty to tell you what that is. But I can assure you it's something that will get Emperor Hirohito's undivided attention. And hopefully bring a quick end to this damn war.

Puffing out his cheeks the admiral turned to lean on the table, arms outstretched, hands down. Except for the sound of waves breaking on the nearby beach, silence ruled the hut. While their leader pondered, nobody moved. Nobody breathed.

Finally he turned back around.

"Gentlemen... I pray we never have to give the order to invade Japan. Thank you, Petty Officers Kelley and Williams, you've been most helpful."

And with that the lieutenant ushered Lee and Willie out of the hut.

EIGHTY-EIGHT

LOST IN THOUGHT on their way back to their barracks neither frogman said a word. As they were passing the mail hut Willie was the first to speak.

"I don't know why the admiral thanked me. I didn't say a damn word. I felt like an idiot standing there with my thumb up my ass."

"Sorry about hogging the conversation," said Lee.

"Hey, better you than me. Besides, you did me a favor. All that brass looking over our shoulders made me nervous. My knees were knocking so bad I'd have made a fool of myself the second I opened my mouth."

"I know what you mean," grinned Lee. "When Admiral Heffner asked me that first question I thought I was gonna piss my pants."

"Hell, I did a little. And he wasn't even looking at me."

As they rounded the corner Lee slowed to gaze out across the beach. The bay was calm—no surf to speak of—but far out to sea a line of towering thunderclouds was lining up, tinting the rising sun crimson. *Red in the morning, sailors take warning.*

"Looks like a storm's on the way," he said, his mind ten thousand miles away.

"Yep, there'll be no diving today," nodded Willie. After a few seconds: "What did you think of the admiral, Lee?"

"That's one smart man. And I sure as hell wouldn't want to be in his shoes."

"Not with the painful decision he's got to make. It's gonna affect thousands of lives. Yours and mine included."

"Something tells me the final say-so will come from someone higher up than him. Maybe even the president. I sure hope to hell and back that the *alternative* they're working on is something big."

Willie cleared his throat. Swallowed hard.

"It better be. Do you really think it will cost a million American lives to invade Japan?"

"At least that," said Lee.

"Then I pray ol' Harry S. gets it right."

Something *big* turned out to be the Manhattan Project. It culminated in a towering mushroom cloud that leveled two square miles of sand dunes at the Alamogordo Bombing Range in New Mexico. And sent out shock waves felt as far away as California.

On July 26, 1945 the Allies issued the Potsdam Declaration. In it was an ominous prediction. It promised "prompt and utter destruction of Japan" if its leaders did not surrender immediately. And unconditionally. Japan's military council promptly ignored it. That left only one question on the table. Should America use her new and hopefully ultimate weapon to end the war in the Pacific?

Never one to pass the buck, when that thorny question landed on his desk at first President Truman hesitated. After searching his soul he ordered the atomic bomb to be dropped on Japan. On the sixth of August a lone B-29 bomber—named the Enola Gay after the pilot's mother—took off from the remote island of Tinian. Several hours later, after an uneventful flight, she opened her bay doors and let loose an atomic bomb called Little Boy, the most devastating weapon ever created by man. In the blink of an eye half the population of Hiroshima was vaporized. When Japan failed to respond a second atomic bomb—this one called Fat Man—was dropped on Nagasaki. With the same devastating results.

Nine days after the dust cleared, Japan finally surrendered. To the relief of soldiers and sailors all over the Pacific. A thoroughly crushed Japan would need General MacArthur's guidance for several years, but not what was left of Mac's Navy. No more islands to conquer meant no more beaches to chart, so frogmen were released early. And that included Lee Kelley, who hopped on board the first troop transport headed for the states. On the voyage home a gung ho master chief tried to convince him to stay in the reserves. Having seen enough death and destruction to last several lifetimes, Stump respectfully declined.

EIGHTY-NINE

CALL IT *DÉJÀ VU*—or maybe a case of history coming full circle—but standing five guys behind Lee in the discharge line at San Francisco was an old friend. That same old friend who three years ago had played a vital part in Lee's walking into that Navy recruiting office in downtown Cleveland. And his *not* joining the Marines. Big war, small world—the two Irishmen clapped each other on the back and broke into tears of joy—thankful they'd both made it back in one piece.

"Jack Conners! Is that really you?"

"Lee? Lee Kelley. As I live and breathe. I thought you were killed."

"So did a lot of people apparently. I meant to write you after we graduated from boot camp... but you know how it is. Things kept coming up."

"Same here. I guess the war got in the way."

"Yeah... I guess so."

A different time, a different place. Close friends then, strangers now. Sometimes it was difficult to walk down the old streets. With a war knifed into their friendship, it was strange trying to pick up where you left off. Too much had happened in between. For several seconds the words they wanted to say—the ones they felt they needed to say—hung awkward in their throats.

"So," ventured Lee finally. "How was submarine duty?"

"I was on two subs and they were both colder than a witch's tit," said Jack. "I wore long johns all the time but I never could get anywhere close to warm. Froze my butt off... just like I did at Great Lakes."

"See any action?"

"All we did was patrol up and down the East Coast of the United States. Never even fired a live torpedo. But it did have its ups and downs." Trying to reconnect with humor.

"Good ol' Jack Conners," laughed Lee, more comfortable now. "I see you haven't shucked your love of bad puns."

"And I see you're still short," grinned Jack. "How about you, Stump? Did you make it through frogman school?"

"Barely. If it hadn't been for Hillbilly and Frenchie I'd have washed out."

It was the first time in months he'd said their names out loud and at first it startled him. That and the fact that they'd slid off his tongue so matter-of-factly. As if he expected everyone in the world to know who they are. Or rather, were.

"My two best friends," he said simply. "They didn't make it back. Um... say, did you ever hear from Chuck Vandusen? You know, the guy who almost turned me into a Marine."

"Never did. But I did get a letter from his mom. She told me he died at Iwo."

"Lot of that going around."

"Yeah... I guess we should consider ourselves lucky."

More silence.

"How are they sending you back home after they process us out?" asked Lee.

"My bus ticket says through Chicago. How about you?"

"It's St. Louis for me."

"Just like the Navy," laughed Jack. "Always making things inconvenient for you. Even to the very end. Think we could exchange our tickets so we could ride home together?"

"I'd like that. But with my luck they'd probably screw it up and I'd end up back on Okinawa."

"Yeah, I hear you. No sense in chancing it. Promise you'll look me up as soon as you get back."

"You bet," said Lee as the line moved forward.

But he never did. Not his fault really, things just worked out that way.

EPILOGUE

AFTER LOSING HIS best friends in the war, Lee Kelley returned to Ohio a confused and angry man. The question *Why them and not me?* would haunt him for years. His confusion was only heightened when he found out his spendthrift—and now divorced—father had cashed in all the savings bonds he had sent home for safekeeping. It was money he had been counting on to kick-start his transition to civilian life.

"Sorry, son," said the elder Kelley, not all that ashamed of what he'd done. "But you should have been more specific in your instructions. I thought all those bonds were for me. I was going through some pretty rough times back here, you know. And they sure came in handy."

Lee's reunion with his mother didn't go much better. He was mortified to learn that while he was fighting for his country overseas she'd been masquerading as a Gold Star mother, claiming to have lost her only son somewhere in the Pacific. When he walked through the door in his uniform—alive and kicking—she was forced to make up an awkward excuse for him, and especially her now skeptical friends.

"It's a miracle! Thank God! We all thought he'd been killed. You know how screwed up the services can be when it comes to paperwork. I guess it was an honest mistake."

But Lee knew better and saw right through her. Ever since her days in Vaudeville his mother had loved being in the limelight. Somehow the role of grieving mother suited her.

"What the hell, Mom? Both you and Dad knew I was alive all this time."

"I'm so sorry, Lee," she finally confessed. "Somehow I let things get all twisted around. At first it was only a little white lie, a miscommunication, if you will. But after a few weeks I got used to all the attention I was getting. The way people looked at me with respect. With both you and your father gone, I kinda needed that."

Not exactly the welcome home he'd anticipated from either of his parents—or deserved—it didn't take long for Lee to once more pack his bags, and set out on his own.

Trying to put the last four years behind him, Lee gritted his teeth and enrolled in Akron University on the G.I. Bill. While earning his bachelor's degree he worked part time at Goodyear, where he built up his biceps by throwing around forty pound tires. To make ends meet he also took a second job at the Chrysler plant sledgehammering balky car doors into place. Having seen first-hand how they were built, for the rest of his life he would never drive a Chrysler, Dodge, or Plymouth.

While at Akron his gift of gab and out-going personality led to the presidency of his fraternity. It also garnered him an eventual job offer to work for General Dynamics, one of the early giants of the newly formed space industry. During the early stages of his career Lee assisted in a joint program with the Northrup Corporation, testing the ill-fated SNARK guided missile. With so many of the skittish craft crashing into the sea, the coast off the southern tip of Florida became known as "SNARK-infested waters."

Eventually Kelley worked his way up through the ranks in the more successful ATLAS program. Over a ten year period he traveled to dozens of college campuses to hire qualified graduates. He was personally responsible for the recruitment of thousands of personnel—in both America and Europe. Known for his sophisticated palate and knowledge of fine wines, often times he was charged with *babysitting* hard charging astronauts and eccentric rocket scientists—making sure that at the end of the day they were tucked safely into their beds and ready for tomorrow's flight.

Due to his time in Vaudeville—or maybe in spite of it—throughout his life Lee nurtured an appreciation of fine music. From classical, to jazz, to Broadway musicals. During his later years he attended at least ten productions of his favorite—*Phantom of the Opera*—and loved every one of them. His love of jazz would lead to a friendship with James Moody, the great jazz saxophonist.

Unwilling to agitate bad memories, for the rest of the twentieth century Lee refused to talk about his actions in the Pacific. Only recently was he willing to open up and let a glimmer of his pain out. When asked about America's current involvement in the Middle East however, he had few reservations.

"When I see our soldiers and sailors coming back from Iraq and Afghanistan missing arms and legs... it breaks my heart. So young, so broken of body and spirit... their lives and the lives of their families devastated. It just doesn't make any sense to me. Those people over there have been fighting and killing each other for centuries. And will be for hundreds of years after we're gone. Didn't we learn anything from the Russians? Oil can't be that important. Not at the cost of so many young American lives..."

Lee "Stump" Kelley passed away in his home a few days before Halloween in 2013—he was trying to make one last Christmas. Although it was not an easy death, he went out as he had lived, fighting all the way. Just like he fought the Japanese in the Pacific. Leaving this world with few regrets—to paraphrase his favorite singer—he did it his way.

They say a life well lived should never be mourned. And Lee Kelley definitely lived his life well. On November 6, 2013 Stump's ashes were interned high up on a hill out on Point Loma at the Fort Rosecrans National Cemetery. His final resting place overlooks San Diego bay and the beaches where he trained as a frogman. It was my honor to give his eulogy. I ended it with the following:

"Here's to you, Lee. From one sailor to another... may you forever have fair winds and a following sea."

Many thanks to Sue Esper, without whose help and computer expertise this effort would have run into a brick wall.

CPSIA information can be obtained at www.ICGtesting.com
Printed in the USA
BVOW02s1610020415

394477BV00002B/4/P